# DEATH LEGACY

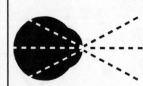

# DEATH LEGACY

## JACQUELINE SEEWALD

**THORNDIKE PRESS**
*A part of Gale, Cengage Learning*

Detroit • New York • San Francisco • New Haven, Conn • Waterville, Maine • London

LIBRARY OF CONGRESS CATALOGING-IN-PUBLICATION DATA

Seewald, Jacqueline.
    Death legacy / by Jacqueline Seewald.
        pages ; cm. — (Thorndike Press large print romance)
        ISBN 978-1-4104-5158-3 (hardcover) — ISBN 1-4104-5158-5 (hardcover)
    1. Large type books. I. Title.
    PS3619.E358D43 2012b
    813'.6—dc23                                           2012019732

Published in 2012 by arrangement with Tekno Books and Ed Gorman.

Printed in the United States of America
1 2 3 4 5 6 7 16 15 14 13 12

This novel is dedicated to my husband, Monte, who supports me in every possible way. A special thanks to family and friends as well — in particular Andrew and Daniel, and their wives and children, as well as my cousins Myrna and Max Spinrad.

# ACKNOWLEDGMENTS

I want to acknowledge the help and support of Alice Duncan, a wonderful editor and writer.

I also appreciate the help and support of the Five Star editorial staff, in particular Tiffany Schofield and Tracey Matthews. Thank you for believing in me and my work and going the extra mile.

Call no man happy till he is dead.
— **Aeschylus**

# CHAPTER ONE

"Here's the check we talked about."

Michelle Hallam's eyes opened wide as she read the amount. "And we still have no idea who our mystery client is?"

"None whatsoever. As you see, the check's drawn on a Swiss bank account. They do have a reputation for discretion," Henry Biggs said, his cultured, upper-class English accent resonating.

His dark blue eyes focused on her intently. "Do you want me to lurk about?"

"No, you have other matters to deal with." It was important that she carry out her responsibilities independently. Otherwise, how could anyone in the agency respect her? She hadn't been an MI6 operative like her uncle or her father. It was incumbent upon her to earn the respect and confidence of her associates by being thoroughly competent.

"Well, do take care."

"Of course." She handed Henry back the check. "Please deposit this."

Henry took it and left as quickly as his massive frame allowed.

She'd been asked to meet the unknown party by herself at this hotel precisely at two o'clock in the afternoon, to wear a yellow dress and order a Napoleon brandy at the outdoor café overlooking the pool. There were unusual clients from time to time, but these requests struck her as eccentric, and her opinion became stronger when the client failed to show at the appointed time. Bugger cloak-and-dagger nonsense!

At two-thirty, she ordered fillet of sole. The waiter suggested the chef's special salad, and she agreed. She supposed the client deserved her patience. Besides, she loved the South of France and this hotel in particular. There was no need to rush away. She was dining out on the terrace by the swimming pool overlooking the sea. The view was spectacular, the summer breeze intoxicating. The hotel, built up on a hill, gave a perfect view of the sparkling beach below. Sunlight pirouetted gracefully on the shimmering aqua waters of the Mediterranean.

Removing her floppy saffron hat, she

placed it carefully on the chair opposite her, keeping the small handbag containing her tools of the trade nearby on the fine white linen tablecloth. While waiting for her meal, she studied the sea, noting that the storm clouds which had threatened earlier in the day had disappeared without depositing so much as a single drop of rain. She admired the beautiful fresh flowers set in decorative brick casements all around the pool. What a shame she couldn't stay longer. She was reminded it had been quite a long time between holidays.

Michelle had finished her meal when she first became aware of being watched. She looked around and saw a handsome man studying her. He was seated two tables away.

She glanced at him covertly. He had dark brown hair and eyes and what appeared to be a thoughtful expression on his face. Although he was well-built and muscular, something about the long forehead suggested that he was more scholar than athlete. She returned his bold stare now, directing her gaze into his eyes. Yes, she could see a keen intelligence in those dark orbs, and there was strong character implied in his chiseled, well-defined features.

He gave her a dazzling, potent smile as steady and sure as a sunrise. She found her breath catching. Was he simply flirting? She so rarely let down her guard that it was difficult to tell. She smiled back in a cool, noncommittal manner meant to show that she was flattered by his attentions, but not interested.

Her uncle had taught her to be careful, how vital alertness was to survival. After the shock of her parents' tragic deaths had worn off, it was her uncle who'd taken her in hand, tutored her in how to bury grief, along with all other forms of strong emotion.

Michelle called for her check. She'd waited long enough for the mysterious client, too long, in fact. It was time to go. Still, she felt the attractive stranger's eyes on her, studying her movements. How uncomfortable he made her feel. Could he be the mystery client?

*"Merci beaucoup, mademoiselle,"* the waiter said with a big smile as he surveyed the generous tip. She got up to leave, but not without taking one last wistful glance at the pool. It really had become a warm afternoon.

Someone came up behind her. She spun around quickly. Him! Her heart was beating rapidly as she waited to see what he would say or do. He was even more arresting up close.

"Care to join me for a swim?" He was a little over six feet tall, topping her by several inches. Dressed casually in faded, cut-off denim jeans and a knit shirt open at the throat, he was broad-shouldered, lean-hipped, and looked young and virile. In fact, he oozed testosterone.

"Have you been waiting for me?"

"Forever, gorgeous." The brilliant smile seemed meant to mesmerize.

He ought to be shot down. She rolled her eyes in annoyance, turned around without further comment and walked rapidly away. He was just a rude American tourist looking for a summer fling after all.

"Wait, I know you speak English. Your French is very good but I detected a British accent when you were ordering. Why won't you go for a swim with me?"

She glanced back at him circumspectly. His look gave her pause. It was a hungry expression, as if he was a starving man and she was a banquet. She shook her head to clear away such a foolish notion.

"I'm not a guest at the hotel."

"Well, I am, so that solves the problem."

"I don't have a bathing suit with me."

"There's a little shop right off the lobby

15

selling them. My treat." His eyes darkened.

"I'm afraid not," she said firmly.

"How about taking pity on a lonely fellow traveler. I barely speak the language." The warm, still air between them vibrated, alive with a hum of sensual awareness.

"Do hire an interpreter," she responded with all the cold hauteur she could muster and resumed walking with determination.

He fell into step beside her, apparently undaunted by her attitude. "You know you want to give in to the temptation just as much as I do. I see it in your eyes no matter how much you choose to deny it."

She tried her best to ignore him, but then he took her arm. The touch of his hand on hers was provoking. She reacted without thought. Trained reflexes took over automatically as she drove her right elbow into his hard abdomen. Then she slipped her right arm around his waist and, grasping his right arm with her left hand, threw him into the pool. *There, since he's so eager to be in the pool, I've given him exactly what he wanted.* She turned to leave.

"Help!" he cried out breathlessly. "I can't swim."

Fear seized her throat like an attack dog. What had she done? She quickly looked around for a lifeguard, but didn't see one.

He cried out again. Doubting his sincerity, she nevertheless kicked off her shoes and jumped into the water. Her arms went around him, grasping him by his neck. Her swift, precise movements got them both out of the deep end of the pool in record time. By then, a small crowd had gathered.

*"Vous êtes mal?"* demanded a young man who was likely the lifeguard.

*"Merci, mais non. Il est bien."*

She went on to explain that her friend had a little too much wine with lunch and needed to lie down for a while. The lifeguard nodded his head knowingly. Meanwhile, the American put his arms around her for support.

He was gasping and breathing heavily. "Can you help me to my room please?"

"Is that really necessary?" She tried to keep the alarm out of her voice.

He coughed loudly and the lifeguard looked back at them again.

"Oh, all right." She helped him through the lobby. The air conditioning made her shiver in her wet clinging dress. At least she'd had the presence of mind to retrieve her purse and shoes, but she'd left the hat behind, floating in the shimmering water. Several people threw questioning looks in their direction. How bloody awful this was!

She always cultivated an inconspicuous demeanor. They were anything but inconspicuous, she and this handsome American.

Luckily, they didn't have to wait long for the elevator. They entered, dripping. He pressed the button for the fourth floor. More puzzled stares from other guests greeted them as they walked down the hall. She was relieved when he finally indicated his room.

"I'll go now," she said tersely.

"No, you can't. Help me inside, please. You do owe me that much. Although I won't insist. My stomach hurts too much from our last encounter. You're some sort of martial arts expert, aren't you?"

She averted her gaze, noting that he framed his question skillfully. He was clever; perhaps too clever?

"I believe every woman should know how to defend herself," she said, following him into his room.

"And then some, in your case," he said with a wry smile. "You ought to slip out of those wet clothes and let them dry." He smiled again, betraying an attractive dimple in his right cheek. His dark brown eyes twinkled slightly as if he could read her thoughts. "I'm a medical doctor by profession, not a voyeur." He went to the bureau, opened the top drawer, and withdrew a deep burgundy robe in terry cloth and handed it to her. "You can change in the bathroom."

She found his conduct suspicious. Was he trying to lure her into going to bed with him? However, she was shaking with chill and did not feel like arguing the matter. If he didn't realize it already, he'd soon discover she didn't believe in casual sex with strangers. She knew she should leave, yet something about him made her want to stay. It was only to understand the motive for his puzzling behavior, she assured herself. Professional curiosity. Her instincts told her there was something more to his motives than sexual chemistry. She did as he'd suggested, changing into the robe in the bathroom, then hanging her wet clothes over the air conditioning vent.

He was on the phone when she came out of the bathroom but put the receiver back into its cradle immediately.

"I hope you like brandy. I've ordered two of them. I think we could both stand some warming up."

She seated herself in a straight-backed chair positioned beside a desk. Both pieces were French provincial. The room was quite nice, light, airy, and well decorated. But she would have expected nothing less at this hotel. It was as modern and luxurious as it was expensive.

He sat down on the bed, having changed into tennis shorts and a white knit shirt similar to the one he'd worn before. The clothes served to emphasize his excellent tan. She was aware that her own complexion was painfully pale by contrast.

"You lied about being unable to swim, didn't you," she said matter-of-factly.

He raised one dark brow in surprise. "How did you know?"

"As soon as I came in after you, I realized you were in no danger of drowning." She studied his smoothly muscled arms. "In fact, you look like a man who can swim quite well and probably does it often."

He gave her a disarming, boyish smile. "You're very observant. I'm from New York, Brighton Beach. I've lived near the ocean all my life and I love the water. Now I have a question for you. If you knew I could swim once you got in the water, why didn't you just dump me and leave?" He seemed to sense her discomfort and didn't push her further. "If you want to take the Fifth Amendment, it's okay. Just one thing though. Were you trying to kill me back there?" He was staring at the side of her right hand. Self-consciously, she slipped her hand into the pocket of the robe. He'd observed the callus on the side of her palm. She stood up and walked over to the window.

"I don't recall when I've met a man as audacious as you."

He responded with an easy grin. "Just my natural charm. I already know two things about you: one, violence comes naturally to you, and two, you're well-educated."

"How could you possibly know that I'm well-educated?"

"You have a classy British accent and you speak French fluently."

"Are you a detective?" Her cool eyes surveyed him with a level gaze.

"Not exactly." He studied her with such frank interest that she felt compelled to turn away from him and look out the window.

"You've a marvelous view of the Mediterranean from here. Nowhere else in the world is quite like it. But then so many things are lovely at a distance. Getting too close can be a mistake. It destroys the illusion of beauty."

"Is that the way you feel about people, too?"

He really did ask peculiar questions.

"I consider myself a very private sort of

person."

"Reserved? Shy?"

"Both I think."

"Do you have close family or friends?"

She was tense and on her guard despite the fact his eyes gazed innocently into hers. "Actually, I have no family."

"What about friends?"

"Many acquaintances, few of whom I could in all honesty call friends."

"You consider yourself a loner?"

"An introvert. I keep my own counsel." Yes, she was a loner, but no need to explain anything more to this probing stranger. No family, no friends, no pets, no vulnerabilities, no Achilles' heel. Nothing to keep her from her work, from what really mattered in life. Others might consider what she did dangerous, but it was forming attachments to people that posed the real threat. Thank God her work saved her from exposure to that sort of agony and pain.

"You're a fascinating woman, but puzzling."

His eyes were so intense that she uneasily looked away. "Perhaps you'd like it if I hopped on a microscope slide for closer inspection?"

"A little too kinky for my tastes." His eyes danced with amusement.

She found herself smiling without meaning to do so.

"But you could hop in my bed anytime." He was eyeing her with longing in a way that made her heart beat faster and heat rise to her cheeks. If it was an act, he was a talented thespian.

Michelle's instincts warned her this was a potentially treacherous situation. She must be very careful. What was this man up to?

# CHAPTER TWO

There was a knock at the door. Their brandy arrived in large snifters and she breathed a sigh of relief. She viewed him thoughtfully. An unusual man. For a time, they concentrated on their brandies and drank in silence. She preferred that. The warmth began to glow in her throat and chest almost immediately. At last the gripping chill dissipated.

"I've answered most of your questions. Now it's time for you to answer mine. Why did you persist in following me after I clearly communicated that I did not wish it?"

The charismatic smile appeared again. "You're a beautiful woman. I'm sure many men have admired you. Some must have even followed you."

She met his gaze squarely, narrowing hers. "Not all that many."

"Now you're being modest. You must

know what a stunner you are."

She was suspicious of his flattery and knew she should tell him to stuff it, but she had to admit he was appealing. Too appealing! "And are you really a medical doctor?"

"I have a diploma that says I am." His voice was mellifluous.

"What sort of a doctor?"

"I specialize in psychiatry."

"That explains it."

He watched her intently. "Explains what?"

"Several things. Your expertise at formulating incisive questions, and also your ability to pay for such an expensive hotel room."

He had a wonderful laugh, as warm as the brandy. "I won't be starting in private practice until September."

"Then you must be very certain of your earning capabilities to invest in such an expensive vacation at this time. Or is your family shockingly wealthy?"

Finally, it was his turn to look uncomfortable. "No rich family. Someone paid me to come over and work here briefly. In fact, someone I hardly know."

"Then we have that in common," she told him.

"Shall we drink to the kindness of strangers?"

She found herself smiling at him again.

"Of course, let's." So saying, she finished the last of her brandy. "What is your family like?" she asked, and then wondered why she'd put the question to him. Why should she care about him, or his family, for that matter?

He put down his glass, and looked her directly in the eye. "After my mother died, my father remarried. I was raised by my maternal grandparents. I was much happier living with them. They're very good people, although old-fashioned in many ways. But I don't think I became independent as early as most men. In fact, this trip represents a kind of symbolic declaration of independence for me."

She found his confession troubling. "You shouldn't tell me things like that."

"Why not?" His dark eyes were quicksand. "I'd like to tell you a whole lot more."

"I have no intention of becoming personally involved with you. I don't want you to consider me a confidante." She had come out sounding a lot harsher than she meant and regretted it, but he seemed to take it in stride.

"I'm sorry if I make you uneasy. I don't mean to. You obviously don't trust me."

"Why should I? You're a total stranger." Their eyes met again; she was the first to turn away from his hypnotic gaze.

"Do you think I'm a stalker, a rapist, or maybe a murderer?"

He moved close to her. She felt his warm breath on her cheek and had an oddly electric reaction that sent heat rushing to her face. She made herself pull away from him, although it wasn't easy.

"I think I might be able to protect myself better if you were one of those dreadful creatures. Charming men are dangerous. You are charming. Therefore, you are a decidedly dangerous man."

"I hope so." He gave her a look that made her blood burn. "Coming from a woman with your talents, that's quite a compliment."

"How is your stomach feeling?" She somehow managed to keep her voice controlled, walk to the bureau, and place her empty brandy snifter on top of a magazine.

"Much better. No internal injuries."

"Good, then perhaps I should be on my way."

"I sense a sudden relapse."

She was convinced that he used his charm in a deliberate manner, fully aware of just how disarming his boyish smile was. "I don't suppose you'll be needing the services of a physician, since you are one yourself."

He moved toward her. "There is something you could do for me before you leave."

"And what would that be?"

His eyes sparkled mischievously. "I'm afraid if I told you, you might try one of those blows on me again."

Perhaps bluntness was called for. "I don't go to bed with men I barely know."

"Too bad," he said with that special smile, and she realized that he'd been teasing her.

"Why don't you lie down and get some rest."

"And end our uplifting conversation?"

His innuendo was clear. He was playing a game with her, she decided. Possibly it was all part of some bizarre mental test. She wasn't certain what to make of him. Yet the attraction between them seemed real enough.

"We didn't meet by chance, did we?" She waited but got no response. "I think I'd better change now."

He stood directly between her and the bathroom. "You know what your problem is? You take yourself too seriously. I thought the English were known for a sense of humor. Wasn't it Sartre who said life is absurd? Didn't you ever feel the desire to do something mad, reckless?" His expression was so intense, so imploring.

Inside, she quaked. She did want him, but she wasn't a fool. "Sartre, as you may recall, was French. Americans who can quote Sartre are definitely not to be trusted. And I'm only half-English. My mother was American by birth." She took several more small steps toward the bathroom, but he continued to block her path. "Please excuse me. You're in my way."

"I wouldn't dare try to stop you. Who knows what you might do to me?" But suddenly his body moved fluidly against her own.

She was in his arms before she knew it, and he was kissing her, his mouth warm and moist against hers, his arms wrapped tightly around her. She stiffened and pulled away.

"I don't believe this is a good idea." Her voice sounded husky and breathless to her own ears.

"It's the best idea I've ever had."

She placed the palm of her hand against his chest, attempting to put some distance between them, breaking the contact. Then she pushed him away, pulling herself free of his embrace.

"I can't," she said in a firm but breathless voice.

He excused himself and went into the bathroom. Instantly she turned to scrutinize the room more closely. She went to the bureau, opened it, and examined his things. There seemed to be nothing out of the ordinary, no weapons of any kind. What would she expect to find? He returned more quickly than she anticipated and caught her.

"And you were . . . ?"

"Looking for some aspirin," she said calmly.

He gazed at her questioningly, one eyebrow raised.

She licked her suddenly dry lower lip. "Real women aren't afraid to go through men's drawers."

He smiled. "Fair turnabout. We guys are always trying to get into women's drawers."

She groaned.

"Okay, I can do better."

"Spare me."

"Haven't you heard puns are for groan-ups?"

"I believe you've missed your calling," she said. "Perhaps you should do stand-up comedy for a living."

"Couldn't handle the rejection. Besides, haven't you heard laughter is the best medicine? I have it on the authority of *Reader's Digest,* and they wouldn't lie." He tossed her a wolfish grin.

"I suppose if you can't cure your patients

you can always make them laugh."

"Does wonders for depression. What do you do, professionally speaking?"

She shifted uncomfortably. "I'm a consultant."

"So who do you consult?"

"I really must be going or I'll miss my plane."

She slipped hurriedly into the bathroom, locking the door behind her. She was trembling all over. Deep breathing, that's what was called for. She took several shaky gasps of air. The filmy summer dress reminiscent of yellow sunflowers was almost dry. She dressed as quickly as her shaking fingers would allow.

He was standing at the window looking out with his back to her when she emerged. She quietly rushed toward the door. There was a perceptible creak as she opened it, and he spun around.

"Wait!" he called out. "Where are you going?"

"To the airport. I told you, I have a flight to catch."

"I'll go with you."

"No."

"You can't go without giving me your name and address. Do you live in England?"

He moved rapidly toward her and she was reminded of a sculpture of the Roman god Mercury she'd studied at the museum. His strides were the sure, easy movements of a natural athlete.

"Better for you not to know anything about me." She started to walk through the door, but he caught her arm. Amazing, even the touch of his hand caused her skin to tingle. "Please let me go. Don't force me to hurt you. I wouldn't like that at all."

"I'd like it even less. But I can't let you go, not like this."

"Don't try to pressure me. It simply won't work."

His hands tightened on her arms possessively. She felt herself becoming angry.

"I ought to have done you some real damage, just to teach you a lesson. I don't appreciate oglers."

"Ogling? Was that what you thought I was doing at the restaurant? My eyes were riveted to your face the whole time, a purely metaphysical exploration, more like goddess worshipping."

"You're bloody pushy and aggressive."

"Never thought of myself in those terms."

His tone was placating, but she could see that he wasn't taking the matter seriously by the amused expression on his face. No one had ever infuriated her to such an extent. Had the kiss they'd shared affected him the way it affected her? The passion he'd stirred had made mush of her brain. What had he felt? Probably nothing more than momentary lust.

"You've got an awfully suspicious nature. All right, stay a woman of mystery if that's what you want. But at least let me give you my name and address in case you want to contact me." He got a piece of hotel stationery and a pen and wrote on it: *Daniel Reiner.*

"I won't take your address."

"Okay, you'll find me listed in the Manhattan phone directory. I'm going to share a practice with a friend. He's already set up an office on Park Avenue."

"A bit pricey."

"Especially for a Brooklyn boy like me, but I've decided to give it a try. You know New York?"

"Quite well."

"Call me day or night. There's an answering service."

"Don't expect to hear from me, Dr. Reiner."

"Why not?" His eyes were so earnest, so inviting.

Perhaps she had misjudged him. "You're

too young for me," she said in a near whisper, which was all she could manage.

"I'm nearly thirty. That probably makes me older than you."

"I wasn't talking about physical age." With that, she left him, hurrying away as if the devil were chasing her. And perhaps he was.

# CHAPTER THREE

Daniel never thought he'd see or hear from his mystery woman again. Being a reasonably sensible man, he tried to put her out of his mind. Since his days were busy, doing so wasn't all that difficult. It was the nights that gave him problems. There were dreams, vivid and erotic, filled with her. And when he woke up in the morning, he'd find himself reaching for her, aroused, hard as granite, longing to have her in his arms.

What was that quotation? Physician, heal thyself. He knew an obsession when he fell over one. He could have discussed it with a colleague, but he preferred just holding on to it. He could have satisfied his physical needs if not his psychological one with a host of eager and desirable women. So why didn't he? Holding out, waiting for a woman who claimed to have no interest in him, didn't make any sense at all, did it? But he couldn't stop thinking about the way he felt when he had her in his arms. And she'd wanted him just as much; he was certain of it. Thinking about her that way, did that make him sick?

No, there had been incredible chemistry between them. When he kissed her, he felt as if he'd been hit by a thunderbolt. He hadn't imagined it, and he wasn't going to doubt himself. Maybe she could try to deny their attraction to each other, but he would not, could not.

When summer turned into autumn, he despaired that his mystery woman would never contact him. He tried dating a few other women, but felt no real interest. Finally, one day in late October when the rain was coming down in gunmetal gray torrents, something happened that made her burst through his mind again like dammed waters at flood stage.

A new patient came to see him. She appeared to be in a highly agitated state. He tried to set her at ease as quickly as possible. His assistant handed him her form to peruse. The woman's name was Nora Jane Parker, fifty-two years of age, married, and the mother of two adult children. She had never visited a psychiatrist before. He saw that the space requesting the name of a referring physician had been left blank.

"Mrs. Parker, who referred you to me?"

She wrung her delicately flowerlike hands. "Someone who said she thought you were the sort of doctor who could help with my problem." She leaned forward in her chair and then spoke in a barely audible whisper. "You will be discreet, won't you?"

"All conversations between doctor and patient are held in the strictest confidence." He spoke in his most reassuring, professional manner. "Our communications are privileged."

She smiled and seemed a bit more at ease.

"Just for the record, may I have the name of your friend?"

"I'd rather not say. You don't know her name anyway."

"Yet she knows mine? How come?"

Mrs. Parker seemed nervous again. "She said you'd met each other under unusual circumstances this summer."

He suddenly felt a rush of excitement, a peculiar surge of anticipation. "This woman, does she possibly have red-gold hair and green eyes, and is she approximately in her late twenties?"

Mrs. Parker nodded her head. He could read distress in her watery blue eyes, as if she were upset because she'd somehow conveyed to him information he wasn't supposed to have. He knew that he ought to stop there, but he couldn't.

"And this woman's name?" He saw Mrs. Parker's reluctance but urged her on. "It's important that I know."

"Her name is Michelle Hallam. She's going to be very displeased that I told you."

"You did the right thing," he assured her. "Mrs. Parker, may I call you Nora? Ms. Hallam and I are on good terms. There's no reason I shouldn't know. Don't worry about it."

"All right, if you say so, Doctor. But Ms. Hallam values her anonymity."

"I understand. Now let's talk about the reason she suggested you see me."

"I hardly know where to begin. I'm not even certain that you can be of any help to me. My problem isn't likely to be similar to any you've ever encountered before."

"Let me be the judge of that," he said reassuringly. He encouraged her to recline on the couch, but she refused.

"I prefer sitting in a chair. It's so difficult to discuss this with a stranger as it is." She wrung her delicate hands again. Her voice was soft, with a trace of Southern gentility.

He could imagine her sitting beneath a magnolia tree sipping mint juleps on the veranda of an antebellum Southern mansion.

"Just tell me whatever you feel like saying. I'm here to listen. Where and when did your problem originate?"

"I think I ought to start at the end rather than the beginning."

He gave her an encouraging, accepting smile. "Whatever you prefer."

She took a deep breath and then let it out in a shaky gasp. "You see, Doctor, a few months ago, I was told by the police that my husband was dead. They said it was likely that he committed suicide. But I didn't believe them then, and I don't believe them now. I think I'm being lied to. In fact, I think everyone involved has been lying to me."

"You believe there's some sort of conspiracy?" He started to take notes. Was this woman paranoid, possibly suffering from delusions of persecution?

She looked up at him, and he could see tears welling up in her eyes. "I suppose I've just convinced you that I'm some sort of a lunatic. Are you ready to call Bellevue?"

"No," he responded in a gentle, soothing voice, "I want you to tell me your reasons for thinking the way you do. I'm willing to listen to anything you want to say."

"Thank you, Doctor. You see, there were just too many things that didn't make sense." She sat stiff and straight, biting down on her lower lip.

"Go on."

"Well, about a year ago, James — that was my husband — he started behaving very oddly. We had what I always considered to be a very solid marriage. It lasted over thirty years. James was a fine man, a good husband, a devoted father. He was in his middle fifties, and everything seemed to be going very well for him. Then he became nervous and irritable, as if he were very worried about something. He wasn't himself at all. One day, he announced that he was leaving me. The next thing I knew, he was living with a very young woman. No reasons, no explanations."

"These things do happen, Nora. We just have to go on with our lives and learn to accept them."

She shook her head. "You had to know James. It was all so incredible. He was not an impetuous man by nature. None of it made any sense. And then he retired from his job quite suddenly. He loved his work. He was so devoted."

"What did he do for a living?"

She lowered her eyes. "He worked for the CIA."

The woman caught him by surprise with that disclosure. "In what capacity?"

"I couldn't really say. I mean, I was never actually certain."

The tension in her voice warned him not to prod her any further on the subject.

"Why do you think he changed his life-style so drastically in the final year of his life?"

"I don't know. Oh, you're probably thinking what most people did, that he was just experiencing dissatisfaction with his mundane life and wanted to have some fun before it was too late, but James wasn't like that at all."

"Is it really important to you to know why he left you?"

"Of course, it is!" Her eyes misted.

"Suppose, just suppose, he left for the obvious reasons. Is it a possibility?" He kept his tone gentle, nonthreatening.

She shook her head vehemently. Her short, frizzy gray hair, tinted a pale shade of robin's egg blue, barely budged an inch.

"I lived with that man for a lifetime, and I know something was troubling him, something he couldn't talk about, something he might have been afraid to confide." Her eyes were circled by iridescent purple shadows. "I want to tell you about how they say he died."

There was a stillness in the room, and then she began to speak in a soft, almost childlike voice. "He bought a sailboat. He liked to go sailing. He was very good at handling his sloop. That was where he died, on board the boat." Tears were running down her face. She looked like a blasted white rose whose petals were slowly beginning to fall away.

He took her hand. "If this is too painful for you, we can talk about it another time."

"No, I must go on. I need to discuss this with you. We lived in Maryland. Since our estrangement, since he left me, I sold our house and moved in with my daughter here in New York. My older girl and her husband have a lovely converted brownstone in Brooklyn Heights. I have my own small apartment in the building and they have theirs. I don't intrude on them, but still, it is nice to know that Katherine and Brian are around. My husband remained in Maryland living with that dreadful girl. One Sunday morning, he took his boat out on the Chesapeake. He was never seen alive again. The sailboat ran aground the following day. He wasn't on board. The weather was excellent. He knew how to handle the boat. The question of an accident was far-fetched. The coast guard informed the Maryland State Police, who in turn notified the CIA, and then me.

"One week later, the coast guard located a man's body in the bay. The man was clad in a T-shirt and jeans. James had been described as last being seen dressed that way. Two diving belts were strapped just below the armpits and at the waist. The body was full of gas, which allowed it to float to the surface in spite of the weighted belts. The CIA man who was in charge of the investigation, a Mr. Kirson, did the courtesy of paying me a visit when I arrived back in Washington. From the beginning, he seemed certain that the man they found was James. He was sure that James was dead. Mr. Kirson told me that there was a gunshot wound in the head that was clearly self-inflicted. I don't know, maybe I should have just accepted what he said at face value, but I couldn't. James wasn't the sort of man who would kill himself. For one thing, he was Catholic. It went against his religious beliefs. And no one let me see the body."

"There may have been a good reason for that."

Her eyes met his. "Mr. Kirson did say the

body was badly decomposed, that he was protecting me."

"But you didn't believe him?"

"I just couldn't accept what he said. It wasn't so much the words. That part actually made a lot of sense. It was his manner. I never trust a man with a dirty smile."

"I don't understand."

"He seemed to be holding something back. I don't know, maybe I have become paranoid after all, but it seemed to me the man was lying."

"Was there anyone involved in the investigation that you considered honest?"

"Not really. The experts confirmed what Mr. Kirson said. He even showed me a wristwatch that I'd given James some years ago and said they found it on the body. Mr. Kirson urged me to dispose of the remains quickly. His suggestion was cremation. At first, I refused, but he convinced me that it was best. He even handled all the arrangements for me. But since then, I've had some second thoughts."

"Why's that?"

She sighed deeply, wearily. He could see the subject was terribly painful for her.

"About a week ago, I had a call. It was a man's voice, in kind of a hissing, insinuating whisper. I think it was purposely disguised. He said: 'James Parker was not your husband. James Parker never existed. There was no James Parker. The man who called himself James Parker is still alive.' I asked him where James was. Then he said something even stranger than what he'd said before: 'Your husband has gone home. He is not dead, but you will never see him again.' I begged him to tell me where James was, but he hung up. The conversation still haunts me."

Was there ever such a call? Was it merely wish fulfillment, or could it have been a dream? He decided to reserve judgment for the time being.

"You believed this man?"

"I don't know. He could have been some sort of crank. I realize that. There are so many sick people in this world. Except he sounded so convincing. Besides, he confirmed some of my own doubts and suspicions. I've been torn apart. You see, I don't know exactly what James did for the agency, but he was far more important than Mr. Kirson led me to believe. Mr. Kirson told me James was just a minor bureaucrat, that his job was ordinary, white-collar work."

"And you think he lied?"

"The air was redolent of mendacity."

"What makes you say that?"

Nora Parker dabbed at her watery eyes with a twisted tissue. "James took several trips to what was then the Soviet Union some years ago. They wouldn't have sent him there if he were a mere clerk, would they? We always lived a simple life, that's true. But James had put away quite a bit of money in savings — for our old age, he used to say. I never asked any questions. However, I knew he'd received several promotions. Important people would come over and spend time with him in his study. Occasionally, we'd be asked to elegant parties, and he was always treated with respect.

"In this last terrible year that I've been without James, I've had too much time on my hands to dwell on the past. I'm not sure I did the right thing at all. I shouldn't have given him up without a fight. I am in agony, Dr. Reiner. I feel to blame for what happened. Maybe I just want to believe James is alive even if he isn't."

"You told all of this to Michelle Hallam?"

"Yes. You see, I asked her to help me, too."

"In what way can she help you?"

Mrs. Parker looked uneasy again.

"I suppose I can tell you. Michelle operates a private consulting agency that specializes in discreet inquiries, among other things. It used to be run by her uncle until

46

his death not long ago. Michelle's uncle was at one time an important figure in British intelligence. James knew the man and respected him. We had him to dinner on occasion when James was working with him, and he left us his card. I understand he passed away not long ago. His niece has operated the firm since then. I've employed Michelle to represent me because, thanks to her uncle, she has connections all over the world. She knows how to obtain sensitive information. She's also bright and committed. If anyone can find out the truth about what happened to James, I believe it would be her."

"I don't understand why she recommended that you see me."

Nora Parker lowered her eyes. "I haven't been able to sleep very well lately. Even pills and tranquilizers don't seem to help very much. I keep wondering if it was my fault that James turned to someone else. Do you think it was?"

"No, I don't, Nora. It's never any one person's fault."

She began to weep softly. He gently patted her back in a gesture of comfort. Most psychiatrists believed there should be no physical connection between doctor and patient. Daniel wasn't one of them. Small, physical expressions gave comfort.

"As you yourself realize, all the facts are not known. In fact, they may never be known. You are just going to have to learn to deal with the possibility that you'll never learn the full truth. And there's no point accepting blame you don't deserve."

Before the hour was up, he wrote her a tranquilizer prescription but refused to issue her sleeping pills. Nora accepted that gratefully. She seemed much calmer by the time the session ended. He felt optimistic about alleviating her depression.

Nora Parker's story stayed with him as he left his office for the day. More than ever, he wanted to know his mystery woman. At least now he finally had a name and some information about her.

It was still raining as he walked toward the lot where his car was parked. His mind was preoccupied as he drove across the Brooklyn Bridge. It was a dark, gloomy day. The sky and sea merged together, both brain-matter gray. The bridge, like a long spinal cord, connected Manhattan to Brooklyn. He glanced in his rearview mirror several times and noticed the same car was sticking close behind him all the way.

He disliked being tailgated. It was some sort of a black limo, and the glass was tinted so that he could not make out the driver's face. He didn't think about it again until he reached Ocean Parkway and found a spot near his grandparents' apartment building. Then he looked into the mirror and happened to catch sight of the very same limo pulling over not more than half a block away.

# Chapter Four

It struck him as an odd coincidence that the same car should be there. Weird. Then again, strange things happened. He shrugged and thought no more about it.

His grandparents lived in a high-rise apartment building just off Ocean Parkway. The wide, tree-lined avenue had one- and two-family brick dwellings interspersed with huge apartment buildings. Like Manhattan, there were always people around, walking, talking, shopping. Brooklyn reverberated with life. People of many nationalties and religions lived and worked here.

As he entered his grandparents' apartment building, he could smell the old-fashioned cooking odors. He heard footsteps almost directly behind him, but when he turned to look, he saw no one.

He rang the bell to the apartment and was greeted with a warm kiss from his grandmother. After that, he forgot all about Nora

Parker and Michelle Hallam. He had a fine dinner with his family and relaxed.

Over roast chicken and potato pancakes, his grandmother launched into her favorite topic. "My friend Sarah has the most beautiful niece, a very charming girl who just happens to teach the emotionally disturbed. You and she would have so much in common. Maybe you would like her phone number?"

"I'm sure she's terrific, but I never talk shop when I'm away from work. I like to forget about it." That wasn't completely true, because he couldn't always forget about his patients or their problems; still, he did try.

His grandmother didn't push him, realizing that he just wasn't interested in meeting any of the "nice" women she selected for him. He knew, of course, that she hadn't given up; he'd only won a temporary truce. His grandmother was nothing if not tenacious. Pit bulls could take lessons from her.

It wasn't until nine o'clock when he was leaving the apartment building that he thought again of the strange tale that Nora Parker had told him. He considered it as he walked toward his car, caught sight of what appeared to be the same black limo, and heard footsteps behind him again. Being raised in the city, he was always alert to muggers. He didn't bother to look at who might be following but jogged hurriedly to his car. Driving back toward Manhattan, he glanced into the rearview mirror and caught sight of the black limo. Totally outrageous, he thought, shaking his head. Who could possibly be following him? And why?

There wasn't any phone number listed in the Manhattan Directory for Michelle Hallam, no private number, not even a listing for her firm in the yellow pages. Somehow, he hadn't expected there would be. But if anything, he wanted to find her again more than ever. His only link to her was Nora Parker.

Mrs. Parker showed up for her second appointment the following week. She didn't seem any more relaxed than she had been before, and that puzzled him. The tranquilizer prescription ought to have helped. Yet she appeared more depressed and despondent. He considered the possibility of using antidepressant mood drugs, but decided to hold off for a while. His gut feeling was that her real problem wasn't a chemical imbalance.

Nora Parker talked more freely, her

thoughts returning to the beginning of her marriage to James Parker when they were happy together. Toward the end of the hour, he asked her about Michelle Hallam.

"Did you see Ms. Hallam again?"

Nora Parker shook her head, her eyes avoiding his.

"Does she have an office near here?"

Nora answered in the affirmative, and he pressed her still further, knowing it was wrong to take advantage of her fragility and trust but unable to help himself.

"What's the name of her agency? Where's it located? It's all right to tell me. I'm going to have to confer with her about your problem."

Finally, still reluctant, Nora Parker trusted him with the information he was seeking.

The following day was sunny but cold. He decided to walk from his office on Park Avenue over to the Citicorp building on Lexington Avenue, where International Consultants had offices. It was only a ten-block walk down to the area between 53rd and 54th Street. A perfect day for a walk. His last patient left at four; that gave him just enough time to get over before the offices closed at five. He was determined to talk to Michelle Hallam if she were there.

He reached her skyscraper office building feeling exhilarated by the brisk exercise.

International Consultants maintained an attractive but small suite. Nothing fancy or ostentatious, simple elegance, just like Michelle Hallam herself. There were two secretaries and a number of telephones in the outer office and only two rear offices from what he could observe. He asked to see Ms. Hallam and was promptly told by the receptionist that it was impossible to see Ms. Hallam without first making an appointment. The young woman's manner was pleasant but firm. He was not going to be put off. He again demanded to see her. But this time the young woman responded that Ms. Hallam was out of town and could not be reached. She offered to take a message. Her eyes didn't meet his.

He felt dissatisfied and demanded to see whoever was in charge. He knew lies when he heard them. The secretary buzzed someone and explained the situation. Finally, he was led into the office of a Mr. Bertram, who kept a potted rubber plant in one corner and had classical music piped in from the other. In point of fact, Mr. Bertram looked neither like a music lover nor a business executive. His rough-hewn features appeared to be chiseled out of granite. His nose was distorted and had very likely been broken at some vague time in the distant past. Mr. Bertram was also a very large man, well over six feet five inches tall. He had the stance of a boxer and the charisma of a hit man.

"I came to see Ms. Hallam," Daniel asserted to the man who towered over him.

"So I hear. I believe you've already been told she isn't in her office. If you state your business, sir, I can arrange to give her your message." The voice sounded like gravel. The *sir* had been expressed with a sneer.

Daniel refused to let himself be intimidated by the man's menacing glare. "I'm Dr. Reiner. Ms. Hallam knows me. In fact, she referred a client of hers to me for treatment. I think it's essential to that patient's well-being for us to confer as soon as possible."

"Like I said, I'll give her the message." Bertram's eyes were laser blue and very cold. Daniel shivered inwardly.

"Can't you just give me her phone number or address?"

Bertram sighed as if his patience were wearing thin. "*Sir,* we don't do things that way here."

Bertram's exaggerated politeness infuriated him. "I still want her phone number."

"I am not authorized to give out that information. With all due respect, I would lose my job if I did give it to you. Rules are rules." He buzzed for a secretary. This time a wholesome, red-cheeked girl of little more than twenty appeared.

"Nancy, please show Dr. Reiner out. You may be very certain that Ms. Hallam will hear of your visit. What she chooses to do about it is entirely her affair. Goodbye."

Daniel restrained a strong urge to punch Mr. Bertram in his crooked nose. But common sense prevailed. Mr. Bertram did not look like the sort of man he could win an argument with. And he had no desire to end up in a hospital bed or charged with assault.

Daniel left the office and stood outside in the hallway, wondering what to do next. Bertram had spoken to him in a patronizing manner as if he were a mentally deficient child. Somehow, he had the distinct impression that the man had protested too much. He decided to walk over to the area near the elevators and wait inconspicuously to one side. It was nearly five; he'd wait until five-thirty. Daniel set his jaw at a stubborn angel. He didn't feel like giving up easily.

The secretaries left first. Then at five-twenty, he was rewarded by the sight of his mystery woman escorted by Bertram. She

56

was as beautiful as he remembered, even in her neat, conservative, navy blue business suit. He felt a jolt of unexpected desire charge through him. As the elevator arrived, he quickly moved into it, just behind them so that when Michelle Hallam turned around, they were face to face.

She stared at him with unflinching green eyes that were like emeralds of fine cut and quality. Her hair was the color of spun gold blended with copper, cut short and tightly curled. He decided she would have stood out anywhere she went.

"I'm sorry, Michelle. I thought he left."

She turned to Bertram. "Quite all right. Dr. Reiner is a very persistent and resourceful person."

"Can we go somewhere to talk? Have a drink with me? Dinner? Anything you like." Did he sound like he was begging? When had he become needy?

"I'm sorry," she said. "I'm leaving for the airport now." Her voice was chilling, that of an ice princess, but he had the feeling it was all facade — or was that just what he wanted to think?

"You could let me go with you instead."

"I'm afraid not."

He studied her carefully. It was her lips that made her seem sexy, he decided; she had a lush, heart-shaped mouth. There was strength of character in her facial features as well. A certain look that informed others she was someone to be reckoned with.

She was a class act, coolly sophisticated. It wasn't just the crisp upper-crust British accent that spoke of breeding. It was everything about her, from the slim, regal lines of her body to the imperial assertion of her chin. He'd never met anyone like her.

"If you don't want anything to do with me, why did you send Nora Parker to my office?"

She wouldn't answer or even look at him.

"Is this guy bothering you?" Bertram asked pointedly.

Michelle shook her head but didn't speak.

Daniel decided to press his advantage. "I need to talk to you about Nora Parker if I'm really going to help her."

"All right, when I get back, I'll contact you."

"I'll be waiting."

He couldn't take his eyes away from her, admiring the small, pert nose that upturned so slightly, and the pearl-like teeth, which were unusually perfect for an Englishwoman. He desperately wanted to pull her into his arms and kiss her the way he had in France. Only he wanted to do a lot more than kiss her. He would have liked to strip her naked and bury himself in her. He could just imagine how she'd react if he actually came right out and communicated his feelings to her in just those words.

When the elevator arrived at ground level, he felt deflated. Watching her walk away from him was like a physical blow. He followed as she got into a taxi cab Bertram hailed. Maybe he really ought to talk to Morris Lerner; his partner might be able to analyze this obsession he had for the woman. Must be a form of masochism.

A moment later, he found himself wondering if the black limo he saw at a distance could possibly be the same one that had been following him. Somehow, he was certain it was. No, he was not exhibiting a form of paranoia. There was a definite connection here, a sinister one.

Instinctively, Daniel realized Michelle Hallam was involved with dangerous people. He ought to walk away, forget her and never look back. But he couldn't. His desire for her was a palpable thing with a life and breath of its own. God, he wanted her! He'd never felt this kind of passion for a woman before and somehow knew he never would again. Without thinking, he pulled open the

door of Michelle Hallam's cab and jumped
in before it could move away.

# CHAPTER FIVE

When Michelle turned and saw Daniel Reiner in the elevator of her office building, she felt drawn to him as if he were a magnet. She was elated but at the same time upset. She'd told herself the attraction was merely physical. He was an immensely appealing man, and totally different from anyone she knew. But even if he were unique, she knew getting involved with him would be a serious mistake. Nevertheless, the chemistry was potent and difficult to ignore.

It wasn't her fault that he proved difficult to discourage. Telling him she'd see him when she returned from her trip hadn't worked: the impossible man impulsively hopped into her cab and rode along with her to the airport. She refused to speak to him, finally offered a curt goodbye, and quickly tried to break away. That should have worked, too, but it didn't. And now here he was actually sitting next to her on the flight to D.C.

"You must be totally mad," she said in a tense voice.

"Absolutely stark raving. The good news is I'll be able to certify myself." He smiled as if pleased with himself.

She narrowed her eyes, ready for war. "You needn't act so smug. And how did you get on this flight anyway?"

"It wasn't sold out. Lucky for us, don't you think, sweetheart?" He gave her a self-satisfied look.

The man was infuriating. "You are delusional. And I am not your sweetheart."

"That's a matter of opinion. The lady who was supposed to be sitting here thinks I am. She was more than willing to swap seats when I explained how we'd had a lover's quarrel that we needed to patch up. Most women are suckers for a good romantic story."

Michelle folded her arms beneath her breasts. "Some women perhaps."

He let out a deep sigh. "But not you? You're a hard case."

"I can't begin to tell you how foolish you are. What about your responsibility to your patients, *Doctor?*" She spoke with biting sarcasm.

It hardly seemed to faze him. "Got that

covered. I phoned my partner and explained the situation."

"And let me guess: he offered free therapy."

Daniel laughed. "Ouch, direct hit. No, he just asked if you were worth it."

She raised her brows. "And you said?"

"That you were passable. Okay, maybe I said you were drop-dead gorgeous — or was it stop-and-stare sexy."

She must not let his compliments or his charming smile get to her. "Are you suffering from mad cow disease? When we land, you must take the next plane back and hopefully seek treatment."

"Wrong. Oh, and haven't you heard? There's no cure for mad cow disease as of now. But we can have the weekend together."

"You're the one that's got it wrong, Dr. Reiner."

"Call me Dan or Daniel." He tried to take her hand. She pulled back. If she let him touch her, her resolve might weaken.

"Dr. Reiner, I am not contemplating an affair with you. I have serious business down in Washington related to the Parker case."

"What makes you think I don't? Incidentally, there's been a limo following me around ever since I started treating Mrs.

Parker."

Warning bells went off in her head. "Did you see the license plates?"

"Never thought to look."

"Might they have been diplomatic plates?"

He shrugged. "Couldn't say."

She sighed deeply. "I made a serious error in judgment sending Nora to you. You had best stop working with her immediately. I don't want you getting in any deeper."

"Deeper into what?"

When she didn't answer, he took her hand and placed it tightly into his own. "I've been in this since I found out you sent her to me. And no matter what, I don't think it was a mistake." He lifted her hand and one by one kissed each of her fingertips.

She wanted to stop him, willed him to end his ministrations, but found herself unable to speak and began to shiver. For all his easy ways and joking manner, there was an intense sensual core to the man. She turned away, not trusting her reaction to him. Then she removed her hand, aware that it was trembling.

"Nora needs my help just as she needs yours. So I'll be hanging around." He sounded very determined.

"All right. I'll drop you at a motel for tonight. Then I'll pick you up tomorrow so we can discuss this in more detail."

"And where will you be staying?" He looked at her pointedly.

"That does not concern you."

"I beg to differ." His gaze was direct and hot.

She turned away from him again. Being with him confused her, and she couldn't afford that. She would lose her concentration and possibly make mistakes.

"Are you going to deny there's something going on between us?"

She refused to turn back and meet his gaze. Biting down on her lower lip, she managed to keep silent.

"If you really didn't want to see me again, then you wouldn't have sent Nora to me, would you? I've thought about you every day since we met. Have you been thinking about me, too?"

She certainly hadn't behaved sensibly about him, not from the moment they met. And the truth was, she'd thought about him many times since then.

Michelle's mind was preoccupied during the rest of the flight. She closed her eyes and pretended to sleep, but she was fully aware of his presence beside her. When they landed, she picked up her car from long-term parking and drove him straight out to

Route 1, depositing Daniel in a motel off the highway in Alexandria, Virginia. He did everything he could to persuade her to stay with him, but she had the good sense to refuse him. She knew very well that he wanted to go to bed with her. She wasn't ready for that; maybe she never would be. She ignored his look of hurt and disappointment as well as the seductive bedroom eyes that roamed over her body.

Right now, she had pressing business to consider, and that came first and foremost. She'd promised Nora Parker to unravel the mystery of her husband's death — if he were actually dead at all. In any case, she was resolved to examine the matter in depth. Being with Daniel would only place him in unnecessary danger. She'd realized that as soon as he told her about being followed. The intimacy he desired could only create problems for both of them.

"Stay with me," he implored.

"I didn't ask you to come with me. Please don't make a nuisance of yourself." With that, she left him, forcing herself not to look back.

The drive over to Langley the next morning was unexpectedly pleasant. It was still early enough in autumn that the sun was warm, yet the foliage was already beautiful. Michelle found driving through the Virginia countryside restful. However, she did not particularly enjoy visiting the CIA's sprawling complex, even if it was almost entirely surrounded by natural beauty. It was a huge place — more than a million square feet of space set on 140 acres, a bit too gigantic for her tastes.

She was allowed to drive through the gates without question. But security took over as soon as she crossed the main building's threshold. Armed guards asked her business and required she write down on a special form her name, address, and citizenship status, as well as the name of the person she'd come to see. A personal escort took her to the CIA Security Division.

It might have been any business office in America. She observed many people who were obviously happily devoted to the task of collecting and collating information. White-collar workers bustling around, lots of attractive, young people. So clean-cut and idealistic, these young Americans. She would not have liked working in such a place, but she could understand how others would.

Her armed escort brought her to William Kirson's outer office. From that point, life became rather dull. Kirson kept her waiting over half an hour. She tapped her gloved hand impatiently on the secretary's desk and asked when Mr. Kirson would be free, but the girl simply put her off. The delay could only mean that Kirson was less than eager to see her. She paced but then sat down again. She crossed her legs and then uncrossed them. Finally, Kirson buzzed his assistant, and Michelle was allowed into his private office.

The windowless room immediately made her feel claustrophobic. As was typical of Kirson, he did not bother to stand up. He was puffing on a foul-smelling cigar. The smoke immediately made her stomach feel queasy. His feet were up on his desk, and he was talking on the telephone. Michelle viewed him with ill-concealed distaste. She knew him from former days; he was a man she preferred not to deal with whenever possible. But there was no choice this time. Kirson had been in charge of the Parker investigation.

"Always a pleasure to see you, honey." He blew smoke in her face.

*Sexist swine.* He watched her grimace with obvious enjoyment.

"I believe this building is required to be smoke-free. Are you given special privileges?

Never mind. You appear to be a law unto yourself. However, if you do not put out that odious thing, I will have to regurgitate my breakfast all over you."

"No call for that, honey bun." He ground his cigar in an overflowing ashtray. How appropriate, since he reminded her of a human ashtray.

"Now what was it you came to see me about?" Of course, he probably knew, but she would have to go through the formalities anyway.

"I'm here in regard to the death of James Parker."

He smiled at her through crooked, nicotine-stained teeth. Dear Lord, how the man repelled her!

"That, little lady, was settled some time ago. Damn mess, too. What's your interest in it?"

"Mrs. Parker isn't satisfied with the thoroughness of the investigation. She asked me to look into the matter."

Kirson stood up and removed the Colt revolver he wore holstered cowboy style, absently twirling the weapon. "Hell's bells, that is one nervous old mare. She don't know what she's talking about. I told you, the case is closed."

Lesser people would have been intimidated by "Wild Bill" Kirson's ill-tempered manner, but Michelle had been trained to remain cool and in control.

"Mrs. Parker does have some rights in this matter. After all, she is the man's widow."

"Soon to have been an ex from what I understand."

"Nevertheless, on her behalf, I would like to examine the files on the investigation." Her tone was calm but compelling.

Kirson stamped one leather-booted foot on the floor. "Can't do that. Strictly classified, and you damn well know it."

"I have security clearance."

"I know all about your influential friends. Being related to royalty don't mean crap around here, honey. This is America. All men are equal here. Time you limeys found that out. Far as we're concerned, you don't have nothin' special going for you."

"My, how petulant we are."

"Don't give me any of your snotty upper-crust superiority. It don't do diddly around here. How come you're handling this yourself, anyway? I thought you were the boss lady now. Run out of flunkies?"

"I'm doing a favor for Mrs. Parker."

"Since when are you such a soft-hearted gal? Must be a real big fee." He leered at her, leaning forward so that she was forced to pull back to avoid his sour-smelling breath. He smiled, seeming to enjoy the fact that he was making her uncomfortable. "You don't need to look at any files. I'll personally fill you in on anything you need to know. Just ask me for it real nice, darlin'."

He moved toward her, and she backed away.

"Real cold fish, aren't you? All business. That the way you want to play it?"

"I don't wish to play at all." She tried not to let her voice betray her disgust.

"All right, honey. I prefer my women younger and sexier anyhow."

"Lolita, no doubt."

"Y'all got that right. Give me a sweet, hot little virgin anytime."

She kept calm; this was all just part of the game. The man was very shrewd beneath the good ol' boy facade he cultivated. Michelle knew all about him. Kirson was one of the Agency's chosen. He had intellectual depth that he carefully hid to gain an advantage, and he wasn't afraid to use dirty tricks as well as dirty language when he felt the occasion called for it. She considered him a formidable adversary. The sadistic bastard was crafty.

"Who was James Parker, really?"

"Nothing I can tell you that I ain't already told his widow."

She took a step toward the door. "There are others I can ask, you know."

"Well, do it then. Parker was just a small time clerk for the Agency, a nothing, a nobody. He got the itch, if you know what I mean. So he dumped his old lady and took up with something fresh. When the bimbo dropped him, he deep-sixed himself. End of story."

She shook her head. "What audacity."

He took a fresh cigar from a humidor on his desk and stared at her out of sharp, light blue eyes. Then he gave her a chilling smile.

"We could discuss the case over a couple of drinks. You know anything about pleasing a man? If you use that clever mouth of yours just right, well, maybe I might remember something else."

She was certain he was baiting her. "No thanks, I'll do my own digging."

He whooped with laughter. "Got you, didn't I?" He twirled his pearl-handled revolver around again for emphasis. "Could be some wet work involved in this. You prepared for that? Mrs. Parker, she offering you enough to risk your life for?"

"If Parker were just an unimportant clerk as you made him out to be, why would I

72

have any reason to expect bloodshed?"

"There are people, misguided people, who might have gotten the wrong idea about Parker. If you go poking your nose into what don't concern you, well, there's no telling what you might turn up. Stick your hand into a snake pit and you're likely to get bit."

"Thanks for the advice."

"Don't say I didn't warn you." He gave her a final ugly smile.

"Good day, Mr. Kirson, and do give my regards to your long-suffering wife." She could hear him chuckling as she closed the door behind her.

She hadn't really expected his cooperation anyway. Asking for it was just a formality. She had the name of the doctor who performed the autopsy on Parker's body. That was a matter of public record. She'd start there.

She was pensive on her drive back to meet up with Daniel. Her instinct told her that Parker was important and that Kirson was deliberately lying — but why? Of course, she was well aware that the tactic of giving misinformation was a common intelligence procedure worldwide, but there had to be a reason it was being employed. Her intuition told her something was very wrong.

# CHAPTER SIX

Daniel frowned. "I wore a hole in the rug pacing back and forth. Where have you been? I thought we were going to have breakfast together."

"I had to see someone at Langley. I didn't think you had clearance."

He arched his brow. "I don't. But obviously you do."

She nodded, offering no further explanation.

"Have a good night's sleep?" His tone was insinuating.

"Not particularly."

He narrowed his eyes. "Neither did I. Have a feeling we would both have slept like angels if we'd been together."

"Oh, I doubt that very much. Likely you would have behaved like a devil."

"Some people find devils very entertaining." His hand pressed against hers.

She'd never felt so physically aware of a

74

man and found it disconcerting.

"So where did you sleep last night — and with whom?"

Heat rose to her face. "That does not deserve an answer."

He slipped his hand around her waist, and she took in the masculine scent of him; it further disturbed her equilibrium. "We're going to spend the rest of the weekend together."

"As it happens, I'm working. You want to help me with Nora's problem? Fine, you can come along with me. But understand. This is strictly business. I refuse to become personally involved with you."

He gave her an I-know-better smirk and a brief salute. "We'll have to see about that."

She ignored his cocky grin. But when he held the door for her as she slipped into the driver's seat of her Corvette, his hand momentarily caressed her face and her cheeks began to burn.

Dr. Gerald Reynolds was Maryland's chief medical examiner. He was a calm, cold man with a waxed mustache who looked more like an undertaker than a medical doctor. Michelle extended her gloved hand politely as she explained her reason for requesting the interview. She also introduced Daniel as a medical doctor, which seemed to impress him. Daniel, for his part, followed the conversation with quiet interest.

"I remember the Parker case. It hasn't been that long, only a month or so. All sorts of law enforcement people hovered about on that one."

"Could I ask why?"

"You might well ask, but I don't think I can tell you." The doctor's face was expressionless.

"Who precisely was here?"

"Officers from the Maryland State Police, then the CIA, and finally even some people from NSA."

She furrowed her brow. "The National Security Agency? Why would they be interested?"

"I believe someone did say that Parker had worked for them."

She felt a sense of mounting excitement. "Strange, I thought he worked for the CIA."

"I didn't ask. They're not the kinds of people you ask questions."

She understood that very well. "Would it be possible for me to consult your records?" she inquired pleasantly.

"You'd need authorization." He seemed apologetic.

"I believe I can get it."

"Well, even if you could, the fact is" — the medical examiner paused to nervously clear his throat — "most of the information I used in making the ID was secondhand."

"Sorry, I don't quite follow. Is that because the family was not allowed to view the body?"

"That was out of the question." The medical examiner stroked his mustache. "You see, a visual identification could not be made. The body had been in the water too long."

He was trying to be kind, to spare her the gruesome details, she thought.

"What means did you use to identify the body as that of James Parker?" Daniel asked.

"It was difficult, but I was under pressure to get it done quickly." The medical examiner seemed uncomfortable.

"Fingerprints?" Daniel inquired.

"When I tried to take them, the skin simply peeled off." He viewed Michelle compassionately. "You seem like such a refined young woman, are you certain that you really want to hear more about this?"

"Yes, unfortunately, it is necessary for me to find out as much as possible."

"I eventually had to amputate the hands and send them to the FBI crime lab. They did the match. Strange though. At first I was told that there were no prints on file for James Parker. I had to ask them to recheck. But two days later, they came up with prints for a 'Jim' Parker."

"I suppose even the FBI can be inefficient at times," she said with an encouraging smile.

"Yes, but that wasn't the strange thing. You see, the description of the man didn't seem to fit. The prints belonged to a male described as five feet seven inches tall."

"And the corpse was a different height?" Daniel interjected.

"Decidedly. I judged him to be well over six feet tall. I took the measurement myself at six feet two inches."

"Quite a disparity. What then would be your conclusion, Doctor?" she asked.

The medical examiner met her direct gaze. "I would have to say in all honesty that I cannot be certain the corpse I examined was that of James Parker."

"Thank you, Doctor, I appreciate your candor more than I can say. This information will be meaningful to his widow. Also, can you tell me if death was caused by suicide?"

The doctor viewed her out of the corner of his left eye. There was a brief, uneasy silence. "I'm of the opinion that the man was murdered. I performed my tests very carefully, tracing the path of the bullet through the brain. I found no evidence to support the theory that the wound was self-inflicted." He coughed and then rubbed his mustache thoughtfully. "I probably shouldn't be telling you any of this, but as long as I've gone this far already, I might as well speak my mind. I told those security people just what I'm telling you. They didn't seem at all interested."

"Kirson didn't?"

"Not him or the others. But it's plain to see that a man who plans to commit suicide doesn't weigh himself down with diving belts."

She thanked him warmly. He took her hand, gloved in soft leather, and did not seem eager to let go.

"Was there anyone else involved in making the identification?" Daniel asked the question, looking displeased; he was very much aware of the way the ME was holding her hand.

"A dentist was also involved."

"I would so appreciate it if you could give me his name and address," she said sweetly.

A smile was the charm; he left her only to return a few minutes later with the information written out in neat handwriting.

"Please feel free to call or come by again any time, Ms. Hallam. We could discuss the case further. You seem to have a clear grasp of forensic science."

She thanked him again and left, knowing she would not return again except on business. The odor of the morgue lingered in her nostrils.

She caught Daniel's disapproving expression as they got into the car. "Something bothering you?"

"You were awfully friendly with that guy."

"Ah, I see. You actually have the audacity to be jealous."

"And what if I am?"

Michelle shook her head. "Madman."

"You're right. I am crazy. Crazy about you. You're so damned sexy."

"Me? Sexy?" She gave a throaty laugh, expressing her astonishment.

"You're the hottest woman I've ever met."

She hardly knew how to respond to such a compliment. "Time to visit the dentist."

"Then you better hold my hand," he said. "I've always been afraid of going to the dentist."

"I'm not your mother."

"Don't I know it." He stroked her hand, then brought it to his mouth and kissed her palm.

She fisted her hand, pulling it away. "I need all my digits to drive properly."

Parker's dentist was located in Silver Spring. Michelle did not expect much cooperation there. For one thing, Agency people were required to use doctors and dentists that were CIA approved. She decided to visit the office without calling ahead for an appointment. Ordinarily, she did not consider this proper procedure; however, she did not want the dentist to have an opportunity to prepare himself in advance. Catching him off-guard would be to her advantage.

As she hit the open highway, she became aware of being followed. In the rearview mirror, Michelle saw a large, black car following at a moderate distance. At first, she wasn't sure that she was actually being followed. Just to check, she exited the highway quickly without signaling. Yes, the black car was staying with her. She swung around and came back on the highway. She did what she could to lose the other auto, but it stayed with her all the way into Silver Spring. An uneasy feeling took hold in the pit of her stomach.

"What is it?" Daniel was studying her profile.

"We're being followed. No, don't turn

81

around. Don't give them the satisfaction."

"You have any idea who's following us?"

"I can only guess."

Dr. Garrison Taylor, DDS, was a handsome man in his early thirties. He had a full head of tawny-colored hair and large white teeth, which were an excellent advertisement for his business. His nurses and secretary were all young and pretty, and they obviously adored their boss — but not to any greater extent than he apparently adored himself.

Michelle was forced to wait a very long time to see him and was not in the mood to be flirtatious, which he evidently expected of all females. She kept her tone brisk, businesslike, and impersonal.

"It seems that you were largely responsible for making the identification of James Parker. May I ask as to the means you used?"

"I relied on a matching of the upper dental plate found in the corpse's mouth. It happened to be one I made for Parker."

"Was there a scientific procedure involved?" Daniel asked.

The dentist seemed annoyed with the question. "I looked at it."

Michelle made an effort to sound friendly. "Yes, of course, you would have to look at

82

it, but don't you make a great many dental plates?"

"Certainly," he conceded.

"And don't other dentists make similar plates?"

"Look, I don't know what you're out to prove, but that plate belonged to James Parker."

"And it couldn't have belonged to anyone else?"

"No way!" the tawny lion roared. It was clear that he was thinking who was she to question his judgment?

"Would it be possible for me to see Mr. Parker's records?" Daniel took over again and kept his tone calm and polite, but the handsome dentist eyed both of them with hostility and mistrust. Had someone warned him in advance?

"It's impossible to see those records. They were destroyed in a recent reorganization of the office."

"They no longer exist? How convenient," Michelle said.

"What's that supposed to mean? Look, I don't have to talk to you. And I don't like your attitude. I don't know what you're after, but you won't find it here."

She gave him a chilly smile. "That, sir, is perfectly apparent." She left the handsome dentist to his devoted admirers, not willing to waste any more of her time on this apparent dead end.

Back in the car, Daniel began talking about their conversation with the dentist. "I know you're suspicious, but Dr. Taylor might very well have been telling the truth. After all, there's little difficulty in placing a dental plate in a corpse's mouth. Even assuming that Parker was alive and wanted the corpse to be identified as himself, he could very easily have fixed his own plate into the victim's mouth."

"But then why were Parker's dental records destroyed?" She shook her head. "It doesn't make sense." There was obviously something more, something she hadn't learned yet.

Michelle looked in the rearview mirror as she started the car and saw that the black limo was still there. Who was following her and why? The Parker case entailed a lot of frustrating questions and few answers.

Daniel's hand brushed her thigh. "Let me know when you get tired of working. I have some better ideas for how we can spend the rest of the day, and they're a lot more pleasant." He gave her a teasing smile, but his eyes burned hot as meteors entering the

84

earth's atmosphere.
Michelle felt an involuntary shiver.

# CHAPTER SEVEN

Still being followed, Michelle set out to see Captain Douglas Maclaren of the Maryland State Police. He'd originally been called in to investigate the case. She knew Maclaren by reputation, knew that he was supposed to be a tough but honest law enforcement officer.

As she and Daniel waited for Maclaren to finish a phone call at his desk, Michelle decided his reputation appeared to be justified. He had a look of absolute integrity. Solidly built, he was dressed in an inexpensive, short-sleeved white shirt and conservative gray slacks. His hair was cropped short, his posture straight, and he wore a no-nonsense expression on his face. He appeared incorruptible. Then again, she knew never to trust appearances.

"Thanks for waiting so patiently," he said, putting the receiver back into its cradle. He glanced at them appraisingly, shook hands politely with Daniel, and then smiled at her.

"So you're a PI, huh? You look too classy."

"Let's just say I do discreet inquiries for select clients. Right now, I'm looking into James Parker's demise."

"Well, I'll help if I can, but don't expect too much." The muscles of his large biceps rippled as he pulled his chair closer to hers.

"Are you aware that although the identification of Parker's body was officially made, it was never conclusive?" She studied him, waiting for the policeman to reply.

Maclaren let out a soft whistle. "Hey, lady, you don't mess around, do you? You stab right to the heart of the matter."

"My time is valuable, as I assume yours is."

"I gather not as valuable as yours." He gave her a self-deprecating smile.

"You are aware, of course, that the FBI prints don't match those of the corpse?"

"Now wait a minute, they came up with some prints. Trouble was, they were for a Jim Parker, age eighteen. Some guys are still growing at that age."

"Yes, but how many inches?"

He shrugged. "Was there anything else?"

"Perhaps you could tell us?"

He leaned toward them. "Well, yeah, there was something. The original address for

Parker proved to be nonexistent, so I couldn't check back any further. I asked the Bureau for current prints on Parker, but FBI personnel responded current prints were not available for evaluation because they had been destroyed four years earlier in a periodic updating of the files."

Daniel's brows raised, but he remained silent.

"Interesting, since Parker's dental records were also destroyed. Don't you find it just a tad peculiar?" she said.

Maclaren scratched his short-cropped head thoughtfully. "Listen, lady, there were some very heavy people breathing down my neck on this one. I didn't get much of a chance to look into it. CIA security people took over."

"A man named Kirson?"

"Yeah, that was the guy."

"Thank you, Captain, it's possible that I will be back."

He gave her a broad, toothy smile. "I sure hope so."

She turned to Daniel as they reached the street. "Captain Maclaren seems co-operative."

"If that's what you want to call it." Frown

marks appeared around his well-formed mouth.

She shook her head, surprised at his reaction. "You could have spoken with him, too."

"He wasn't interested in me. That was clear enough."

"The man was just being polite and friendly."

"Too friendly." He took her arm possessively.

When they reached her car, she saw a big black automobile parked just up the street. She felt a chill slither snakelike down her spine. Quickly, she got into her Corvette.

"Speaking of friends, ours are waiting for us," Daniel said. So he'd noticed, too.

"Well, if they want to follow us, that's fine," she said.

"It can't be the same car that was following us in New York," Daniel observed, "but it's for sure the same kind of vehicle. Gives me the creeps."

Michelle silently agreed.

Michelle's Washington office, like the one in New York, was small. Her needs were simple. The people who used her services rarely appeared at the office, so there wasn't any need to impress them.

Her secretary had neatly typed the list of people involved in the Parker case, just as Michelle had requested. She looked at the names, addresses, and telephone numbers. The name Charlene Bennett seemed to stand out. She was the woman Parker had been living with. Michelle dialed the phone number, and after four rings it was answered by a woman's voice. Michelle hung up immediately.

"Let's go," she said to Daniel.

"Where to?"

"Banbury Cross, perhaps."

"Have I told you that women who talk whimsically in nursery rhymes turn me on?"

She felt his warm breath on her neck and quickly moved away. "I have a feeling there are few things that don't turn you on."

He kissed her gloved hand, and she felt the heat right through the leather. "Everything you do excites me."

She hurried out of the office without offering a response.

Back on the highway, she glanced at her watch. It was four o'clock. Teatime in London, she thought longingly. She was not unhappy in America; it had become a second home to her. Still, it would have been nice to take time out for a cup of tea, and she would have done so if she were not working at an American pace and anxious to see if she could locate Charlene Bennett quickly.

The Bennett woman had a garden apartment in a good neighborhood located in Arlington close to the Beltway. Michelle had to ring the doorbell several times before a tentative voice called out from the other side. It took a good deal of persuading to convince the woman to let them in. Michelle observed there were strong locks on the front door. Obviously Ms. Bennett was concerned about security.

Ms. Bennett turned out to be surprisingly young. Michelle estimated her age to be somewhere between twenty-five and thirty. Her flaming red hair was blatantly unreal. She wore heavy, dark eye makeup, which made her look appallingly cheap. Yet she had a good figure and was relatively attractive. The atmosphere in the apartment was heavy with cigarette smoke.

"I'm sorry to trouble you, but this really is important."

"Yeah, to who?"

"Mrs. Parker, as I told you."

Charlene Bennett eyed her distrustfully, screwing her smallish eyes into narrow slits.

"You being paid?"

"Of course."

"Then you ain't doing no favors."

"I always expect to be paid for my services, Ms. Bennett. I'm a professional."

The redhead threw back her head and laughed bitterly. "Yeah, then you and me got something in common. I'm a professional, too." She began to pace the room nervously. "What do you want to ask me? I don't have much time."

"It won't take long. This is for your time." Michelle opened her purse and removed a hundred-dollar bill from her wallet, handing it to the young woman. There was a definite relaxation in the room after that.

"Mr. Parker must have loved you a great deal to leave his wife and live with you."

"It wasn't exactly like that." Charlene Bennett avoided eye contact.

It was clear that the girl was uneasy again. She picked up a pack of cigarettes and quickly lit up. After a few puffs, she resumed the conversation.

"You want one?"

Michelle shook her head. "I wonder if you could describe James Parker for me: height, weight, any distinctive characteristics."

Charlene looked surprised and twirled a strand of stiffly sprayed hair.

"Didn't you already get that kind of stuff from his wife?"

"Yes, but I'd like your description. How tall was he?"

"He was a big guy, at least six feet, maybe more."

"And his weight?"

She puffed irritably. "I don't know. He wasn't fat or skinny, just kind of medium."

"Do you have any pictures?"

"No, he didn't like having his picture taken, had a real thing about it."

"Did his death shock you?"

"I didn't expect it, if that's what you mean. But we were already through, so I don't know what was going on in his head."

"Why did the two of you break up?"

"That's personal. Look, I don't want to talk about this anymore. Could you just leave?"

Michelle didn't think the offer of more money would get results at this point. She exchanged a look with Daniel. He seemed to understand what her look implied.

"I understand how you feel," he said in a sympathetic tone of voice.

"Do you?" Charlene seemed to be responding to him.

"This has been very hard on you."

"It sure has. Not that I should feel bad about him dying. He moved out on me."

"He must have had feelings for you."

Charlene shrugged. "Maybe, but he was talking about making up with his wife. Go figure. And it wasn't as if we argued or anything."

"Did he ever discuss his job with you?" Michelle asked.

"No, he was real secretive. We didn't do a lot of talking — we did other things."

"Did you love him?"

"Me, hell no! I'm too smart to love a guy. Parker was okay, better than most, but I didn't care about him. Like I said, I'm a professional."

Michelle took another hundred-dollar bill from her purse and placed it on the coffee table next to the pack of cigarettes. "Spend it on something to relieve your grief."

Michelle left her card and they went out into the fresh air. She could still feel the cigarette smoke in her lungs.

"So what did you think?" Daniel asked as they walked back to the car.

"That you're very good at getting people to talk."

"We're a good team," he said, gently squeezing her hand. "She seemed to be telling the truth."

"Still, Parker involved with a prostitute . . . somehow that doesn't feel right. Yet, one never knows. However, I had the distinct

94

impression that Charlene was holding back information." She resolved to question the woman again, but only after a more thorough investigation.

"I'm starving. What about you? Why don't we go get some dinner?" Daniel said.

"Yes, all right," she said distractedly, still thinking about the case.

"I know how you manage to keep that model-slim figure of yours. You just forget to eat, don't you?"

"Sometimes, when I'm very busy."

"Well, eating is my second favorite thing."

"Second favorite thing?"

He gave her a suggestive smile.

"Quite the Don Juan, are we?"

"Not really, but we could work on that together."

She decided not to play his game and concentrated on her driving. He in turn fiddled with the CD player. As she drove along the Beltway in the early evening, the autumn twilight turned into lavender velvet with a pretty sash of pink ribbon wrapped around it. She was reminded of a lovely party dress her mother had bought her when she was still very young. But that was in another lifetime. She caught herself in a moment of nostalgia and carefully put the memory out of her mind, neatly folding the thought away like old clothes that have outlived their usefulness. Dwelling on her childhood only made the old feelings of pain and horror return. She couldn't afford to think about her parents. She turned her mind to the present and glanced in the rearview mirror. She didn't see the black limo but had the uneasy feeling that it was still with them.

Michelle returned to her office on Connecticut Avenue NW, not far from where Harry Truman had lived before becoming president. She had bought into a high-rise condominium that particularly suited her needs. The upper-level apartment was small but comfortable and modern. The lower level she had prepared for business with sound-proofing in the private offices, while the outer, larger office served as a reception area where both secretaries worked. The arrangement was less formal than in New York, but it seemed to work out equally well.

"So where is the main office of International Consultants, here or in New York?" Daniel was looking at the neat lettering on the door.

"Our main offices remain in London. Two men are in charge, one who runs the business in England, the other who runs it for the Continent. They both worked with my uncle. The operation was long established there and had been operating successfully long before I took over. In America, it's been quite different. The whole idea of setting up an office in New York and another in Washington, D.C., was mine. In point of fact, our London people disapproved."

"So you're usually behind a desk doing administrative work rather than out in the field?"

"That's correct."

His probing gaze made her uncomfortable.

"Why are you personally investigating this case?"

She shrugged uncomfortably. "Nora is special. We're related by blood. She was my mother's cousin and also her friend."

He took her hand and caressed it gently. "So you have a sense of family loyalty."

She snatched her hand away. "Don't make me out to be something I'm not. I have no emotional ties. I can't afford them."

"Why not?"

"Shall we go inside?"

Anita was still in the office typing when they arrived. She was a plump girl with a pleasant smile. The secretary gave Daniel a speculative look. When he smiled at her, she blushed shyly.

"It's after five. You ought to go home," Michelle told the girl.

"I'm almost done."

"Did Ray call in?"

"Yes, he's wrapping up that case he was doing."

"Good, I may need him for the Parker investigation. Any calls for me?"

"I left messages on your desk. You had two visitors, though."

"Who?"

Anita's eyes blinked momentarily. "These men, FBI types, you know, crew cuts, gray suits. They called me 'ma'am.' " Anita giggled. "They were kind of cute really."

"Catch any names?"

"No, they just said that they'd be in touch."

"Thanks, be off then."

"See you in the morning."

"I'll be going back to New York on an early flight."

"When you come back then." Anita smiled sweetly.

Michelle liked the girl. She was reliable and responsible. What she didn't like was the way Anita looked at Daniel. But why should she care? There was no real involvement between herself and Daniel.

After locking up the office, she shut off

the lights and went upstairs to her apartment. Daniel followed her.

"Mind if we eat here?" she said. "I'm too tired to go out again. The girls keep my refrigerator stocked."

"No problem," he said with an easy smile.

There were pears and yogurt in the refrigerator. That would do for her dinner, but what about Daniel?

"I'll make my own supper," he said as if he could read her mind.

"Please feel free. I hope you don't mind, but I must work out for a little while."

It was extremely important to maintain her agility and flexibility. She disciplined herself never to miss a day of training even when she couldn't visit the gym or dojo. Uncle Ted had trained her to believe that skill in martial arts was not merely a hobby but could be a question of physical survival. Through the ritualistic performance of regular exercises each day, she strengthened not only her body but her mind. The discipline had taught her both modesty and self-control. She left Daniel and went into the room she had equipped for her workouts, quickly changing into shorts and a T-shirt.

She was sweating freely by the time she finished her workout and decided it was time for a shower. She heard a knock at the bathroom door.

"Dinner's waiting," he said.

"Thanks. I'll be out as soon as I've showered," she told him.

"I have a talent for scrubbing backs."

"I'm sure you do, but I'm self-sufficient."

"Your loss."

It probably was, she conceded.

He had a tuna salad on toast ready for her when she returned to the kitchen area.

"Are you trying to impress me with your culinary skills?"

He ran his hand along her jaw, sending a rush of excitement through her. "Whatever it takes. You smell good."

She seated herself at the table. And he seated himself beside her, legs touching.

"You'll find me handy to have around." He tucked damp hair behind her ear and set her nerve endings tingling.

They were finishing the meal when the office phone began to ring. She got to it quickly.

"I'm calling to warn you," a voice on the other end said.

"Warn me about what?"

"You better stop digging into the disappearance of James Parker. They'll stop at nothing to keep the secret."

The whispered words insinuated themselves into her ear.

"What secret are you talking about?" She switched on the tape recorder.

"I can't tell you that. Just stop asking questions. Otherwise, they're going to kill you."

The voice was gruff, obviously masculine, and most assuredly disguised.

"Who are *they?*" she persisted.

"You don't really expect me to tell you that." The line went dead.

Who was he, and how did he know so much? Would she be able to find this man? She played the tape back for Daniel.

"What do you think?"

He shook his head. "More questions here than answers. But I could tell something for certain. That man wasn't threatening you. He was definitely warning you, and he's very afraid."

"Do you mind staying here for the night?" she asked.

"I was hoping you'd ask." His eyes ran over her body hotly.

"It's not what you think. I want to make certain of your safety. Involving yourself by coming down here with me was not the smartest thing you've ever done, Dr. Reiner. But I think it's best if we stay together."

"I couldn't agree more."

"My couch is fairly comfortable."

"We'd sleep better together. I have it on good authority that I don't snore."

"And whose authority would that be?"

"My grandmother." He gave her a wicked wink that had her shaking her head in exasperation.

"I have a feeling this is going to be a long night."

"I'm thinking the reverse."

"I'm going into the bedroom. I have to clear my mind with my nightly meditation. TV and couch are yours."

She left him and closed the bedroom door behind her. Kneeling, she attempted to focus the energy of her mind. Her yoga exercise was meant to make her mind become an unrippled pond in a forest. Her thoughts imaged smooth water, reflecting all objects within range. She relaxed. In this peaceful frame of mind, she was prepared for sleep.

Then the telephone rang once again. Her mood shattered like broken glass as she hurried to answer.

"If you want to know what happened to James Parker, you will return to Charlene Bennett's apartment immediately." She heard a click before she could answer. The voice on the other end was muffled and male, but she could tell that it was not the same person who had phoned earlier to warn her. There had been the suggestion of a foreign accent.

Michelle realized that whoever phoned obviously knew where she had been during the day. She questioned whether she should even go out again, but curiosity got the best of her.

Daniel was listening to the news when she returned to the living room dressed in black jeans and turtleneck.

"I thought we were through for the night."

"*We* are, but I've got to make a return visit to Ms. Bennett's apartment."

His dark eyes were bright and alert. "The phone call you got? I did hear the phone ring."

"Yes, something's going on."

Daniel got to his feet and put on his suit jacket. He looked rumpled and tired. "I need to pick up a razor, so I'm coming with you." He rubbed the stubble on his chin, which would have made most other men look disreputable but just seemed sexy on him.

"We can do that in the morning."

"I prefer now." He took her arm, and she gave up trying to argue with him.

■ ■ ■ ■

They were cruising down the Beltway back to Arlington within ten minutes. When she checked her mirror, she found that the limo was with them again. She looked for license plates but saw none. With some concern she noted the other vehicle was getting too close for mere surveillance. She had a premonition and gunned her engine. The blue Corvette was not exactly new, but the engine was powerful and well maintained. The large black automobile was keeping right up with them. There were few other cars on the highway now. Suddenly, the limo pulled into position beside them. She knew what was coming. The limo was going to try sideswiping her car. She felt a hard jolt of impact. The heavier automobile tried to force them over the guardrail and into an embankment. Her reflexes were quick. Righting the car, she took off at top speed, leaving the other car in a cloud of dust.

"Were they trying to kill us?" Daniel's voice was raw with shock.

"There's a cell phone in my handbag. Reach in and dial emergency. Maybe we can get some police to assist us."

Daniel did as she asked. Her heart was

pounding. Moments later, the black car was beside her car again. She wished she could see into the vehicle, but the glass windows were tinted dark.

"Hold tight," she said to Daniel.

Foot far down on the accelerator, she took the Corvette lunging forward and began a zigzag pattern back and forth across the road. Finally, she had to straighten out as other cars entered the Beltway. Her nemesis closed in again, but she opened up full throttle. Without warning, she cut off at the next exit that led to a busy shopping center.

"This time, we really lost them." She breathed a deep sigh of relief. "What about the police?"

"I hung up. Didn't get through quick enough."

"Just as well," she said.

Someone obviously wanted to frighten her, possibly hurt or kill her. But why? She hadn't gotten any information about Parker that could threaten anyone. Kirson had warned her, too. Was he now taking executive action against her? He wasn't above that sort of thing, as she well knew. But she wasn't that easy to get rid of. Uncle Ted had schooled her well.

She drove back to her office-apartment, pulling the car into its assigned space in the underground lot. She checked the back of the car. The dents on the side and rear were appalling. Beneath the trunk, she found what she suspected she'd find: a small transmitter had been attached. She showed it to Daniel, and then ripped the device out and threw it into a garbage can. As they turned to walk toward the elevators, the large, dark car came seemingly out of nowhere rushing rapidly toward them. The bright lights blinded her eyes as she pushed Daniel, and they tumbled out of the car's way. Perspiration poured from her body as they ran into the security of a waiting elevator.

"Whoever these people are, they're deadly earnest," Daniel said grimly.

They didn't talk again until they were inside the apartment with the door securely locked.

Daniel turned to her. "I could think of easier ways to earn a living. How about skydiving instructor?"

"With or without a parachute?" She offered a wry smile.

"Listen, I'm just an old-fashioned kind of guy. Call me crazy, but I'd like to see you in a safer profession."

"Really, this is not typical of my work." Why wouldn't her hands stop shaking?

"How about I try phoning the police again?"

"No, don't. Let it go for now."

"Someone just tried killing us again. Don't you think we ought to report it?"

"Actually, I think it was meant as a warning."

Daniel pulled her down beside him on the couch. "Well, it worked for me. I am thoroughly warned. Once the adrenaline rush wears off, I'm going to start shaking. I need you close to me, very close." He placed his arms around her.

"Fear is a powerful aphrodisiac for some people," she commented.

"Give me Swiss chocolate any day." There was a twinkle in his dark eyes. It was good that he could maintain his sense of humor. "You are shivering."

"As you said, adrenaline crash. I suddenly feel very cold."

"I believe I can rise to the occasion."

She gave him a dubious look. "You have a dirty mind."

"What did I say?" he asked innocently.

He began rubbing his hands up and down her arms in a tender, soothing manner. She closed her eyes, relaxing and enjoying the physical contact, the intimacy. His mouth brushed hers; then his tongue began tracing, outlining her lips. He kissed her more deeply, fully. She wrapped her arms around him and took comfort from his warmth, curling her body around his.

That night, her vague dreams turned into a nightmare around dawn as a faceless stranger in a sinister black car crashed into her Corvette and pushed it over a cliff. She was locked inside, unable to escape, the car rolling over and over and then bursting into flame. She woke up shaking, the taste of death in her mouth.

Daniel, who lay beside her, immediately was awake and alert. "What is it? What's wrong?"

She shook her head. "Bad dream. Nothing worth talking about."

He pulled her against him. "As your therapist, I suggest you talk about it, describe it to me. It'll take the sting out."

"No, just hold me."

"What you need is to be loved by me."

She pulled away from him. "We didn't make love, Daniel. We had sex. It was wonderful. But there is a definite difference." She'd never felt the kind of sexual attraction she felt for him with any other man, but she would not tell him that.

"Sounds pretty cold." She felt his body stiffen.

She glanced at him through half-closed lids. "I'm not looking for emotional commitment. If you are, you're sleeping with the wrong woman."

"Right." He got out of the bed and left the room, closing the door behind him.

She did not bother to try to go back to sleep.

# CHAPTER EIGHT

Michelle Hallam was sitting on the desk in his office when Daniel returned from lunch. He stared at her in amazement, not quite ready to trust his eyes. He hadn't expected to see her again.

"How did you get in here? I thought the office was locked."

"It was, but I managed." She gave him a cryptic smile.

She was dressed elegantly in a russet-colored suede dress and matching jacket with cream-colored gloves and boots of calfskin leather. He decided that she could easily pass for a high-fashion model with her imposing height and trim figure. The red-gold highlights in her hair danced in the afternoon sunlight.

"How would you like to accompany me to the symphony tonight?"

"I'm strictly a rock music fan."

She looked surprised. "The ballet then?"

He shook his head again. "Definitely not."

"Now look here, Dr. Reiner, I've dropped everything to accommodate you. Is it possible for you to be a trifle more agreeable?"

"I didn't think you wanted me except to use as a boy toy." He was still angry at her and didn't care if she knew it. He folded his arms over his chest.

Her eyes locked with his. "If you'd rather I leave . . ."

"I didn't say that. On the other hand, I don't think I should let you boss me around."

"I see, so you're arrogant as well as aggressive." She gave him a look that was glacial.

He was tempted to say that if anyone was arrogant it was her, but thought better of it. "I'm not into ballet."

"Then we'll go to a Broadway show. That's my alternate plan. I've got tickets for a smash hit." She pulled a small envelope from her purse. "It's a mystery fraught with Freudian overtones. Just your sort of thing."

Patronizing, he decided; she was definitely planning to treat him like a pet poodle. "Not interested. If I spend an evening with you, I want to really be with you." He moved toward her, only to have her pull away.

"You're still annoyed with me, aren't

you?" Her lower lip curled up in a pout. For just a moment, she looked like the innocent child she must once have been. Such a sensual and provocative mouth, he was finding it difficult to maintain his stance of severity toward her. "I just flew back from D.C."

"District of crime? Must be a good place for your kind of business since you spend so much time there."

She overlooked his smart-mouth comment. "You're the first person I came to see." She put her hand very gently on his arm.

He tried to ignore the way that slight touch excited him. "Did you find out anything more about what happened to Nora Parker's husband?" He decided to change the topic to something neutral.

"It's all becoming rather complicated. I had hoped to have the matter straightened out by now, but it simply isn't sorting out. Has Nora been coming to see you?"

"Yes, she came for several sessions during the past week."

Michelle smiled. "That's good, don't you think?"

"Why did you send her to me?"

Her face flushed slightly. "I checked up on you and found out that you're very good at helping people deal with their problems. Perhaps you could tell me what she's told you."

"It wouldn't be ethical."

She sighed deeply. "We're on the same side in this."

"I'll just say I think she could be holding something back. I haven't been able to help her deal with her guilt feelings in regard to her husband's death. She keeps closing up, as if she feels personally responsible."

Michelle's eyes looked keenly into his. "Do you think it's possible she killed him or had him killed?"

"No, I don't."

Her lips curved into a Cupid's smile. It made him want to kiss her; instead he forced himself to concentrate on what she was saying.

"I don't believe she had anything to do with his death, but I had to ask anyway. I can't see her contacting me if that were the case. Are you finding any improvement in Nora's condition?"

"Unfortunately, I haven't. But we've only begun therapy. It all takes time." He cleared his throat. "And time is something Nora may not have a lot of."

Michelle stared at him. "What precisely does that mean?"

"Nora is deeply depressed. She might even be suicidal."

Michelle bit her lower lip in a troubled manner. "We must help her. I'll visit her this afternoon."

"I'll come with you," he said.

She stared at him in surprise. "Don't you have patients to see?"

"I only had one for this afternoon and she cancelled, so I'm yours for the day — and the night."

"We'll discuss that later," she assured him in her cultivated, commanding voice.

"I thought you wanted me as a sex slave." He studied the way her skirt revealed long, shapely legs. "Or are you sitting that way just to torture me?"

"It's you who are obsessed by sex, not I." She gave him a hard look, but there was deep color in her cheeks.

"We haven't been in contact for over a week and then you show up here today and strike a provocative pose on my desk." He moved toward her. "What's your intent? You're sending me mixed messages. Should I start calling you Delilah? Are you requesting my special services?"

She scrambled off his desk and agilely moved toward the door. "I don't appreciate your sarcasm."

"Who said I was being sarcastic? I thought you were vamping me. I was offering to service you out of the goodness of my heart. That is all you want from me. Am I right?"

"You've made your point, Dr. Reiner. And may I say you are being both vulgar and crude. Let's keep this a business association from now on. Shall we visit Nora?" Her eyes glittered.

As far as he was concerned, that was just fine. Okay, so he was lying to himself. He gave a long, hard final look at the desktop before leaving his office.

Nora Parker looked ill. There were deep, iridescent purple shadows under her eyes. Daniel also thought she was too thin. Her frizzy, short gray hair was unkempt and she was sitting in a stained bathrobe at three in the afternoon. He was disturbed by what he observed and could tell by the frown on her face that Michelle was troubled as well.

"I'm so glad you both came," Nora said.

He thought she seemed sincere.

"Do I have to pay extra for a house call, Doctor?"

"This one's free," he said in a gentle voice.

"My New York office gave me your message," Michelle told Nora.

"I didn't mean to bother you. I know you

have other clients to take care of as well. I just wanted to know if you'd found out anything new about James."

"Not yet. Did you hear from that man again?"

"The one with the awful voice? Yes, he phoned."

Michelle raised a sculptured brow with interest. "What did he say?"

Nora wrung her hands nervously. "Michelle, perhaps you better stop looking into my husband's death."

"Why?"

"That man, he said something that frightened me terribly." Nora reached over and took Michelle's hand. The bony fingers looked slightly arthritic, resembling bent twigs. "He knew about you. He said if I didn't stop you from probing, you'd be killed." Nora began to weep softly. "If anything should happen to you, I'd be to blame, just as I'm to blame for what happened to James."

"Rubbish!" Michelle said scornfully. "Perhaps that fellow means well and perhaps he doesn't, but I intend to find out what really happened to your husband. Besides, I don't feel I've even earned your advance payment."

"That money is yours, regardless. I'll pay

the rest whenever you want it."

"I never accept money I haven't earned. Actually, since you're family, I shouldn't have accepted a penny."

"No, I don't want you doing this investigation merely as a favor. It would shame me."

Daniel listened thoughtfully without speaking. He realized how little he knew about Michelle and how different their two worlds were.

Nora turned suddenly to him. "Dr. Reiner, I'm afraid I really am going crazy."

He felt a sense of alarm. "What makes you say that, Nora?"

She shook her head and began to cry. "I'm to blame for all the trouble."

"Why do you think that?" He gently took her trembling hand.

But she continued to cry and wouldn't answer. He helped her to her bedroom and got her to lie down and rest. She looked exhausted. After a short period of him holding her hand, Nora drifted off to sleep. He quietly left the bedroom and rejoined Michelle in the living room. Before he could speak to her, there was a knock at the door. He answered it quickly, hoping that Nora would not be disturbed.

The young woman standing in the doorway was relatively attractive; there was a resemblance to Nora, although the woman's complexion was fairer and her figure fuller.

"I'm Katherine Matthews," the woman at the door said to Daniel. "I'm glad you're both here. My mother hasn't been herself at all lately. My husband and I are both very concerned. My sister lives several thousand miles from here, so she can't help. I don't know how to handle the situation. Mother was always high-strung, but she had it all together. Since she and Dad split up, she's been a wreck. After we heard that he died, she seemed to go totally to pieces."

"She needs you with her as much as possible right now," Daniel told the young woman.

"I don't like to intrude on her privacy." Katherine Matthews's eyes didn't meet his.

"You won't be intruding."

"I suppose I could take some time off from my job if you really think that it's necessary, Doctor. Where's Mother now?"

"Your mother's resting," he informed her. He thought she seemed relieved.

"Good, she was restless all night. We heard her pacing the floor. We sleep right below her, you see. I'll just go then."

"Before you do, I would like to ask a few questions," Michelle said.

"You might as well know that I think

Mother is wasting her money on this investigation."

"Perhaps she is, and I won't continue if I find it's unnecessary. Did your father have any close personal friends?"

"I suppose you're referring to that dreadful woman he left my mother for?" The daughter's face contorted bitterly. "I could have killed him for what he did to her!"

"Did you?" Michelle asked in a level voice.

"Of course not. But I'll never understand him. He had such high principles — or so we thought."

"What about other friends, perhaps someone from the Agency?"

Katherine was reflective. "I believe there was a man, a coworker. Father mentioned him several times. He had great respect for this fellow's cleverness. But the man retired from the Agency before Father did and then they lost touch."

"Still, I'd like to have his name and address."

"Let's see, I believe he's a professor of political science now."

"In Washington, D.C.?"

"I'm not certain, but I could find out. Mother will know."

"Good, I'll phone you for the information."

119

As they left, Daniel thought about what Katherine Matthews had told them. He had seen an unmistakable look of loathing in her eyes when she talked about James Parker. Who else might have hated Parker enough to kill him? Daniel was well aware that a majority of homicides were committed by family members.

"Shall we discuss Nora's case over dinner?" Michelle asked. She eyed him warily.

"Fine," he said. "You pick the restaurant."

It was nearly six by the time he and Michelle arrived at the Midtown restaurant. They had compromised and decided to have dinner at the Caribbean Room, which offered a spectacular view of New York City at the epicenter of midtown Manhattan. Seen through floor-to-ceiling windows, the views covered nearly all points of the compass. To the south, they saw the spires of St. Patrick's Cathedral and imposing Rockefeller Center. To the east was the stunning tower of architect Philip Johnson's AT&T Building, now owned by Sony, and the sharply angled roof of Citicorp Center. To the north, they had glimpses of Central Park and Trump Tower. The view encompassed the soaring facades of steel, concrete, and glass. Even for a jaded New Yorker like himself, it was breathtaking. As far as he was concerned, this was the most spectacular city in the entire world.

Daniel admired the mahogany paneling, blue velvet curtains, and thick leather armchairs in a variety of understated earth tones. There was an air of quiet elegance and Old World stateliness to this restaurant. They were seated at a table for two. The waiter arrived quickly to take their drink orders.

"Splendid, isn't it?" Michelle said, indicating the panorama.

He looked at her thoughtfully. "Wonderful view, all right." He stared into her eyes and felt hypnotically drawn. Then the waiter returned with her order of white wine and his seltzer with a twist.

"To you, my mystery woman," he said, toasting her.

She laughed softly. "Good heavens, I'm not all that mysterious."

"Aren't you? I think it would take me a lifetime to get to know you, but I'm willing."

"You must not say things like that."

"Why not, if they're true?"

She looked away from him and picked up the menu, then buried her face in it. He didn't press her, but after the waiter took their dinner orders, he took her hand firmly in his own.

"I'll keep the chatter amusing and impersonal, if that's what you want."

"Good. Aren't New York psychiatrists supposed to be urbane and sophisticated?" The light caught the highlights in her hair and made her look like a newly minted copper penny, while that certain hardness about her mouth suggested the worldly knowledge of a courtesan.

"I'm not urbane or sophisticated, Michelle."

"Then you must be sensible."

"Not really." He wasn't very sensible where she was concerned. He hadn't a clue to understanding what went on in her head, and that was certainly a shameful admission for someone who dealt with the subtleties and frailties of the human mind. "I have this theory about people and their line of work, which I will share with you. I think a lot of individuals are attracted to an area in which they show a handicap or weakness."

She smiled as if she thought he was joking.

"I'm dead serious. Witness the weak eyesight of many artists."

"Or Beethoven's deafness?"

"Exactly."

"Then using your theory, am I to assume that all psychiatrists are madmen?"

"All except me, naturally. But then you probably won't believe me because I haven't behaved in a particularly sane manner where you're concerned."

She had a throaty laugh. He liked the sound of it.

The dinner was a good one, and she seemed to relax a little and let down her guard. But after the waiter brought her tea and his coffee, Michelle's mood altered again. He saw her stiffen. She was looking over at an older man who'd been seated two tables away.

"What's wrong?" he asked her, but she only shook her head vaguely. Her eyes were fixed on the small, ugly man.

Daniel watched as the man glanced at Michelle, a look of recognition lighting his eyes. Suddenly he was walking toward their table.

"Ms. Hallam, so good to see you again. How lovely you are looking." The man had a strong Eastern European accent. "How unfortunate that your dear uncle passed away. It is good to see you in such excellent health."

She nodded coldly. "One might say the same about you. I didn't realize you were in

123

America, Mr. Nastchenkov."

"I am here briefly in a diplomatic capacity."

"How lovely for you."

The man's face was deeply lined and as plump as a pheasant. "What an interesting coincidence running into you here, would you not say?" The man's light eyes narrowed in a shrewd, calculating manner.

"I've been trained to question coincidence."

Daniel saw a look pass between them that he could not decipher. When he and Michelle were alone together again, it seemed as if the night had lost its charm. Michelle looked distracted and tense. He took her hands into his own. They felt cold as a mountain lake.

"Shall we go?" she asked.

"Don't you want to finish your tea?"

She shook her head. "I've changed my mind about the theater; perhaps we ought to just say goodnight."

"I'll take you home," he said. "Better still, I'll take you to my home. You look like you need cheering up."

To his total amazement, she agreed. They took a cab to his apartment on the fringes of Greenwich Village. She hardly spoke in the cab and still seemed preoccupied.

124

"That Russian fellow upset you, didn't he?"

"Actually, he's part Bulgarian, part Romanian. If you ever see Nastchenkov — that's the name he goes by these days — and he happens to walk in your direction, cross the street."

"That bad?"

She grimaced. "Worse!"

"Don't tell me he's some kind of spy."

"I won't tell you. You're better off not knowing."

# CHAPTER NINE

The cab driver pulled up in front of his building and Daniel quickly paid the man, including a generous tip.

"This is a lovely old building," Michelle said as they walked into the lobby. He studied her reflection in the gilded mirrors.

"You've improved the place considerably." He led her to the elevator. "I have to warn you, my place is nothing to speak of, just a small studio."

"Sounds cozy," she said with a forced smile.

As he put on the lights, she glanced around. "This is really quite charming."

"You have good manners." He took her hand and seated her beside him on the couch. "Can I fix you a drink?"

"No, I'm fine."

"Good, then we're both ready for you to tell me about the real Michelle Hallam."

"You already know all there is." She

turned away from him.

"I don't know anything."

She suddenly looked angry. "Well, Dr. Freud, I suppose this is your way of trying to get to me. You must think I'm very easy because I decided to come to your apartment tonight."

"Sure, I want to get laid. I'm real horny, and all I can think about is getting you into my bed. In fact, you're sitting on it right now." If she could be offensive, so could he!

Michelle rose to her feet. "I'll be leaving now."

He pushed her back to the sofa forcefully. "You're accusing me of something that's obviously on your mind."

She tried to stand up again, but he held her arm in his grip.

"Let go of me this instant!" She was trembling.

He tried to take her into his arms. Before he knew what had happened, she'd flipped him and he landed hard on the floor, sprawled out embarrassingly. He let out an involuntary groan.

"Did I hurt you?" All the anger evaporated from her voice.

He let out a louder groan, this time just for effect. As she leaned over him, he pulled her down on the floor beside him. Suddenly their eyes met and they both began to laugh.

"I was going to ask you to give me a break, but I think you've already done that. Hell, what's a few broken bones between friends — or lovers?"

He brought his mouth down on hers and kissed her. Her mouth was warm and firm against his. They lay on the floor in each other's arms, hugging, kissing, touching. Finally, he unzipped her dress and disrobed her to the waist. He was excited by the small, exquisite beauty of her breasts, kissing and caressing each pink nipple in turn. She arched toward him and a deep moan emanated from her throat. He thought she was responding to him the way he was to her, but suddenly her body stiffened.

"No, I can't," she said, pulled away from him and quickly redressed. "It shouldn't have happened before either."

"Why not? We're two adults and this thing between us is potent."

She turned away from him. "It's best that we don't become involved. Becoming involved would only complicate matters."

"Not for me. But you are one hell of a complicated woman. I want to make love to you. I want you to let me. I just want you." He was as frustrated emotionally as he was physically but holding tight to his self-control.

"My, you're blunt."

"I told you I wasn't sophisticated. If you were expecting poetry, you're with the wrong guy."

She got up and paced around the room. "I ought to leave. I don't know why I decided to come up here in the first place."

"Yes, you do." He took her hand and led her back to the couch. "Let's just sit and talk for a while. I promise to behave. Honor bright."

She smiled in a way that told him that she didn't quite believe what he said.

"I care too much about you to try to force something you don't want." He decided just to relax with her and try some conversation. His instincts told him she was a very reserved individual, suspicious of people generally. "So what brings an English-woman to the United States?"

"As I already told you, I'm half American. My mother originally came from Amherst. She met my father in London when she was taking a graduate degree."

Good, at least she was willing to talk. "But you were raised in England."

"Oh, yes, that I was, but I was born here. My parents traveled a great deal. Father was in the diplomatic corps. When they were killed, I was sent to live with Father's only relative, Uncle Ted."

He didn't ask her about her parents' death; the sadness and sense of loss were clearly written on her face. "You're an only child?"

"Yes, and you are, too?" She gazed at him intently.

"That's right. Lonely, wasn't it?"

"After my parents died it was. But my uncle really was a remarkable man. He was a bachelor who knew very little about children, yet he was always patient and kind. He had to travel quite a lot. He knew a great deal about the world. Occasionally I went with him, although he never allowed travel to interfere with my schooling. He saw to it that I got an excellent education."

"He sounds like quite a man."

"That he was." Her huge green eyes were as elusive and mysterious as the sea. She seemed far away from him as she spoke of the past. "He lived very well. But there came a time when he found out that he was ill. It was then that he decided to teach me everything he knew so that I could take over his business. When he died, he left me something more important than money. His legacy was a way of life, a philosophy few people would have the courage to follow or live by. He actually tried to leave the world a better place."

"I don't know if I'm exactly following you."

She smiled in her cryptic manner. "I was rambling a bit, wasn't I?"

"Michelle, your uncle was some sort of espionage agent, wasn't he?"

Her face was suddenly devoid of all expression. "My uncle was involved with that sort of thing at one time."

"And you?"

"No, of course, I'm not a spy." She laughed lightly. "Let's just say I provide needed services for discriminating clients."

"You're being evasive."

Her eyes were fixed on the floor. All he could see were curly auburn lashes. "We do work for governments sometimes. But we take on many different cases. The firm is completely independent and not politically affiliated."

"Your work is dangerous, isn't it?"

She still would not meet his gaze. "I'm good at what I do. As I told you, I had an excellent teacher."

"So you actually are involved in intelligence work? Spying?"

She laughed again in that sexy, throaty

way of hers. "I just told you. I'm not a spy. I merely do private investigations. Of course, intelligence agencies occasionally do hire professional people. Sometimes their operatives don't blend into a particular situation, so they subcontract. People like myself who hold dual citizenship, and particularly those who are bilingual, are constantly in demand. We're adept at collecting information."

"So you're an information specialist?"

"Precisely."

"Isn't that something of a euphemism?"

She met his eyes finally. "You find my line of work distasteful?"

"It does take some getting used to," he admitted.

"A typically American reaction. The British have the Old World attitude. They prefer to keep the subject of espionage locked up in a drawer labeled 'things one doesn't talk about.' The truth is, I'm not an espionage agent in the sense you might think, because I don't steal secrets."

"That's reassuring. I already know you don't advertise in the yellow pages."

"We work strictly on a referral basis. Few people know who I am or what I do. Uncle Teddy felt discretion was the key to survival."

"And you're helping Nora because she's a

relative and a friend." He took her hand in his.

"I have no friends," she said, pulling her hand away. "I can't afford them. Emotional involvement is a dangerous complication in my line of work." Her eyes were suddenly icy jewels, faceted, sparkling emeralds with nothing to catch hold of. He found himself almost shivering.

"That man with the thick accent we met earlier, he was an espionage agent, wasn't he?" He saw her eyes darken.

"In a manner of speaking. Dimitri used to work almost exclusively for the KGB. These days he's branched out and does contracts for the highest bidder."

"He looked so harmless."

"Appearances are deceiving. Nastchenkov is a cobra. He is a cold-blooded, calculating assassin."

Daniel felt a sense of alarm. "Are you implying he had some purpose in being at the restaurant when we were there?"

"It was a warning."

"What sort of a warning?"

She shrugged. "I'm not certain. Possibly to stay out of the Parker matter."

"You seriously think this man might try to kill you?"

"Not at the moment, but you should know

that he is a murderer. His nickname in some circles is Vlad the Impaler." Her eyes met his squarely.

"Because he's part Romanian?"

"Perhaps because he enjoys torturing his victims. He's been described as a vampire on occasion."

"You know some very scary people, don't you?"

"Some years ago, there were two defectors. They came to live and work in London. Both worked for the BBC. The first one — let's call him Alexei — he was a young man in excellent health. One day, he failed to show up for work. A friend dropped by his flat and found him dead, face down at the bottom of his stairwell. The police dismissed it as an accident. When the second defector, Georgei, died, they were forced to change their opinion."

"Why?"

"It seems Georgei was walking near Waterloo Bridge, when in front of a crowded bus stop, he suddenly felt a sharp pain in his left thigh and turned to see a short, heavy-set man carrying an umbrella. The man quickly muttered an apology in a thickly accented voice. Then he disappeared into a waiting car. That evening, Georgei developed a high fever. Three days later, he was dead, but not before telling people that he'd been stabbed by a poison-tipped umbrella. The autopsy performed on Georgei revealed no poison. However, the doctors found a tiny platinum-iridium pellet with two holes drilled in at right angles under his skin. The holes could easily have provided an access route for a toxic substance, either bacterial or chemical and quite likely untraceable."

He whistled softly. "But why?"

"Because the broadcasts of these two men proved something of an embarrassment to the Russians. It's done all the time. Nastchenkov is a master at thinking up unusual methods of assassination. He once liquidated two exiled Ukrainian leaders in West Germany by squirting prussic acid in their faces from a fountain pen, thus making the symptoms appear to be those of simple heart attacks."

"I can't believe what I'm hearing. Couldn't the authorities prove anything against him?"

She smiled a hard, cynical smile. "Knowing and proving are two different things. Besides, Nastchenkov is what we call a *legal* spy. That means he has diplomatic immunity. The worst that can ever happen to him is simply to be declared *persona non grata* and politely asked to leave the country."

They talked on late into the night. He suggested that Nora might be right about leaving the investigation of James Parker's death alone. But Michelle was stubborn.

"When I make a commitment, I stick by it. It's very important in my line of work to honor my obligations."

"Your most important responsibility is to yourself."

"It's a matter of principle."

He found himself admiring her strength and determination. Before the light of dawn, they fell asleep wrapped in each other's arms.

He awoke with sunlight lapping happily through the one real window in his studio. It felt right to find Michelle enclosed in his arms. He stayed for a time, luxuriating in the pleasure of holding her warm, sleeping body. Then he gently lay her down across the sofa bed as he went to shower and change. He'd slept very little, but he felt remarkably rested and alert.

He was scrambling some eggs as she arose. Two slices of wheat toast were popping up as she entered the small kitchen area rubbing her eyes.

"Go wash up," he said, "while I put out

the plates."

She returned as he sliced fresh oranges.

"I must look frightful," she said, sitting across from him.

He placed his hand under her chin.

"Actually, I was just thinking how much more beautiful you look without any makeup."

"Ridiculous," she said with a laugh.

"Absolutely true. Gives you a fresh, girlish look."

"That won't do. My clients would quickly lose confidence in me. They expect a mature woman to handle their affairs. No, I better get my makeup on before I leave."

"At least you allowed me a glimpse of the woman beneath the mask."

"I confess to being at my most vulnerable at this hour."

"Is that a promise?" he said in a teasing voice. He gave her a quick kiss on the lips before she could object, then handed her a cup of coffee.

They ate breakfast in relative silence.

"How was breakfast?" he asked as she finished.

"You're quite a good cook. Wish I could say that about myself."

"Glad I could please. Incidentally, I'm good at a lot of things." He took her hand

and kissed it.

"Your cooking is what I value at the moment. Mind you, I could have done with a rasher of bacon along with those eggs."

"Never touch the stuff."

"Spoken like a true doctor. However, in my occupation, one need never be too concerned about longevity."

"For the record, I'm still very hungry, but not for food."

She groaned. "I expected something more inventive from such a clever man."

He took her into his arms, breathing in the warm, female scent of her. He tilted her face and fit his lips to hers. Her lips were soft and sweet. He tightened his hold on her, molding his body to fit against hers and she responded by moaning softly into his mouth. The fire between them took on a life of its own. She might not want him drawing too close emotionally, but once he breached the barrier, her true passionate nature came through.

The sound of the phone ringing jarred them.

"You'd better answer that," she said, pulling away from him. "It could be important."

He went and lifted the receiver, but as soon as he answered, there was a click at the other end. "Wrong number, I suppose."

Her eyes wouldn't meet his. "I'd better go," she said. He watched her gather her things together as he stacked the dishes in the sink.

By the time he had dressed and was ready for work, she was leaving. His heart lurched at the thought of parting with her.

He grasped her hand. "You can trust me. I have feelings for you. There isn't anything you could say or do that would cause those feelings to change."

Her eyes darkened like the sea at night. "If only that were true."

His kiss brought a response from her, but then she pulled away. "We should have met a long time ago, you and I." Then the door closed and she was gone.

He hurried down the hall after her. "Wait! You're not getting away from me that easily."

"I have to get back to my apartment, change, and catch a flight."

"Why don't I cancel my morning appointments and we can spend more time together?"

"Out of the question. We both have promises to keep."

He searched her face thoughtfully. "I'll get you that cab."

"All right," she agreed.

In the elevator, a silence developed between them, as if they were strangers. When
they got out on the street, he looked for a
cab, but there were none around, so they
began to walk. His building bordered
Greenwich Village, close to Washington
Square. They walked around near the Arch
of the park, where there were always people.
Two boys were throwing a Frisbee, and a
couple read poetry on a bench. They seemed
oblivious to the homeless men tented on
the ground.

"They've got a great art show here every
year," he told her, not certain what else to
say. They finally reached Washington Square
North, just west of Fifth Avenue, and were
standing in front of a very grand row of
Greek Revival houses that dated back well
over a century and a half. "We'll find it
easier to get a cab here. They're always out
along Fifth Avenue."

Michelle had just turned for a moment to
admire some porcelain and pottery in a
store window when he heard the sound. She
seemed aware of what it was before he did.
It started as a plinging noise that hit the
airwaves. He recognized it as nothing more
specific than a vibration of sorts. Michelle
grabbed him, pulling him down beside her
behind a parked car. He marveled at the

strength of her hands and the speed of her reflexes.

"Stay down," she said. The plinging sound repeated, coming toward them from some point in the distance. There was a crash of metal and glass in front of them. The car shielding them was sprayed by gunfire.

"They're using silencers," she whispered. "Don't move." From her handbag she removed a gun.

"Are you planning to use that thing?"

"No, I rather thought I ought to let them kill us instead."

"I'd find that remark amusing if my heart weren't pounding so damned hard."

The sound came again, shattering the tranquility of the airwaves above their heads. A few minutes passed, then Michelle peered out.

"They're gone," she said coolly. "We can go." She slipped the gun back into her purse. "I think someone picked up two men rather hurriedly just down the block. I suppose they thought it wise not to linger."

"Were they really trying to kill us?"

She shrugged. "I don't know. Perhaps it was just another warning addressed to me."

His knees were shaking as he stood up. He did not want her to see how unsteady he was. She turned to him and seemed to

141

understand what he was feeling.

"I'm sorry, Daniel. It really would be much better for you to forget about me entirely."

"No, I won't do that," he responded decisively.

"It would be safer for you," she emphasized.

At that moment, a cab came by and he stepped out into the street to wave it to a halt. Before he would allow her to get into the cab, Daniel pulled Michelle into his arms and kissed her thoroughly. She tried to pull away, but he didn't let go of her hand. "I've made a decision, I'm going with you."

"That is insane!"

"Maybe, but I'm not letting you go through this alone."

"You are wild, reckless."

"You think so, do you?" The impossible man actually looked amused by her pronouncement.

"Considering the nature of your work, Doctor, I find it truly disturbing. There's a decidedly self-destructive streak in you."

He cocked one brow. "And you're not reckless?"

She tried to tamp down her temper. "I have been trained to be cautious. I am ruthlessly careful. If I'm not, the results could be fatal. I don't run risks. You, on the other hand, treat what we're doing like a juvenile lark, and quite frankly, you stand a good chance of getting us both killed. The people we are dealing with are not amateurs. You are placing us both in danger."

For a moment, his expression was grave and thoughtful. "I see. Then it's a good thing I have your experience and maturity to rely on, isn't it? Because I'm not letting you go alone, no matter what arguments you give me."

"You're being obstinate and childish."

"Stop nagging. It doesn't suit you." With that, he grabbed her into his arms and gave her a bone-melting kiss.

"Is that your method of winning every disagreement?"

"Why not? It does seem to work."

# CHAPTER TEN

They argued on the ride to her apartment.
They argued at the apartment. They continued to argue all the way to the airport. The
man was impossible.

Kennedy International was crowded with
people, but her flight was on schedule. Michelle was still arguing with Daniel as they
boarded the plane. How he was able to get
a ticket on such short notice amazed her,
but he somehow managed it.

She tried very hard not to remember how
wonderful it had felt being in his arms. It
scared her to realize how attracted to him
she was. She knew she had to put that out
of her mind. It was all right for most women
to get emotionally involved, especially with
a man like Daniel, but not for someone like
her. A relationship could only end in disaster
for both of them. Uncle Ted had remained
a bachelor for a reason. She had to find a
way to end Daniel's connection to the Par-

ker case as much for his safety as for her own. She'd used poor judgment getting involved with him.

Michelle took her seat and looked around. The first-class section was fairly crowded. She watched with interest as a man in a crumpled, ill-fitting suit approached a group of foreign businessmen. She couldn't be certain, but the man had the demeanor of a diplomat. He talked in a soft, confidential whisper, glancing around furtively. The businessmen responded in excited speech. The man who had approached them appeared to have Slavic features. She pegged him as Eastern European. He gestured to the businessmen to be quiet and follow him. Suddenly, they were all jumping up, nervously grabbing papers and briefcases and then hurriedly leaving the plane. What could the emissary have said to make them depart so rapidly?

Then she realized what it must be, had to be. Her body tensed as she approached the flight attendant.

"We're about to take off. You'd better take your seat."

"Those men, do you know what reason they gave for leaving so hastily?"

The attendant gave her a puzzled look. "No, but I did hear one of the gentlemen say something about an emergency."

"I want to talk to the captain immediately. We cannot take off. I believe there is a bomb aboard this aircraft."

The girl's face paled visibly. "Is this some sort of joke?"

"I assure you it is not." Michelle kept her voice calm and quiet, but her tone and intent were serious.

"I'll get the captain."

"Michelle, what's going on?" Daniel had come up beside her.

"Someone intends to blow up this plane. We're getting off right now."

"Are you sure?" He looked at her in shock.

"I have well-honed instincts. Trust me on this."

"I never argue with women's intuition."

"Let's hurry, shall we?"

There was no point hanging around for explanations. She'd warned them; that was sufficient. She did not want or need publicity. And what if, by some stretch of the imagination, she was actually wrong? She certainly didn't want to be accused of being paranoid or, worse still, creating bomb scares.

Back inside the airport, Michelle arranged for another flight. Before boarding, she called Bertram to tell him what had happened, asking him to make inquiries later to find out if her suspicions were verified. He promised to let her know as soon as possible.

Daniel made his own reservations. He simply refused to leave her. The man was infuriating.

"This has become too dangerous. I don't want you with me. I promise to arrange for backup, some people with more experience in the field than I have. But I cannot allow you to endanger your life this way."

"I'm an adult. I can go where I want, make my own decisions." He gently caressed her cheek with the palm of his hand. "Don't worry about me."

Her skin tingled where he touched her. Why did she react to him that way? It was absurd. "I'm trying to do what's best for both of us. Can't you see that?"

"I think you're scared. I don't think you're as tough as you make out. I think you need me." The warmth of his eyes was almost her undoing.

She managed to shake her head. "You're wrong about me. I don't need you. I don't need anyone." She tried to walk away, but he took her hand.

"We'll see about that."

■ ■ ■ ■

She took her seat on Flight 307 in something of a daze. If there actually had been a bomb on the other flight, she had to assume it had been meant for her. But surely whoever was behind this wouldn't choose to kill a whole planeload of people just to murder one individual — or would they? It seemed insane, and yet she knew very well that such things did happen.

Daniel sat solemnly beside her. She had not succeeded in shaking his resolve to stay with her. He took her hand and steadfastly held it. She knew he was lending her moral support even if they spoke very little. During the flight, she developed a bad headache and realized its source was tension. But the trip itself proved uneventful. By the time they landed in Washington, D.C., Michelle was wondering if her reaction hadn't perhaps been a tad paranoid.

At the office on Connecticut Avenue, she found Ray Howard waiting for her. As she had with Bertram, she had carefully and personally selected Ray to work for International Consultants. He was a likable, highly competent operative. A huge, hulking figure with skin the color of café au lait, Ray resembled a great Kodiak bear. As a marine, he'd won the Silver Star and Purple Heart. Michelle had complete confidence in his integrity and ability. She introduced him to Daniel, and the two men shook hands in a congenial manner.

"That friend of Parker you asked me about did retire from the Agency. He teaches at Georgetown now. The Matthews woman didn't get her information quite straight though. The guy's field is international relations, not political science. Seems he teaches at the School of Foreign Service."

She glanced at the neatly typed fact sheet Ray handed her. "Did you happen to get a line on what this man did for the Agency?"

"The Agency's strictly closed to us on this subject."

"Not surprising. I'm going directly over to the university. I want to talk to this chap myself."

The blue Corvette had already been repaired. She drove out to Georgetown, admiring the picturesque old homes that lent a unique atmosphere to this section of the District. It was beautifully situated on the Potomac, with colonial architecture giving an historic feel to the area. She continued to drive through the old-fashioned, narrow streets, which were well-shaded by stately trees. Neither she nor Daniel engaged much in conversation on the drive. She began to relax and enjoy the simple tranquility of driving through beautiful scenery.

Up above on the Heights, many fine residences stood imposingly with their impressive gardens. The campus itself was steeped in history. She drove past the Healy Building, a massive structure in Flemish Renaissance style, which was the principal building on campus. She parked in the area designated for visitors, and they began to walk, passing the bronze statue of the university's founder, John Carroll, a Jesuit educator.

After stopping some students to ask for directions, they walked toward the Old North Building, which contained administrative offices. It was dark inside, and there was an odor of decay typical of old buildings. The plaque said that it had been built in 1793, and Michelle remembered reading something about Washington and Lafayette both coming here to address the university students.

They were able to find out from a secretary that Dr. Latimer was currently teaching a class. Hurriedly, they found the lecture hall and seated themselves at the rear. Most of the people present were young and fresh-faced, absorbed in listening and note-taking. Occasionally, the professor would turn to write some term or phrase on the blackboard. He spoke in a clear, well-modulated voice, and her immediate impression was of a clever, perceptive man.

Conservatively dressed in a Harris tweed jacket and black trousers, Professor Latimer looked every inch the scholar. When the class finally ended, Michelle and Daniel waited for the students to depart and then approached him at the lectern.

"Doctor Latimer?" She extended her gloved hand and introduced Daniel and herself. "I am looking into James Parker's unfortunate demise."

He gave her a smile, but his blue eyes behind his dark-framed glasses sparkled coldly, like a mountain lake in winter. "And how can I be of help?"

"You were a friend of James Parker, I believe?"

"An acquaintance."

She frowned at his lack of candor. "You were both employed by the CIA."

"We lost contact some time ago."

"Do you have a little time you could spare us? I just have a few questions."

"Very well then." Professor Latimer seated

himself behind the old, wooden teacher's desk situated on the platform, while Michelle and Daniel remained standing.

"Do you think James Parker committed suicide?"

Latimer seemed slightly startled. He removed his eyeglasses and pressed his fingertips against his sinuses.

"James was not the sort of man who would take his own life. He had enormous vitality."

"What do you believe then? You must have some theory as to what happened to him."

Suddenly Professor Latimer moved toward her, his voice dropping to a confidential whisper.

"If he is dead, James Parker was murdered."

"You say *if* he is dead. What do you mean by that?"

"You ask the most perplexing questions. I am only speculating. You must understand that. I really know nothing."

Her posture stiffened. Instinctively she knew that he was lying, though she had no idea as to the reason behind it. "You don't believe James Parker is dead. Please explain." Her eyes met his directly.

Latimer let out a deep sigh. "Yes, I do believe he is alive."

"You are the man who called Nora, aren't you?"

For a moment, he didn't reply. "I don't think I should discuss this with you any further. Doing so could be dangerous for me."

"Nora is going to pieces. Knowing the truth would make all the difference to her."

"I hardly think so. As Thomas Gray said: 'Where ignorance is bliss, 'tis folly to be wise.' "

"Isn't there also something in the Bible about 'know the truth and the truth shall set you free'? Obviously you're concerned about Nora or you wouldn't have phoned her. And you did phone me as well, didn't you?"

He would not look her in the eye. "You needed to be warned."

"Why?" she pressed.

Latimer shook his head.

"Can't you see my only real protection is in knowing the truth so I can plan a proper course of action."

"All right, I'll tell you what I know, but we can't talk here anymore. It isn't safe." He glanced around uneasily. "Let's go for a walk."

They left the building and walked out on campus. She exchanged a grim look with

153

Daniel as they fell into stride beside the professor. The sky was a brilliant blue, and colored leaves fell freely through the crisp air.

"I've been followed lately," he said. "I observed someone watching me on several occasions. I believe I'm under surveillance, and I don't want to take any chances."

She didn't bother to inform him she was being watched, too, reasoning that it would only frighten him further.

"We're willing to talk to you now or any time and place you choose."

He glanced around then shook his head. "Not here, not now. Shall we say the Capitol at three o'clock tomorrow? I'll be in front of the restaurant that's open to the general public. We can take a walk and chat then." He hurried off into the library building, leaving them to find their way back to visitor parking on their own.

"I didn't like the fact that he put us off. But there aren't any better leads."

"I think he does intend to meet us," Daniel said in a reassuring manner.

"I hope you're right."

"Hey, I am a doctor of the human psyche as you may recall." His eyes sparkled with good humor.

"After all we've been through today, I

can't believe you can be in good spirits."

He shrugged. "I don't like the alternative."

As she got into her car, Michelle realized she was suffering from a headache again. She pressed her hand against her forehead.

"Want me to drive?" he asked.

"Thanks for the offer, but I'm all right."

"What you need is one of Doctor Dan's special neck massages, guaranteed to relax away your troubles."

"That sounds very good, but right now, I believe we could both do with a bit of brew." She decided to stop off at a little pub on 36th Street and Prospect NW. It was filled with Georgetown students and a few of the professors as well.

"Friendly atmosphere," Daniel said.

"I ought to check in with the office before we get served," she said. She left Daniel, who took charge of ordering, and found a private corner to use her cell phone.

"Any messages?" she asked her secretary.

"A man called and identified himself as a Colonel Atwood. Very authoritative voice. He demanded to speak only to you. When I told him that you were out, he said you should call him back. He's from the National Security Agency." Anita sounded awed.

"Did you catch the number?"

155

Anita read it off, and Michelle made the call immediately. Colonel Atwood had obviously given some instructions concerning her call. She got through to his secretary on the first try and was given an immediate appointment. She wondered at the man's eagerness. It must have to do with the Parker matter, but she was puzzled about the connection.

She joined Daniel at a small, intimate table and appreciatively sipped the glass of white wine he'd ordered for her. This Atwood chap could wait. She liked this cozy place with its warm atmosphere. She realized that she very much liked sitting here with Daniel. Watching his handsome, manly features as he smiled at her made her feel that all was right with the world after all. Everyone around her, including Daniel, seemed to be drinking beer; she could not imagine why. But they all seemed very cheerful. The room, little more than a basement really, had a charming atmosphere. There was an enormous bar with beer mugs dangling from the ceiling. Old World War I recruiting posters and vintage sports prints lined the walls. Oars of victorious Georgetown University rowing teams hung over a fireplace. It was noisy but congenial and pleasant. She thought that this was the sort of place she would have enjoyed being at and sharing with Daniel often. But then she caught herself. What was she thinking? Any long-term relationship with him was simply impossible. She was being lulled into a false sense of security; it was nothing but a dangerous illusion.

By the time she had finished her wine, a group of students had started singing, and many of the other customers were joining in. They lingered briefly as she glimpsed a world where life was relatively simple, a life that she would never really know or share.

"Feeling better?" he asked.

"Much," she lied.

"Want me to find out if they have chicken soup?"

"Whatever for?"

"It's like penicillin, according to my grandmother, a general cure-all."

"A placebo?"

He smiled at her. "Not exactly. There are actually physical benefits."

"All right, Doctor, if you say so."

He shook his head at her, a lock of dark hair falling attractively over his forehead. "You're a card-carrying skeptic, aren't you? My grandfather has a chicken-soup story."

"Is that whom you get your particular sense of humor from?"

"Right, I come by it honestly. It's a matter of genetics."

"You're going to force me to listen to your god-awful story, aren't you?"

He took her hand, removed her glove, and rubbed her fingers against his cheek. "It seems like the least I can do after you've led me on such a merry chase around the airports."

"As I recall, you weren't invited."

"True enough. But I'm a sucker for a damsel in distress."

"I'm hardly that. Actually, I think you're the one in need of a bodyguard," she said. She was enjoying their little verbal sparring match more than she should.

"You're just trying to make me forget about telling you my grandfather's chicken-soup story." He kissed each of her fingers in turn.

She retrieved her hand from his grasp. "Please do something about your finger fetish. I think we'd better go," she said with some regret. Outside, she readjusted her eyes to the glaring light of day.

"You and I make a great team. We work well together."

She shook her head. "I have to go somewhere that demands security clearance. I'll drop you at my office."

"Fine. I ought to check in and see what's going on back in New York anyway. You sure you can manage without me for a while? I wouldn't want white slavers to carry you off."

"You have the most absurd sense of humor."

"But you love it, don't you?" He kissed her on the tip of her nose.

"Just stay in the office while I'm gone, and behave yourself around my secretaries."

"Does that mean you're jealous?" She knew he was teasing her.

"No, I just don't want you distracting them from their work."

"A man can always hope." He gave a mock smile that almost caused her to laugh.

Michelle let Daniel off at the office and then drove out to Fort Meade, Maryland, where the National Security Agency was located, fifteen miles northeast of Washington in the bucolic Maryland countryside. The complex here was actually larger than the one occupied by the Central Intelligence Agency. NSA headquarters was protected by three fences, cyclones with electrical and barbed wiring.

Security guards escorted her to the Office of Security Services. Colonel Atwood, it would seem, was the soul of efficiency; his administrative assistant buzzed her in as soon as she identified herself.

She was in the presence of a very tall, lean man of ramrod-straight military bearing. He wore an austere gray worsted suit. His shoes were polished to a perfect shine. His steel-gray hair was smoothly slicked back. His eyes arrested her. They were hazel, flecked with dots of green. He offered her a chair, but he remained standing, his hands clasped behind his back in an at-ease position.

"Miss Hallam, so good of you to come on such short notice. It is a pleasure to meet you at last. I had no idea that you were so attractive." He shook her hand vigorously. "I sent some of my people to your office, but as you seldom seem to be there, I decided to use a more direct approach. Besides, it was high time I met you personally. We had need of your special talents not long ago. I almost hired you then. I regret now that I didn't."

"May I ask why you decided against our firm? Professional curiosity, I assure you."

"Bad advice from what we considered to be an impeccable source. Obviously we were wrong."

She smiled at his flattery. "Obviously."

"You've never been here before."

She shook her head. "Quite a gigantic place."

"We're sanguine about enlarging our facilities further. That's why we're on over eighty acres."

"You haven't told me yet why you wanted to see me."

"I have information to give you. In turn, I hope you can tell me a few things. I want to discuss what you've learned about James Parker's death." He glanced at her from the corner of his eye. "You look surprised."

"What is your interest in the matter?"

"Let's just say that I'm willing to put you on retainer. I want to know what you find out."

She chose her words with care. "I'm certain you have greater access to information than I ever could."

His owlish eyes were grave. "Not really, Miss Hallam. You see, it was the CIA that investigated Parker's death. And we were not satisfied with the results."

"May I inquire what concern this is of NSA?"

He smiled again, but his eyes remained solemn. "A perfectly reasonable question. James Parker was, as you already know, an employee of the CIA. However, some years ago, he was selected to act as coordinator for a super-secret project started by the director of the CIA. The director wanted better and more realistic assessments of Russian military capability. He believed that the in-house staff of the CIA had become too complacent about Russian strategic power during the era of Glasnost. He decided to bring in experts from outside and give them access to major secrets regarding not only Russian strength but that of the United States as well.

"Parker was chosen as cocoordinator, quite a plum assignment, a real step up for him. To facilitate his role, he was assigned here to NSA. Dr. Robert Latimer was also brought over to act as a consultant on the project. Both men had been specialists on the old Soviet Union. Have you ever heard of Laslo Rems?"

She turned the name over in her mind. "Sounds familiar, but I don't seem able to make any identification."

"No particular reason you should. Rems was a very gifted professor from Yale who worked for us some years ago. He died under mysterious circumstances. It seems he owned a boat, a sloop. He took it out for a sail and supposedly committed suicide." His eyes met hers, and she realized he was waiting for her to react and comment.

"You think he and Parker met the same fate?"

"The thought did occur to me. In fact, that's one of the reasons I want to hire you, Miss Hallam."

"I prefer to be called Ms."

"Of course. James Parker had access to a great many secrets, as did Rems at the time of his death. I am concerned that there may have been, and still is, a serious breach of security. You are probably aware that our basic work here is in the field of cryptography — codes and ciphers. Our area is highly specialized and technical. We use electronic code machines and computers. Our security is very tight. However, we are not infallible. Someone could have sold us out."

"Parker?" She raised her brows.

"Possibly. That is exactly what I want to know. It's a matter of national security. Obviously, the CIA is busy covering up to protect its own people. There may be a security leak here. I can't be certain. Your firm has a spotless reputation. I want you to investigate. I'm prepared to pay you very well."

"I'm flattered, but I have to refuse."

Colonel Atwood frowned at her; he looked ruthless and intimidating at that moment.

Then, as if aware of what she'd observed, he smiled pleasantly. The smile flashed a lot of pearly white teeth; shark's teeth, she thought.

"I had great respect for your uncle. He was a legend. I know he had people working for the CIA from time to time, all experts in black ops, like yourself, I presume. We have a decided need for that kind of expertise here and now."

Black ops? Was he looking to hire assassins? If so, why? "Under ordinary circumstances, I would be willing to discuss your offer. However, I already have a client with an interest in this matter."

"Nora Parker. Yes, I know about that."

"Then you understand it would constitute a conflict of interest."

The colonel paced the room stiffly, hands behind his back. "Your ethics are commendable. I understand, although I cannot say I am pleased with your decision. Let's leave it at this, shall we? If you need help at any time, don't hesitate to call on me directly. What you've undertaken is highly dangerous. I promise to assist in any way I can."

She thanked him and then left. It was good to know that there was someone she could turn to for help if necessary. He was an entirely different person from Kirson, thank heaven. However, Uncle Ted's tenet burned in her brain: *Trust nobody.*

# Chapter Eleven

As Michelle drove back to the office, her cell phone rang, and she adjusted her hands-free headset.

"I thought you ought to know, Michelle, they did find a bomb on that plane you were on." Bertram's words jarred her. "How did you figure it out?"

"Educated guess."

"And your Doctor Reiner, is he being something of a pest?"

"No, actually he's not. He's trying to help me."

"Well-meaning amateurs are nothing but trouble. I'd dump him if I were you."

"I'll keep that in mind."

Of course Bertram was right. She would have offered the same advice herself. Daniel Reiner was becoming her Achilles' heel.

Daniel was pacing the office when she returned. "You were gone a long time."

She remembered Bertram's comment and decided not to discuss her meeting with Atwood. It was nothing that Daniel needed to know about. "I had to see someone," she said vaguely.

"You don't trust me, do you?" He had a hurt expression on his face. It was almost childlike, and she thought he must once have been an adorable little boy.

But she refused to let him make her feel guilty. "You don't belong here. You know I don't want you here. And the less you know about my business, the better off you'll be." To her own ears, her words sounded cold and hard, but, she reminded herself, absolutely necessary. Besides, keeping him in the dark was for his own good.

"I'm not going back to New York until you do."

"You're quite ridiculous. You do know that, don't you? What do you intend? To handcuff me to you?"

"If I had a pair of cuffs, I'd use them."

"Bloody absurd!"

"Kinky maybe, but not absurd." He smiled, turning his lethal charm on power wattage.

She shook her head, refusing to be placated.

■ ■ ■ ■

For the rest of the day and evening, they hardly spoke to one another. There were other cases piling up on her desk that needed to be looked at and assigned. She closed the door to her office, swallowed aspirin and water, then concentrated on her workload. Ignoring Daniel was her best course of action. Maybe he would finally take the hint and get out of her life.

But she found Daniel upstairs in the apartment when she retired from the office for the day. He'd been busy, she observed. The table was set with an Irish linen cloth, plates, glasses, and flatware. There was a centerpiece of red roses. Classical music was playing on the stereo. And something smelled awfully good. She began to salivate like Pavlov's dog. Food was not one of her priorities, but she suddenly found herself truly hungry.

Seeing Daniel at the stove caused her to gasp. There he was naked except for an apron tied around his waist, stirring a pot of spaghetti. And looking so sexy her bones felt in danger of melting.

"What do you think you're doing?" Her

voice was shrill.

"Cooking my specialty. I do Italian very well, Brooklyn-style. Your secretaries helped me. Anita picked up a few things. I thought it would be a nice surprise."

"You used my secretaries on company time?"

"They thought it was very romantic." The smile was devastating. How did he manage to look handsomer each time she saw him?

"I should dock them both on their salaries."

"Don't be so grumpy, sweetheart. Why don't you come over here and sample my sauce."

"You're not wearing any clothes." She felt like a fool stating the obvious.

"That's a blatant untruth. I've got this apron around me, don't I?"

The warmth of his eyes sucked her in, luring her. "Why are you nude?"

"I can tell you're great at interrogation. I'm protecting my clothes. Spaghetti and meatballs get messy. You don't mind that I borrowed this apron, do you? It's frilly for my tastes, but it was the only one I could find. In fact, I'm surprised I found even this. Women don't wear aprons anymore, do they? Symbolic of subjugation, I suppose. And you're such a liberated woman. But I

169

don't mind being subjugated as long as it's by you. Still, if you don't like me wearing it, too effeminate for your tastes, I'll just remove it." He started to untie the apron.

"No," she quickly assured him, "do leave it on. It's quite becoming on you, actually."

"Good," he said with a teasing smile, "I was sure you'd get used to it. Maybe I'll start a new trend."

"Somehow I doubt that very much."

"Dinner's almost ready. Why don't you relax, change into something comfortable while I serve the salad."

"I'm fine, thanks," she said stiffly.

"Liar. No, you're not. Plus, I promised you a massage and never gave it to you. You're wound tight as a violin string." He moved toward her.

"Please, don't touch me." She retreated from him.

"What are you so afraid of, Michelle, *ma belle?*"

"Bertram's right. You're nothing but a pest." God, she sounded bitchy! She felt like crying but kept a tight lid on her emotions.

He placed his hands theatrically over his heart. "Ouch! Direct hit. You consider me a liability. I understand. I disagree with you, but I do understand. I don't know martial arts. On the other hand, I do know other things."

"Could it be you were president of your debate team?"

"Some people think I have a way with words and ideas. Right now, I think you're one of the walking wounded and won't admit it. Let me help you relax." His mellifluous voice was rich and soothing. He almost had her convinced.

"Daniel, what happened between us the last time we were here was a mistake for both of us. We don't want the same things. It must never happen again."

"Wanting you is not a mistake for me." He reached out and took her hand, pulling her toward the couch, then seated her on his lap. "Maybe it's time I took this thing off," he said.

The apron went with an easy toss. She took a deep breath, feeling beneath her the hard evidence of his desire. She arched her back against him. It was perfect rapture.

"Ride me," he urged.

And she did. She rode him hard and long until they both shattered into myriad glittering shards, until they breathlessly fell together lying sweaty and tangled in each other's arms on the sofa.

Much, much later, they ate overcooked

spaghetti and slightly burned meatballs in relative silence. No meal had ever been so delicious.

Punctually at two o'clock the next day, she and Daniel drove over to Capitol Hill. Driving along Pennsylvania Avenue, it occurred to her that the Capitol was the symbol of the stability of American government. She was going to meet a man there who knew about a plot that sought to destroy everything the Capitol stood for.

"If it's any comfort to you," Daniel said, "my patients are being taken care of. Of course, I'm going to owe a lot of favors for a long time to come."

"It's all so unnecessary." She let out a deep sigh.

"Not to me," he said, squaring his jaw.

"You shouldn't be here. This is my case and my area of expertise."

"I don't intend to get in your way. I only intend to help you."

"There's an old saying, isn't there, about the path to hell being paved with good intentions."

It took quite a while to find parking, but it was still only two-thirty. She glanced at the art treasures in the circular hall of the rotunda. Together, they admired the great

172

paintings of Gilbert Stuart, Rembrandt Peale, and John Trumbull.

By two-forty, they were standing in front of the restaurant in the Capitol building waiting for Professor Latimer. She studied the fine tile flooring; the elegance of the white marble government buildings suited her taste for formal excellence.

People came and went. It was nearly three P.M. now. She thought about the excellent soup the restaurant served and wished she could stop in for a bowl.

"Hells bells, if it ain't my favorite fancy English lady!"

She turned to see Wild Bill Kirson leering at her. A cowboy hat was perched on his head, and the ever-present cigar, now unlit, was crunched between his nicotine-stained front teeth. Suddenly, she lost her appetite for lunch.

"Why are you here?"

"Free country, I do believe. Say, my wife's out tonight. Maybe you and I could go somewhere." He gave her a dirty laugh. Then he looked over at Daniel, and his expression sobered. "All right, that's not quite the truth. Tell your boyfriend I don't really have the hots for you. He looks mighty angry, and I don't want to have to punch his lights out."

"Who's the creep?" Daniel hands were fisted.

Michelle held his arm tightly. "Mr. Kirson, what is the CIA's involvement in the Parker matter?"

"I came here out of the goodness of my heart to deliver you a message. Your friend the professor, he ain't gonna meet you here today after all."

"How did you know about that?" She could have easily punched him herself.

"Hey, honey, it's my job to know things, remember?"

"Why won't he be coming?" She warned herself to control the anger that was building within her.

"Man got real scared. People keep followin' him around. He ain't got the proper stomach for this business. You'd be smart to get a little frightened yourself, darlin'. Drop this damn-fool business. Otherwise, you won't be hired by the Agency again. Fact is, you may never work for anyone again."

Inwardly, she called him an ass; outwardly, she remained poised and aloof. She would not let him get to her. "Planning to put more bombs on airplanes?"

He laughed loudly. "Hell, we're the good guys. We don't do things like that. It's President's orders." He removed the cigar

174

from his mouth and spat on the fine tile floor. "Why don't you ask your pal Nastchenkov what he's been doin' with himself lately? Might be real enlightenin'."

"Why the cover-up, Mr. Kirson?"

"Parker's dead, honey. Let him rest in peace. Ain't gonna bring him back with this nonsense of yours."

"NSA thinks national security was compromised. You are a patriot first, are you not, Mr. Kirson?"

"NSA? Damn those spooks! Just poking around looking for trouble as usual. It's nothin' more than a pissin' contest. They'd like to show us up. That way them people get bigger appropriations than us. Hell, they already get a bigger slice of the pie."

"Perhaps they deserve it."

"They ain't no friends of yours, honey lamb. Now me, I'm different, in spite of your uppity attitude."

"Did you know that Mrs. Parker thinks her husband could still be alive?"

Kirson's face turned white as a peeled summer squash. "You ain't gonna drop it, are you?" He chomped down on his cigar again. "Goodbye, honey. Oh, and just in case I don't see you again, good luck."

Latimer never showed up, just as Kirson

had said he wouldn't. But they waited around until four o'clock anyway. Then they stopped at a small café and had a bite to eat. Daniel looked a bit worse for wear. He was quiet and preoccupied. He seemed troubled. She herself was quite dejected. They barely conversed.

Michelle drove them back to her apartment, kicked off her shoes, and put Brahms's Fourth Symphony on the sound system. Daniel loosened his tie. She observed that his suit looked rumpled, but somehow on him the casual effect was attractive and only served to make him seem more virile. His dark hair fell in luxurious waves across his elongated forehead. She itched to run her fingers through it, but realized what a mistake that would be. Instead, she fixed a pot of herbal tea for the two of them. She promised herself she would be civil to him and nothing more. It was for the best, after all. The sensible thing to do. The music and tea soothed her; she would soon be ready for her exercises. When she finished, she would take a warm shower and prepare her mind for meditation.

It was then that the office phone rang in the apartment. She looked at the clock on the wall and realized that it was nearly six

P.M. Anita and Carol were long gone. She lifted the receiver.

"Ms. Hallam?" She recognized Professor Latimer's cultured voice immediately.

"Why didn't you come?"

"Isn't that rather obvious?" he responded coldly.

"We have to talk. Do you want to come here?"

"No, and not tonight. I've had enough anxiety for one day. Tomorrow morning at the Washington Monument."

"What time?"

"When it opens at nine. I'll meet you at the top. I won't wait, so be on time." He hung up abruptly, leaving her with the impression that Professor Latimer was a very frightened man.

The next thing she did was call Bertram back in New York. She knew he would still be at the office. Unlike Ray, he no longer had a family. Bertram had made the mistake of marrying a young, attractive woman who loved the good life. She'd eventually left him for a younger, richer man. Ever since then, he devoted his evenings and his days to his job.

She wanted to discuss what had happened today with someone who could advise her. Bertram, like Uncle Ted, was wise in the ways of the intelligence community. His advice was to follow through, meet with Latimer, and push the professor for answers.

She turned and found Daniel watching her. "Bertram believes we should try to meet Latimer tomorrow morning as the professor requests."

"I don't know," he said worriedly. "Something doesn't feel right about this."

"You don't have to go with me."

His eyes met hers, and she felt the electricity spark from him.

"If you're going, then so am I."

# CHAPTER TWELVE

They came early to 15th Street and Constitution Avenue NW to be assured of parking. Briskly she and Daniel walked to the center of the Mall area where the Monument was located. The tapered shaft, faced with white marble, cut cleanly through the brilliant blue autumn sky. They made their way toward the famous obelisk, aware there was still time to spare. Already tourists were lining up for the first elevator ride to the top.

"Please wait down here," she said to Daniel. When he looked at her questioningly, she tried to convince him. "You'll be my backup. Just in case."

"All right," he agreed, looking around uneasily.

She managed to get a place in the first car. At the top, she went and looked out at the view from the windows. She was patient and composed, waiting for the arrival of the professor.

Several men came toward her. Immediately, she was alert to the possibility of danger. They were very good and very fast. Suddenly, something cold and metallic was thrust into her ribs, and she gasped.

"Come along quietly or die here and now." The menacing message was hissed into her ear.

As he stepped off the elevator, Daniel immediately began looking for Michelle. He checked his watch and realized he'd been waiting downstairs for almost half an hour. She'd asked him to remain below as a precaution, but he suspected she just wanted to keep him out of possible danger. He thought he would be more help if he came up and met with her and the professor.

He heard a commotion and turned around. Michelle was involved in some sort of altercation. He saw her right arm, bent at the elbow, come up to swing back into a man's solar plexus. A second man was grabbing at her, pinning her arms to her sides. She raised her left knee high and drove her heel down into his left instep. The man let out a guttural groan. Lifting her right knee this time, she bent forward and drove her foot back into his knee in what appeared an effort at dislocation. The sound emitted this time was clearly one of agony. But the first man was at her again.

Daniel regained his composure and went charging at the assailant, fists flying. His fist connected solidly with a jawbone. The impact jarred him.

"What are you doing here?" she gasped.

"Thought you might need a little help." He pushed the man away from her as hard as he could. But clearly the fellow had good balance, because he regained his former position. Daniel saw the unmistakable glint of a metal object in his hand.

"Look out!"

Michelle agilely kicked the weapon from the man's hand. Then she struck a chopping blow at the side of his neck with her extended right hand. The man fell unconscious, the blow seeming to have blocked the flow of blood to his brain momentarily.

"I didn't need your help."

"Obviously not."

A woman near the elevator let out a shriek. Other people began to gather around, staring at Michelle and the two immobilized men.

"Come on, we've got to get out of here," Michelle said, grabbing him by the hand.

"You know what happens to deer that get frozen in the headlights?"

They began running down the stairs. My God, there were so many! He was totally winded and exhausted by the time they reached the bottom landing.

"Why wouldn't you do as I asked?" Her voice came in gasps.

"Sorry, *mein Führer.*" He traced her elegant cheekbone with his forefinger. She looked beautiful flushed and panting, even if she was angry as hell with him. "Maybe in England you're known as *she who must be obeyed,* but this here's a free country, partner, and I plan to make my own decisions."

"Don't you hear what I'm trying to tell you? When you put your life in jeopardy without thinking, you're actually making things more difficult for me as well."

He put his arms around her. "I thought you didn't care about me."

"I never said that." She lowered her long coppery eyelashes, refusing to look at him directly. "What I said was that I could not have a relationship with you, at least not the kind you are seeking."

"You know the theory of relativity? The crux of it is that everything is subject to change in the universe."

She shook her head at him. "You really hear exactly what you want, don't you? The longer you stay with me, the more your life is in peril."

"The way I see it, we all have to die sooner or later. There are worse ways to go."

"Bull! Death is always an indignity. You, as a medical doctor, should know that. I can't believe you've blinded yourself to the truth with some bizarre romantic notion."

"You're very sexy when you talk tough." He brushed the lushness of her lips with a gentle kiss.

"God, not now. Those men might still be nearby. I need my wits about me. And there's the professor. He might still come. I don't want him frightened away again."

"I'm staying with you. Maybe later we'll have a chance to really talk."

Professor Latimer came toward them and grabbed Michelle's arm. "Here you are. I thought I might have missed you."

"Why weren't you at the top of the monument?"

"I was afraid to go up. There were some suspicious-looking men lurking about."

Michelle appeared to accept his explanation.

"Come on, I've got my car parked illegally. You'd better hurry up!" This Latimer fellow was short on manners and temper, Daniel decided as they quickly followed him.

Latimer had the engine started before Daniel could even shut the car door. Then the professor accelerated like a race-car driver.

"I suppose you were aware that you were followed?" Latimer's tone was patronizing in its inflection of hostility.

Daniel took an instinctive dislike to the pompous professor. "Could be you were the one being followed," he said.

The professor didn't respond. Taking a determined series of turns, Latimer kept checking his rearview mirror often. Finally, he seemed satisfied.

"Where are we going?" Michelle asked.

"For a drive in the country."

They did not communicate again while he drove. Latimer's concentration on the road was total. He kept checking for tails in a manner that bordered on paranoia. He drove south to Alexandria according to the highway signs. From there he took Washington Street until it became the George Washington Parkway. Daniel watched the view as they drove about nine miles, past marshes and woodlands along the river-banks to the parking lot outside the entrance to Mount Vernon. Latimer parked the car and shut off the engine with an air of finality.

"You seem to be quite the sightseer," she remarked.

"The perfect place for a private meeting. Usually, they won't try anything out in public."

Who were *they*, Daniel wondered.

Tourists were everywhere, but no one bothered to glance at the occupants of the late-model, dark blue Accord.

"All right, what can you tell me about James Parker?"

"Why don't you have your friend take a walk?" Latimer suggested uneasily.

"I'm working on this case with Michelle. I know everything."

"That's correct. Daniel is quite perceptive about these matters. Please continue, Professor."

"All right, I suppose I must trust you both. I'll tell you what I know. James was a fine man, but even a fine man can be led astray."

"And you think that's what happened to him?"

Latimer did not respond to Michelle's question, but she didn't seem perturbed.

"You worked for NSA as well as the CIA, didn't you?"

The professor removed dark-framed glasses from his eyes. Daniel noticed that the lenses were unusually thick.

"I was an analyst."

Obviously the man was less than eager to talk.

"And what exactly did Parker do for the Agency?"

"Quite a lot." An enigmatic smile crossed his thin lips. "James was a pioneer in spying methods. Contrary to the swill being handed out by the Agency, James was on the payroll at the time of his disappearance. He was a man of real importance. Only a few of us knew just how important."

"But I thought he retired," Michelle said.

"Not so. That was just a cover. In fact, the day James disappeared, there were top-secret reports on board his boat, reports he was working on that no one else had seen as yet. They disappeared along with him."

"Classified documents? Couldn't the agents have removed them from the boat when they searched it?"

"Doubtful, according to what I've heard." The professor closed his eyes wearily. His facial muscles contorted.

"Are you all right?" Daniel asked.

"Your expression of concern is really quite touching. It's just my eyes. Haven't had time to have them checked lately. I believe my sight has changed for the worse. Even with these glasses on all the time, I can't see as well as I should and I'm getting rather unpleasant headaches."

"What makes you think that Parker isn't dead?" Michelle asked pointedly.

"In the months prior to the time James disappeared, many top-secret papers were removed from headquarters. They were sold to our country's enemies, whoever bid the highest. It was only after James was gone that the Agency became aware of what had happened."

Michelle was staring at the professor in surprise. "Are you saying that Parker sold out?"

"Not quite. There's more to it than that. You see, there was a Russian who defected. We've always known that a certain number of defectors were only pretenders. This particular man was strongly suspicious. He was believed to have previously been a Soviet agent by certain people in the Agency. When these people brought forth the charge, they were replaced. Some of us believed this agent was protected by one of our top-level agents who happened to occupy an important position in the CIA bureaucracy at headquarters."

"Maybe the Russian was providing valuable information to the Agency," she said.

Latimer shook his head. "That's doubtful. In any case, the mole was leaking information to the KGB. A secret investigation was authorized by the Agency."

"And the man turned out to be Parker, is that what you're implying?"

"It's a possibility." Latimer sounded impatient. "I can't be certain."

"Then you believe Parker may have faked his own death so that he could disappear because he felt that the Agency was about to discover his true identity, if they hadn't done so already."

"Remember, I didn't tell you any of this. You deduced it for yourself." His tone was sharp.

"Do you think he's in Russia?" she asked.

"One can only surmise."

The professor refused to say any more and drove them back to Washington, dropping them off several blocks away from the Mall. When they were alone, Daniel turned to Michelle, who seemed lost in thought.

"So this Latimer guy thinks that Parker was a mole, a Russian spy planted long ago who worked his way up to a position where theft of classified secrets was possible."

"Yes, and that would go along with NSA

fears as well. But there's one thing that puzzles me; why would Latimer refer to Parker as being a fine man if he actually thought him an enemy spy?"

Daniel was thoughtful. "I think Latimer has more to tell. Notice how he was very careful not to implicate himself in any way."

"Yes, you're quite right. He was holding back information. Is it possible, I wonder, for Parker to have found someone who resembled himself to some extent and then lure that man onto the boat, kill him, and then leave his own dental plate in the man's mouth for identification purposes? That would explain why the body was weighted down with diving belts. Parker didn't want the body to be found quickly, because he realized it wouldn't be identified as his. We could get a look at missing persons reports filed for that time period to try to determine who the real victim might have been."

"If that's what actually happened," Daniel said.

"Sounds like you don't buy the professor's theory."

"Just cautious," he said.

"Daniel, there's also a matter of fingerprints that don't actually belong to the man generally known as James Parker."

"So you think he really was a Russian mole?"

Her lovely face registered confusion. "I don't know what to think. I'll put my staff on digging up some more complete biographical information. I thought the Russians were out of the spying business these days, but perhaps not."

"Doubt that will ever happen."

"I'm afraid you're right," Michelle agreed.

Daniel accompanied her back to her automobile.

"Where are we going?" he asked.

"I'm driving you straight back to the airport."

"Not a chance!"

Her expression turned into a deep frown. "You saw what happened at the monument today. It isn't safe to be around me. I reiterate, your life will be in constant peril."

"I'd say you really know how to take care of yourself." He gave her a quick kiss on the lips, finding he couldn't resist.

"Someday I might not be so fortunate. I can't protect you and me. You're a civilian. Go home, Daniel Reiner. Your patients are in desperate need of you."

"You need me more."

She let out a sigh of exasperation. He took her into his arms and then kissed each

190

cheek playfully, finally resting his lips lightly on hers. The gentle kiss that he had intended became something quite more, deeper, more intimate. She was responding to him, warm and pliant in his arms, then she suddenly stiffened and pushed him away.

"Stop that," she said, her breath coming in ragged gasps. "Go home to your family, your patients, and your friends."

"When you come with me."

"You're totally impossible."

"Just so long as it's total. Look, my partner is taking my appointments until I get back. He also thinks that I'm crazy chasing after you, but I can't seem to help myself. Take pity on a man who's totally lost it over you."

She finally surrendered to his persistence and drove him back to her office. Ray Howard, whom Daniel had instantly liked better than Bertram, was waiting for Michelle. Ray didn't ask any questions; he just instinctively seemed to sense what the relationship was between himself and Michelle. Daniel liked the man's friendly smile and accepting attitude.

Ray was with them when the call from Charlene Bennett came. He could only hear Michelle's end of it, but it was obvious she was eager to meet with the woman.

"I've set up a meeting with Charlene for tonight," she told them, hanging up the receiver. "The lady says she has information to sell."

"Great," Daniel responded, "I'll go with you."

"I'd prefer to have Ray."

"Whatever you say," Ray responded. "You're the boss."

"The three of us can go," Daniel said.

Michelle glared at him. "You're going back to New York this afternoon."

"No way!"

"If there are too many of us, Charlene will get nervous," Michelle said firmly.

Ray looked from her to him and then cleared his throat.

"To tell the truth, my wife's been complaining lately about my late work hours. The woman's insanely jealous. Thinks I'm getting some sugar on the side. I did kind of promise to take her out tonight."

Daniel appreciated Ray's sensitivity to the situation. He wanted to thank him.

"Of course," Michelle said evenly. "I do demand a lot of overtime. I'll go myself."

"With me," Daniel quickly interjected.

Dee Dee's Place was crowded and noisy. The music was at an ear-shattering intensity.

Lots of couples were dancing; others sat at tables drinking tall alcoholic concoctions.

"Come here often?" he asked Michelle.

She shook her head at him. "Hardly my cup of tea, but it is the hottest nightspot in the D.C. area these days. Big on singles action."

"Think Parker came here with Charlene?"

"I can't imagine it," Michelle said.

They sat down at the bar. He ordered ginger ale for himself and white wine for Michelle. There was no sign of Charlene Bennett. When the short, fat bartender returned with their drinks, she asked if he knew Charlene.

"How the hell should I know?" came the rude reply.

"Don't speak that way to a lady," Daniel said angrily.

"I'm certain the gentleman was not intentionally insulting, were you?" Michelle put a crisp fifty-dollar bill on the counter.

"Well, come to think of it, maybe I do know this girl. You ain't connected with vice, are you? I mean you don't look like cops." He eyed the bill with obvious interest.

"We're friends of Charlene. She asked us to come here and meet with her tonight."

"Yeah, a redhead, right? She comes

around to hustle sometimes."

"Has she been in tonight?"

"Not that I noticed." The bartender looked up at them. "Anything else?"

"No, we'll just sip our drinks," Michelle responded.

The bartender quickly grabbed the money off the counter and moved on to another customer. They couldn't really talk; the music was earsplitting, and so time seemed to drag on. A half hour passed and the phone at the counter began to ring. It was several minutes before the bartender got to it. He talked for a few moments, and then came over to Michelle.

"Hey, lady, is your name Hallam?"

She nodded her head.

"Well, someone wants to talk to you."

Michelle picked up the receiver immediately and did more listening than speaking. When she got off the phone, she turned to Daniel. "She wants me to meet her."

They climbed into Michelle's blue Corvette and she drove around for a while just to make sure no one was following. Then they drove out on Route 1 to a motel in Alexandria called The Citadel. Daniel found it a sleazy place, but well-named, since the building was constructed of sturdy stucco in an architectural style reminiscent of the Alamo.

Charlene's room was comfortable enough. She let them in and promptly plopped down on her unmade bed. A glass on the nightstand was overflowing with half-smoked cigarettes. Michelle sat down on a straight-backed chair. Daniel stood by the dresser. He studied the young woman. She looked worse than the last time they'd seen her. She was heavily made-up, but he observed shadows beneath her eyes, and her expression was grim. Her black leather miniskirt was tight-fitting, and her nipples were outlined suggestively by the skimpy red top she wore. Could Parker have really found her attractive? She was young and sexy, while Nora was neither. But the image was one of a cheap prostitute, which caused him to question Parker's reasoning. Charlene just wasn't the kind of woman men left their wives for. It didn't add up.

Charlene chewed her lower lip and glanced over at Daniel. "Why is he here?"

"He's my associate. Remember?"

"Yeah, okay. He's nicer than you, anyway."

"Let's discuss what you're doing here instead of your own apartment."

"I'm in trouble," Charlene said simply.

"What kind of trouble?"

"Someone wants me dead."

Michelle was suddenly silent and still. Then she took a deep breath and spoke again.

"Why?"

"Because this party thinks I'm gonna tell you certain things about Parker and me."

"And are you?"

Charlene jumped up from the bed. "Just how long do you think I'd live if I told you?"

"If you tell us everything you know, I'll guarantee you protection."

"Yeah? And just how are you gonna take care of me?" She lit up a cigarette. He observed that the girl's hands were trembling.

"I have exceptional people working for me. You'll be well-guarded."

"You gotta do better than that."

"What does that mean?" Michelle was totally cool and collected.

"It means money. Lots of money. I need it to get out of here and start over somewhere else."

"Just how much money are we talking about?" The tone was still detached, but the concentration seemed keen.

"A hundred thousand dollars."

"My client cannot afford that sum of money," Michelle said coldly.

"Well, I guess I know who can."

"Greedy little girls end up dead."

Charlene's eyes narrowed. "Are you threatening me or something?"

"Hardly, but if you're considering blackmail, it's a highly dangerous game. Don't deal with anyone just yet. I'll see what I can arrange. Mrs. Parker is not independently wealthy, but she does have some assets. Perhaps we can manage something. Meanwhile, I'll arrange to have someone keep an eye on you around the clock."

Charlene's small eyes screwed into bullets. "Don't send anyone until you get me the money. I mean it!"

"You can get what you're asking for. Just be reasonable. It takes time to put that kind of money together."

"I can't wait very long. All right, fifty thousand, but I want it all in cash and fast."

"I'll be on the plane to New York tomorrow. If you decide not to stay here, leave a number at the office where you can be reached. If you don't leave, I'll come back here with the money."

"I plan to move around, so I'll be in touch."

"All right. We'll be able to do business."

After they got back to the car, Michelle

197

turned to him. "What did you think of her story?"

"She's definitely frightened."

"She and Latimer both," Michelle agreed. "I'll have Ray put her under surveillance. We might learn something."

Back at Michelle's apartment, Daniel had a cup of coffee while she phoned Nora Parker in New York. When she joined him, her sensual mouth was set in a deep frown.

"What's wrong?" he asked.

"It's Nora. Her daughter told me she tried to commit suicide. They've got her in the hospital."

He stood up. "How is she?"

"Touch and go. Feel like going back to New York tonight?"

"I'm ready right now," he told her.

Michelle arranged for a night flight, and they left hurriedly. They napped briefly on route. He held her hand and dreamed of making love to her. The dream was very vivid and when he awoke, the wanting didn't stop. Her head was on his shoulder; the copper of her hair gleaming. Her face in repose looked innocent and vulnerable, almost childlike. He kissed her awake, and she smiled up at him. At that moment, he could almost believe she loved him.

■ ■ ■ ■

They were both very tired by the time the cab pulled up to her fashionable Manhattan apartment in the East Eighties.

"Want me to come up with you?" he asked, knowing in advance what the answer would be.

"I'm in a bad mood for company, Daniel. I just want to get some sleep so I can get to the hospital early tomorrow."

"I'll meet you there," he told her.

In spite of feeling tired, he didn't get much rest when he finally settled in back at his own place. His thoughts were troubled. Had his obsession with Michelle nearly cost the life of Nora, his patient? That would be unforgivable. True, his partner had been available, but Nora's bond was with him. He was the doctor she was counting on.

The following morning was foggy and drizzly. He had slept later than he'd intended. Outside his building, the fog protectively spread itself over the street like a white-plumed egret fluttering its wings over a nest of birdlings. The chill set into his bones. He pulled his raincoat tightly around his body and hailed a cab.

Daniel surveyed the vast hospital complex

after paying the driver. No matter how many times he came to Bellevue, he was always struck by the sheer enormity of the place, fully aware that it was the largest hospital in Manhattan and one of the largest in the United States.

He got right to the job of seeing to his patient. By the time Michelle joined him at the hospital, he could give her a full report on Nora's condition.

"Physically, she's out of danger. Emotionally, that's another thing entirely. She's been asking for you."

"Do you have any of the details?"

"She took an overdose of barbiturates. Apparently, she had a bottle of sleeping pills stashed away for the occasion. Katherine found her sprawled on the bathroom floor. Luckily the paramedics got to her in time."

"Will she be all right?" Michelle's bright orbs were like searchlights.

"Physically, sure. But I can't promise that she won't try again. I'm putting her on anti-depressant drugs. I'll have to experiment a little to find the right one to help her."

"Can I see her now?"

"Yes, but take care what you say."

She gave him a look that said he'd made an unnecessary request.

Daniel followed Michelle into the hospital

room. Nora's face looked pale even against the starched white pillowcase.

"How are you feeling?" Michelle asked as the older woman's gaze came to rest on her face.

"Terrible. It would have been much better for everyone if I'd succeeded in killing myself."

"How awful of you to think that way." Michelle took Nora's weak, unresponsive hand in her own strong ones.

"Everything that's happened is my fault. I can't change any of it, but I thought I could make it right. I even bungled that." Nora turned her face into the pillow. "Michelle, I want you to stop the investigation. Stop it, immediately. Do you hear me?"

"Why?"

"Because something horrible will happen to you, and it will all be my fault." Nora started to cry in anguished, choking sobs.

Daniel tried to comfort her by gently pressing her hand in his own. "Why should anything happen to Michelle?" he asked.

"That man called again. He told me you were in great danger, that they had already tried to kill you and failed, that they would try again, that I must stop you."

"Who are *they?*" Michelle asked.

Nora shook her head weakly. "Michelle, I

never should have asked you to find out what happened. I started something terrible."

"No, it's not like that at all. Please don't worry about me. I'm an adult, just as James was, and I make my own decisions. I have a commitment to see this thing through. I think the implications of your husband's disappearance go far beyond what we might imagine."

"What have I gotten you in to?"

"I'm sorry, Nora, but there is something I must discuss with you now. We have an informant who is willing to sell us vital information for a price. Do you wish to pay?"

"Do you really want me to do it?"

Their eyes met.

"Yes."

"Then you have my authorization. My daughter will write the check for you. I hope I'm doing the right thing. If I shouldn't be here when this thing finally resolves, well, I trust you to do whatever is right."

"You will be here," Michelle said, her voice ringing with conviction.

"I'll see to that," Daniel reassured her.

"I'm very tired now," Nora said, closing her eyes. She looked like an iguana sleepily sunning itself on a rock. But the peaceful image was misleading, as Daniel so well knew. Gently, he adjusted the IV, slowing the flow. Then he followed Michelle out of the room.

"She'll sleep for a while now. Hopefully, the rest will calm her."

"I'm going to call on Katherine."

"Good idea."

He arranged with Michelle to meet at his office at one o'clock.

She was waiting promptly at the appointed time.

"You look beautiful as always," he said with a smile. "I would like to take you out for lunch. Have you any suggestions?"

She was pensive. "There's a little French restaurant I like. They do have an excellent meal, and it's quiet enough so we can talk privately."

He took her hand. "As long as we're together."

The sky above them was a battleship gray as they walked along the street. The threatening weather seemed appropriate to their somber mood. The restaurant, on West 51st Street, was charming, just as Michelle had suggested. André, the owner, personally led them to their table while his rotund wife surveyed them from the kitchen. There was Gallic warmth and hospitality here, and the atmosphere was intimate. They sat in a corner booth by themselves. The room was dark and quiet with French music unobtrusively piped in.

There was a small candle burning. Daniel let the waiter select a beef bordelaise for him, not caring particularly about the cuisine. He held Michelle's hand and didn't take his eyes from her face. She didn't seem interested in food, either. But her mind wasn't on romance.

"Daniel, I am very much afraid that Nora is going to try suicide again just as soon as she possibly can." Her eyes seemed dark and depthless. "What is your take on the situation?"

He soberly contemplated her words. "I tend to agree with you."

"Well, then, can't you have her kept at the hospital for observation, at least until she's in a better frame of mind?"

He wrinkled his forehead in concern. "I've already looked into that possibility. They will only keep her in the hospital for three additional days."

"But why?"

"It's a crowded facility. It serves a big city. They need the bed space. She could harm herself, that's true. But some of those brought in are dangerous to others as well as themselves. It's a matter of priorities." He knew he sounded defensive as well as apologetic. "The new medication may show some results soon. I told Katherine that over the phone when she called earlier. I also tried to convince her to put Nora into an institution after her mother's discharge. I'm afraid I upset her. Did she mention it to you?"

"No, but that does sound drastic."

"I mean it only as a temporary measure, just until Nora comes out of her depression."

"Did she agree?"

"No. Katherine wants her mother back home. Her husband follows Katherine's lead. They've decided to get her a day nurse and have Nora sleep in their guest room. Katherine's already arranged for a leave from her job."

"But you don't think that will be enough?"

"Michelle, if someone is determined to die, they can always find a way."

Her expression was contemplative. "So what you're really saying is that Nora's safety is assured for only the time she remains in the hospital. No more than three days."

"I suppose that's right. She'll be restrained there, and the staff is well-trained, so nothing will happen while she's being supervised. Once she leaves, who can say? But I will be working with her every day, and I'll make certain she gets an extremely competent nurse. Besides that, I can't make you any promises."

Michelle sighed deeply. When their food arrived, she ate with something less than enthusiasm, pushing food listlessly around on her plate, although everything was truly excellent. As they waited for coffee, he took her hand and searched her eyes.

"I've been thinking a great deal about you. Maybe this isn't the right time or place to tell you this, but I care about you very deeply. The fact is, I love you. I believe I loved you from that first afternoon we spent together in France."

She stared at him in shock, and he knew he'd made a serious blunder telling her how he felt. It was clearly too soon and neither the right place nor time. For a man who prided himself on sensitivity to the feelings of others, how could he have allowed himself to blurt out his feelings that way? Then the waiter arrived with chocolate mousse for him, an apple with Camembert for her. Dessert momentarily saved the embarrassment of further conversation.

"I just wish you wouldn't make things difficult for me. I don't want you to love me, Daniel. And I don't want to love any man. Relationships make life much too complicated. So please, don't ever talk this way to me again."

"I don't see why it couldn't work for us."

"It simply is not possible. You and I barely know each other. I need to have my freedom, my independence. Relationships are steel chains forged in guilt. Please, don't look at me that way. I don't think I can bear it. Your eyes are like open graves, and I am afraid I'm going to be buried in them."

He tried not to show his hurt. "Our relationship would be whatever you wanted it to be. I'd never try to control you. What are you so afraid of?"

"There are so many things you can't possibly understand."

"Why won't you trust me?" He took her hand again and tried to kiss it, but she quickly pulled away. "Come on, I'll escort you back to your office."

"No, thank you. I'm better off on my own."

"Your problem, Michelle, is that you're afraid of the wrong things." He hurriedly paid the bill and left the restaurant. He had never felt so miserable in his life. But if he were angry with anyone, it was himself.

As Daniel hurried away down the street, he was so agitated he hardly noticed the short, stout man carrying an umbrella, who purposely followed his departure.

# CHAPTER THIRTEEN

Watching Daniel leave made Michelle feel like crying. But tears were unthinkable. She had not cried since the day she found out about her parents. Even when Uncle Teddy was buried, she hadn't shed a tear. That was what he would have wanted. She had always behaved sensibly until Daniel Reiner came into her life to confuse and complicate it. She mustn't think about him, not ever again!

Michelle attempted to turn her sorrow to scorn. Who was he anyway? She could forget him. She would forget him! How many attractive men were there in the world? Zillions. And Daniel was all wrong for her. She must simply think rationally and close her heart to him.

She returned to the office, determined to conclude the Parker case as quickly as possible. She didn't have a moment to waste. There were only three short days before Nora would be released from the hospital.

The phone was ringing in her private office as she came through the door. She grabbed the receiver.

"Michelle, this is Ray. I had a good man on Charlene, but she managed to skip out sometime before dawn. I don't know how she got out of that motel without my man seeing her."

"Perhaps you can pick up her trail. It's very important. I'll have the money for her. If you can find her, tell her that."

"All right. We got her apartment under surveillance, but I don't think there's much chance of her going back there."

"I agree. She's in trouble and she knows it. There's always the chance she'll contact us on her own."

"I'll get to this personally."

She thanked him and their conversation quickly ended.

Bertram came into her office carrying a container of coffee and Viennese pastries.

"Care to share this with me?"

"I just had lunch."

He sat down, settling his large frame opposite her desk and biting into an apple-walnut pastry with gusto. "I think I found out something you want to know about Parker."

"You've got my undivided attention."

Bertram shoved some typed notes in front of her as he finished chewing.

The door to her office came flying open. Bertram and Michelle had their automatics drawn before their startled visitor could utter a word.

"My God, you're awfully quick with those guns!"

"Daniel, what are you doing here? And why didn't you wait to be announced?"

"We were both pretty upset before. Honestly, I didn't think you'd see me, given the choice."

When he smiled at her that way, she hardly remembered she wanted nothing to do with him. The next moment, she was again startled when he thrust a bouquet of red roses at her. "Gun in one hand, roses in the other. Fits you perfectly." He viewed her with hot eyes.

She kept her cool demeanor, at least outwardly. "Daniel, Bertram has uncovered some information on Parker and we were just about to go over it."

"Good, I'd like to listen in, maybe provide added input."

Bertram looked at Daniel mistrustfully, narrowing his eyes to slits. "Look Romeo, we're about to discuss business here, so get lost."

Daniel turned to Michelle. "I believe I can help. Look, I apologize for coming on too strong earlier, but I know how to separate the personal from the professional."

"You really think he should be here?" Bertram shook his head in disgust.

"I'm as involved in this case as you are," Daniel said, facing the bigger, heavier man without a trace of fear.

"Bertram is right. You really should be kept out of this."

"I'm very much in it." His jaw was set squarely.

"All right, stay, but I want your promise that you won't act on anything you find out. Nora is your patient and should be your only concern." She gave him a meaningful look before turning to her employee. "Bertram, what have you found out?"

"The man who was fingerprinted by the FBI and identified as Jim Parker joined the navy when he was eighteen. At first he was a radio operator; later he was commissioned as a lieutenant. I gather he got some schooling along the way. From there, he was recruited into Strategic Services and spent two years in the former Soviet Union, where he learned to speak fluent Russian. He continued his education, got sent back and forth to Russia on numerous occasions, and got to know the Soviet bureaucracy. More important, they got to know him. Just a guess, but I think he could have started out serving his country and eventually ended up betraying it." He sat back and waited for her to venture an opinion.

Michelle bridged her hands. "There is, of course, another possibility, though admittedly far-fetched. Jim Parker and James Parker may have been two different men. The Russians could have switched men, might have planted an enemy agent to replace the original. Since he spent a great deal of time in the Soviet Union, and they knew him very well, it might not have been all that difficult. Did Jim Parker have any family?"

"No living relatives listed at the time he entered the service. He might have been an orphan."

"Well, then, it is a possibility. Professor Latimer advanced the theory that Parker was a mole, planted by the Russians long ago. We already know that the information on file at the FBI was tampered with. The original description of Jim Parker does not fit the man that the Maryland state medical examiner identified. Even the dental records were destroyed. What do you think?"

Bertram took another bite of his pastry. "You could be right. There might have been two Parkers. That boat of his, it wasn't the little sailboat the Agency led people to believe. The radio equipment was highly sophisticated. It could intercept all kinds of messages. I got that on good authority from one of my old buddies at the FBI."

"Are we talking secret, coded messages?" Daniel asked.

"You got it, Doc. My information from a very reliable source is that there was a suitcase on board the sloop with a number of telephone-line intercept devices. I even talked to an expert in the computer field about this. He said that a device of that nature would allow someone to tap both the CIA and NSA computers for information."

Michelle felt her heart begin to beat rapidly. "Bertram, are you quite certain of this?"

Bertram summoned up his huge, muscular body, looking like a fighter who had just won the world heavyweight title. "Absolutely! For what it's worth, my take is that Parker was spying for the Russians at first, and maybe after they lost interest, for whoever would pay for American secret info. That's why the Agency is trying to push you around. It makes them look really bad having one of their top people turn out to be a traitor. Kirson comes off looking like crap. I think you got this case tied up."

"Not quite yet."

"Hell, Parker's probably living it up somewhere under a new identity."

"Or his remains are sitting silently in an urn over Mrs. Parker's mantelpiece in her Brooklyn Heights brownstone. No, we need facts to substantiate our suspicions. Right now, we've got nothing but theory. Charlene Bennett may hold the missing pieces to the puzzle. I'm almost certain of it. I hope Ray can bloody well find her for us."

"I'll keep on this for you," Bertram said.

He left after that. Michelle wanted to ask Daniel to leave as well. There was a palpable tension between them.

"Don't you have patients to see?"

"I'll be going back to the office in a little while. Look, I know I said some things I shouldn't have earlier. You're not ready yet. I understand."

She was about to bluntly tell him she'd never be ready for the kind of involvement he wanted, but at that moment, he came around her desk and pulled her into his arms. His hands were warm on her back. One hand came to her face to caress her cheek; with his other hand, he held hers against the broad expanse of his chest in an intimate gesture. His engaging smile, crinkling at the corners, seemed to see right through her. His firm jaw was clean-shaven, and his cologne had a woodland scent.

He kissed her longingly, passionately, lustfully, and her eyes drifted shut while he tasted and explored her. Her lips clung to his; her body melted into his body. She forgot all about the Parker case; she barely remembered her own name. Her mind whirled with emotion. Trembling, she pressed closer, hungry for his touch. His tongue teased and excited hers.

"Let me see you tonight," he murmured. He rubbed his hands up and down her arms, making her shiver.

"I have to leave town again."

"Then let me pick you up here after work. I'll drive you to the airport."

"I need to pick up a few things at the flat before I leave."

"Fine, I'll pick you up there. And I'll bring some incredible Chinese takeout so we can eat together before you fly off into the unfriendly skies."

"All right. I have a spare key I'll give you — for tonight only. This is not an indefinite offer. I'm only giving the key to you because I might be in the shower when you arrive. I'm feeling grungy."

He inhaled her scent. "You couldn't tell it from here. You take all the time in the shower you like. I might just arrive early enough to scrub your back. Purely as an unselfish act of duty on my part, you understand. I look on keeping you clean as a top priority."

"Right up there with prescribing Prozac? Your dedication to cleanliness is exemplary, Doctor."

Michelle forced herself to think about business after Daniel left. There were matters to attend to, a message to phone the London office and also one from the Continent. She assumed the administrator's mantle for the better part of the afternoon.

At five P.M., Ray called back.

"Did you locate Charlene?" she asked hopefully.

"Sure did, but it's not what we hoped for. She's in the morgue."

"Dead?" Michelle tried not to sound as shaken as she felt.

"Went and got herself killed."

Michelle felt as if someone had delivered a hard blow to her abdomen. "How did it happen?"

"Auto accident. At least that's what the cops think. Seems she reeked of alcohol.

Her car skidded over an embankment. She was dead on impact. Skull fracture, head smashed in like a peanut in a shell."

"Bloody hell! Who's investigating?"

"Same cop as in the Parker case, Maclaren."

"I'll be back in Washington this evening. Expect me."

With an involuntary shudder, she recalled the black limo that had almost run her off the road. Had Charlene met a similar fate?

It was raining hard when she left the Citicorp Center. Her shoes and stockings were quickly soaked through as she waited for a cab. Maybe she ought to have let Daniel pick her up after all, but that would just be encouraging him further. As it was, she didn't know why she'd agreed to have him come by and drive her to the airport. By the time she got to the apartment, a chill extended through her entire body. She looked forward to peeling off the wet clothing and taking a hot shower.

On entering the apartment, she had a sense of something not being quite right. Her intuitive reaction was to withdraw her custom-made lightweight Colt Commander from her purse and walk quietly around the apartment, examining here, poking there.

No one was hiding in the small apartment. And yet she had the oddest feeling that someone had been there while she was gone. It was the smell that wasn't right, she decided. Every place had its own distinctive odor, and her apartment was no different. Yet everything did seem to be in order.

Slipping the automatic back into her purse, she went into the kitchen and brewed a cup of chamomile tea. She still felt uneasy. But she'd installed a steel door and a Medico security lock with a supposedly pick-resistant cylinder. As an auxiliary, there was an inch-long dead bolt. Even for someone with special skills, it would have taken close to an hour to enter her apartment.

She stripped away her clothing, started the shower water, and adjusted the tap to a comfortable temperature. It felt good being freed of the restraints of clothing.

She was just about to go into the tub when she noticed that there wasn't any soap. Opening the medicine cabinet, she removed a cake and tossed it into the tub. Suddenly, something peculiar happened. A valve shut off the water. As she wondered what was wrong, there was an immediate hissing sound and a thrust of gas came shooting through the showerhead. She was stunned by the realization that if she'd been standing in the shower at that moment, the gas would have hit her directly in the face. Obviously, the momentum of the soap had tripped a device meant to be set off by the weight of her body standing in the tub. She moved swiftly to the bathroom door but it was locked. It had to have somehow been tampered with, because she'd left it unlocked. The small bathroom was quickly filling with gaseous vapor. *I must not breathe it in!* She grabbed her towel, moistened it, and put it over her mouth. Using her right hand, she smashed at the door. It took several hard blows to work through the door. She used her feet to kick a wider area through near the handle. Gasping for breath, she could finally reach around. Yes, the lock from the other side could be released. The door open, she stumbled out of the bathroom, coughing and choking.

She willed herself forward toward the windows. But the one in the bedroom was jammed. She picked up a chair and smashed the legs through the glass with every bit of her remaining strength. Then she hung her head out the window and took a series of deep gasping breaths.

Michelle forced herself on through the living room and kitchenette, opening windows as best she could. In the kitchen, her hands were shaking so badly that she could barely turn on the faucet. Without being able to control herself, she began to retch. The gas fumes had made her violently sick to her stomach. She ran the water, washing her face and rinsing her mouth. Her eyes still burned.

Someone was coming in the front door, she realized with panic. Were the killers returning?

"Michelle, my God, what happened?"

Daniel stood there, strong and caring; he had never looked more desirable. She virtually collapsed into his arms. He pulled her to him and held her tightly. His words meant little, but the sound of his voice was pure comfort and reassurance. He patted her back soothingly and kissed her forehead. Then he wiped the tears from her cheeks.

"I never cry."

"I understand," he said. "But if you did, it's okay. Tears are therapeutic. They cleanse the soul the way the rain out there is washing the dirt off the concrete."

It felt so good to be held securely in his arms. She tried to explain to him what had happened. He set her down on the sofa very gently, as if she were made of fine crystal.

"I'll see if I can't open the windows some

more," he said.

Daniel returned and sat down beside her, holding her close. He kissed the top of her head. Neither of them spoke. After a time, she was herself again, strong, controlled, resolute. She summoned herself up to her full stature. Still coughing, Michelle checked the bathroom. There was no more of the deadly, toxic gas. Whatever had been forced through the shower head was obviously finite in amount and had dissipated. What remained must have shifted through the vents.

She went to the bedroom and quickly dressed, then handed Daniel the traveling bag she kept ready for short trips. She must get to the airport. She would not come back to the apartment until she found out how this violation had been done. It was an ingenious murder attempt, the work of professionals. It smacked of a true artist — someone of Nastchenkov's shrewdness and ability. She was almost certain the crime bore his signature.

An alarming thought occurred to her. What about Daniel? Was he in danger, too? No, they must realize that he knew nothing. But in truth, neither did she. That was what made this all the more frightening and frustrating.

"Can you take me to the airport now?"

"You're shaking. Let me take you to my place instead, and then we'll discuss what to do."

She felt too drained to argue. Her hands were still unsteady as they reached the elevator. Thank goodness they didn't have to wait very long. There was only one other passenger inside, Mr. Janser, the building superintendent. His keys jangled as he moved. It suddenly occurred to her how the assassins had gotten into her apartment, and it was the only possible way. No one had to pick the locks. They had taken a much easier route.

She studied Janser's face. It was as red as a rare roast. There was a foolish grin on his face.

"Have you given the key to my apartment to anyone within the last few days?" She eyed him keenly.

"Course not!" Then his brows furrowed as if a thought had suddenly struck him. "Oh, there was them exterminators."

"What exterminators? I didn't ask to have anyone exterminate my apartment."

"It wasn't just your apartment. They did the entire building. They had some orders from the owners."

That odd smell. So that was what it was.

A lingering odor of insecticide. Of course, she should have pinpointed it immediately. Insecticide was a perfect cover.

Janser leaned forward and lowered his voice to a confidential whisper, although there was no one else in the elevator. "Seems one of the tenants called to complain about cockroaches."

"Did that person identify himself?"

"Not that I know of. Now you know we don't have that kind of a building, but the owners got real upset. That's why they had the whole building done." The super's warm breath reeked like a distillery. She backed away.

There was no point in reprimanding him. He had only been doing his job. She made a mental note to have all the locks changed and the apartment gone over for any other clever little devices that might have been left behind before she would ever set foot in it again. Despite the landlord's wishes, she would never again allow them to have a duplicate key. That had been a near-fatal error on her part.

From Daniel's apartment, she phoned Bertram and told him what happened. He promised to personally hire a reliable locksmith and a crew to clear the apartment. She felt much better after talking to him.

Like Uncle Ted, he was a wise and experienced professional whom she could trust.

Daniel began removing her raincoat. But he did not stop there.

"Why are you undressing me? I'm not in the mood for a sexual orgy at the moment."

He smiled. "I wasn't planning on one, but now that you've suggested it that might not be a bad idea. Don't look at me that way. I just want to examine you, make sure you're all right, see if your lungs are at normal function. Otherwise, I need to run you over to the hospital."

"I'm fine. And I have to leave soon if I'm to make my plane. Let's forget about dinner. I seem to have lost my appetite."

"I'm not surprised about that. I don't believe you should be going anywhere tonight. You can catch another flight in the morning. Your system's had a bad shock. Someone just tried to kill you and damned near succeeded. You ought to get some rest." He pulled her into his arms. "What you need is a good night's sleep and someone to hold you so there won't be any nightmares."

"Doctor's orders?"

"You got that right." His mouth brushed hers gently.

It was she who deepened the kiss, who pressed her body urgently against the vibrant heat that emanated from him.

"Are you planning on giving me a sleeping pill?"

He gave her a slow, sensuous smile. "Sweetheart, I've got the cure for insomnia, and it's not dispensed in capsule form."

A quiver ran through her. He began kissing her with feather-light strokes. Everywhere his lips touched her, Michelle's flesh felt searing hot, as if a fire were burning beneath her skin. He trailed kisses down her neck, her shoulder to her breasts. His mouth was warm, wet, exciting. Her bra was gone before she even realized it.

"Speaking professionally, you've got magnificent lungs. Lucky for you, I know just the right method for keeping them healthy."

"I suppose it's always best to seek professional assistance."

"Always wise," he said in a husky voice. "You never did get to take that shower. Maybe we should take one together. I did promise you a back scrub."

Before she knew what was happening, Daniel had lifted her into his arms and was carrying her into the bathroom. He quickly finished undressing her and did the same for himself. Under the hot, cascading waterfall, they made love, moving together in a slow, passionate rhythm. He wanted her and she wanted him. It had become that simple and elemental. Nothing else seemed to matter at this moment. He took a wash cloth, dampened and soaped it, his eyes never leaving hers. Ever so gently, he applied it to her body, moving the cloth with a circular motion to her throat, then her neck and breasts, to her stomach and finally between her thighs. "I want to love you with every part of my being," he said.

Seconds later, he was drying her and then carrying her back to his bed, where he began his ministrations anew. She felt like a fly wrapped in a spider's silken web. When she finally felt him inside her, Michelle let out a deep sigh of satisfaction. Becoming one with him made her feel safe and complete, whole. He brought her to a shattering climax that left her spent and breathless. Wrapped in his arms, sleep was not long in coming.

# CHAPTER FOURTEEN

Close to dawn, Michelle awoke in Daniel's bed, the warmth of his arms comforting her. Ever so slowly, so as not to wake him, she extricated herself. What was she doing involving him in the danger and madness of her world? He was such a fine man: kind, warm-hearted, with a droll sense of humor. The last thing a sane, sensible psychiatrist needed was to live *la vida loca.* Like a thief in the night, she quickly dressed, grabbed her bag and hurriedly left his flat.

The flight to Washington, D.C., proved thankfully uneventful. She forced herself to eat a light, bland meal on board, aware that she hadn't eaten for a very long time. Her lungs hurt; she was still recuperating from inhaling the noxious fumes of the gas vapor. Odd how none of that had mattered when she and Daniel were together.

She closed her eyes and tried to rest, but

visions of Dimitri Nastchenkov kept appearing. Why was a truly great master of murder concentrating on her? She could admire the man as a stylist without any desire to be his next victim.

Dimitri must have used some sort of paralyzing nerve gas. After her death, she surmised, his goons would simply have returned wearing gas masks, opened the windows, and let any last traces of the gas escape into the atmosphere. After the lethal gas had disappeared, they would have left. It would appear that she'd died of a simple coronary while taking a shower. Death by natural causes: Dimitri's specialty.

Was Parker somehow behind this? Or was he merely another victim? If he were really dead, why would anyone care what she found out? Even if he were in Moscow, why would they care who knew about it? His value as a spy was over. No, there had to be more to his story, and she was missing it. Kirson must know, but he would never tell her anything.

When Michelle arrived back at the office on Connecticut Avenue, Ray was not there to meet her. She went upstairs to the apartment and lay down for a nap, too exhausted to do anything else. She slept badly, her dreams fraught with twisted images of Dimitri Nastchenkov, of cars going over cliffs and bursting into flame. She saw herself dying. She awoke, unable to catch her breath and terrified. She hoped dreams were not actual omens or portents of the future.

Where was Ray? She waited impatiently at the office all morning. When she phoned the house, his wife told her he hadn't phoned or come home the previous night. She sounded worried. Michelle was worried herself. It wasn't like Ray not to report in; he was too much of a professional for that and had too much common sense. Something was wrong. She felt restless, unable to sit and wait any longer. It was time to see Captain Maclaren again. The Maryland police were investigating Charlene Bennett's death, so maybe he'd have some information for her.

The detective squad room was a totally undistinguished place. People came and went like bees buzzing around a hive. A young clerk led her into Maclaren's office and asked her to wait there. She glanced at his desk. It was a battered wooden piece cluttered with many files. He was obviously not a paper pusher. Her first impression of him, as a man most alive in an action situation, was most likely correct.

It was fifteen minutes before he came into his office, and she felt every one of them. She was impatient, aware that she had little time to spare.

Maclaren smiled at her apologetically. "You're lucky I'm seeing you at all today. We're really busy around here."

"I came to discuss Charlene Bennett with you. I'd like to get the details of her death straight in my mind. They bear directly on my investigation."

He obliged her by recounting the facts pretty much as Ray had related them, but with more in the way of specifics. She interrupted at a certain point. "Excuse me. I don't fathom why you consider this an accident."

He flexed a heavily muscled arm displayed to advantage in his white, short-sleeved shirt.

"We've found nothing suspicious, nothing that would suggest anything other than an accident." He looked like the prototype of a policeman, with his shoulder holster tied around the wide expanse of his chest in a businesslike manner.

"Was there another set of tire tracks near where Charlene went over the embankment?"

"It was a rainy night. And there were lots of tracks. No way to tell anything conclusively."

"Forgive me if I'm just a little skeptical about your accident theory. You see, Charlene called and told me someone was out to kill her. She even offered to sell information about James Parker's disappearance, information that would prove damaging to someone. I think her death is part of a conspiracy of silence."

"Now it's my turn to be dubious. Every crackpot in the world has some kind of a conspiracy plot running through their brain. Can you prove any of this?"

She felt furious with him. "I am not a crackpot. Obviously, I can't prove anything since Charlene Bennett is not here to substantiate what I'm telling you. However, there is someone who can give you some information."

"And who would that be?"

"Professor Robert Latimer of Georgetown University. He was a personal friend of James Parker. He was also an analyst for the CIA until he retired. He knows a great deal."

"Is he willing to talk?"

"He's a frightened man. I was thinking more in terms of offering him protection.

You can be persuasive, can't you?"

"We can arrange something."

"Immediately?"

Maclaren phoned the university in her presence. The wait seemed interminable as he was put through to a number of people in a variety of positions and constantly asked to hold.

"Damned bureaucracy!"

"At last we agree about something."

Maclaren grinned at her. Finally, after what seemed an incredible amount of time, he was given the message that Dr. Latimer had taken a sudden and unexpected leave of absence. It appeared illness in the family had forced him to take a week off, but he was expected to return within five days. However, no address had been given where he could be reached.

Michelle felt a terrible sense of dejection. Every turn led directly to a dead-end. Doug Maclaren looked at her and seemed to read her feelings from her expression.

"I'll have his home address checked out. If there's any lead as to where he's gone, I'll find it."

"Then you'll cooperate with us on this case?"

"Sure, we'll look into it." He put his large hand over hers in what she presumed was a gesture of camaraderie.

"This entire thing has gotten way out of control. I have the feeling I've botched it rather badly," she said. She got up to leave, but he stopped her, his hand on her shoulder.

"Hey, it's lunchtime. I got an hour coming to me. Let's eat together, okay? How do you feel about pizza?"

His invitation took her by surprise. Normally, she wouldn't have accepted, but she was feeling vulnerable.

"Pizza would be lovely."

They went to an Italian restaurant where he was a regular. The owner came over and took their order personally. Maclaren ordered a large pizza with everything on it, which made her laugh.

"I hope you have an incredible appetite. I don't eat very much for lunch."

"You could use a little more meat on you," he said appraisingly. "Not that I don't like what I see."

She looked at him thoughtfully, judging that he was in his late thirties. His hair was sand-colored and very straight, a lock falling roughly across his forehead. He had a jaunty look about him that reminded her of a soldier of fortune she had once liked very much.

"I would order a couple of beers, but I get the feeling you're just too classy a lady for beer."

"I would prefer white wine, French, Rhine or domestic, in that order."

"I like a woman who knows her own mind."

For some strange reason, she felt very relaxed, even secure, in his company. There was something about his open manner that immediately put her at ease.

The service was excellent. The waiter and bartender couldn't seem to do enough for Doug Maclaren.

"I'd like to know you better," he said.

"Professionally or personally?"

"A little of both I guess, but mostly personal."

"I'm not looking for a relationship," she told him bluntly.

"You and the doc have something going, don't you? Yeah, I could tell that right away, but no harm in trying."

She decided to change the subject. She studied his powerful build and thick neck. "You're a weightlifter, aren't you?"

He laughed. "Not much anymore. Just a little to keep in shape and keep up my strength."

"You're an athlete then."

"I used to be. Went to college on an athletic scholarship. Thought I'd be a pro football player, but by the time I got my chance, my knees were gone."

"I'm sorry."

His eyes, very blue and bright, smiled into hers. "Don't be. It happened a long time ago. I really like my work. I've never regretted it." He took her hand and held it. "You know, you're pretty hard to figure. I never expected you to agree to eat with me."

"Why shouldn't I eat with you?"

"You're a princess, totally regal. Me, I'm just a working stiff, a regular guy."

"I thought Americans didn't believe in class distinctions."

"Well, I guess we don't. Otherwise I never would have asked you to lunch."

"I have many faults, but I'm not a snob."

The waiter came by and hovered over them. "You like the pizza?" he asked her. "We make the best pizza in Maryland. We use the brick ovens."

"That's right," Doug Maclaren agreed. "Best pizza around."

She hadn't even tasted a slice yet, but she did now and had to agree. "Delicious," she said.

The waiter was all smiles. "See, I told you, but you got to eat it hot." When he walked away, Doug turned to her.

"You don't have to finish if you don't want to."

"No, I like the food."

"You're not married?" he asked her.

She shook her head.

"I didn't think so. You don't act married, and you don't wear a ring. I'm divorced myself. My wife couldn't stand being married to a cop. I was never around when she wanted me to be. I work crazy hours. She hated it. Now she's got herself a nine-to-fiver. Makes both of us a lot happier. Aren't you going to have any more of this pizza?"

She indicated that she wasn't, and he quickly wolfed down the rest. Then he contentedly wiped the tomato sauce from his chin. She couldn't help but like him. He was definitely the sort of man she preferred to have on her side.

"You have a reputation for being a dedicated policeman."

He seemed pleased by her comment. "I give it my best shot. I've heard some things about you, too. You don't seem as dangerous as they say you are."

"That would depend on your point of view," she said dryly. "Has someone been warning you about me?"

"Does that matter?" he asked evasively.

"It might just."

He suddenly seemed uneasy. "I can't really talk about it."

"Why not?"

"Let's just leave things as they are for now, okay?"

"Not quite fair."

"I know your line of work, and to my way of thinking, it only makes you all the more interesting. In fact, it gives us a lot in common."

"Yes, I rather agree with you. We do understand each other. Captain Maclaren, may I go along with you when you visit Professor Latimer's apartment?"

"Call me Mac. I have to tell you, I wasn't exactly planning on making that visit right now, and it's against department regulations for you to come with me, regardless." He returned her look. "Oh, all right. I suppose I could drop by his place this afternoon."

When Michelle returned to the office, she noted there was still no word from Ray. She was more worried about him than ever. She glanced through some paperwork, but it was difficult for her to concentrate.

At five-thirty, Ray finally phoned in.

"Where have you been?" she asked, skipping by the normal amenities.

"It's where I am that's the problem. No time to answer any questions. I'm hip to what's going on. I'm connected. Tell you all about it soon. You're going to be very surprised and very pleased. I just about got it all tied up. Get a big bonus ready for me 'cause I'm sure earning it."

"All right. Just tell me where you are so I can come and help you or send for extra help. It's not safe for you to work alone."

"No, that could blow everything."

"Ray, tell me where you are!"

Suddenly, the line went dead. Had he hung up on her? She couldn't tell. Why wouldn't he simply tell her where he was? Did he really think that he could handle the situation by himself? God, he could be anywhere. She had no idea where to look.

She waited impatiently by the telephone as late afternoon dragged into early evening. She went upstairs to her apartment and went through her normal ritual. First, there were the exercises, followed by a shower and meditation. She followed that with a light dinner.

Doug Maclaren arrived at her apartment at eight P.M. She was surprised that he had come by instead of phoning, but she was honestly glad to see him. He had clearly taken the trouble to go home and change his clothes before coming over. He was wearing a sport jacket and knit shirt now and looked much more casual and informal.

He glanced around. "Real nice place you got here. Very clean. You got great taste in furnishings. You like Oriental stuff?" he asked, pointing to some of the watercolors hanging on the living room wall.

"I like the painting and the philosophy of the East," she told him. She seated him next to her on the sofa.

"Those pajamas look like Chinese silk. You sleep in them?"

"They're for lounging, not sleeping," she explained and thought he looked just a trifle disappointed.

"I'm pretty much of a slob myself, but I can appreciate a woman who's neat and organized."

She offered him a drink, and he readily accepted.

"Beer?" she asked.

"Sure, if you've got it."

"I stock a variety of beverages."

"That's nice to know."

She brought him a bottle of chilled imported ale. While he was drinking it, Michelle pursued the topic of Dr. Latimer's unexpected leave from the university. Maclaren told her what he had found out, or, to her mind, what he had not found out. Mac had not been able to locate Robert Latimer. No one in his apartment building had any idea where he'd gone.

"I put out a bulletin on the guy. I hope to hear something shortly."

Then she told Mac about Ray, about her fears concerning the danger he might be in. Mac listened attentively. He finished his beer and placed the bottle on the coffee table.

"We'll look for your friend, too. Don't worry. From what you've told me, he's no stranger to this kind of business. I'll check into it first thing in the morning." He removed his jacket and his holster, placing them carefully on an end table.

She glanced at his revolver. "Do a lot of elephant hunting with that thing, do you?" She indicated the weapon with a sweep of her hand.

He seemed amused by her comment. "What would a sweet, lovely lady like you know about weapons?" His tone was teasing as he seated himself beside her again on the sofa.

"My uncle was something of a hunter. He taught me."

"Big game?"

"The biggest."

He picked up his revolver, cleared the action, and handed it to her to examine.

"Think I could stop a buffalo with that?" She handled the weapon with expert care and precision as she had been trained to do. "Smith and Wesson. I apologize. I thought it was a Forty-four Magnum. I see now that it's a Forty-four Special, not quite as bulky as I first assumed. But it does have quite a bit of stopping power. Do you need that much? Aren't most policemen satisfied with a Thirty-eight Special or some variation of it? Then again, I believe most law enforcement professionals now use automatic pistols, don't they?" She put the gun down.

"You do know, don't you?"

"A smattering. I've been trained to use both a revolver and an automatic. But even a civilian Glock has a magazine of ten rounds. I'm surprised you don't use one."

"I'm not into plastic. Besides I don't like the safety action. As far as I'm concerned, it's like carrying a rattlesnake in your pocket."

"I often carry a Colt Commander. I like the feel of that."

He gave her an appraising look. "Yeah, you're dangerous all right."

"Perhaps your source was right to warn you."

"You ought to know I love danger. I live for it. You ever get tired of the doc, think of me. I got a feeling we'd be real good together."

He leaned over and kissed her, not tenderly but roughly. She didn't feel a thing — but she should have. He was an attractive, exciting man. If anyone could make her forget Daniel, it was Doug Maclaren.

She knew that he wanted to make love to her. She should welcome him. They really were right for each other. With Mac, there'd be no concern about emotional commitment. There would just be mutual enjoyment. Total compatibility.

But then suddenly without warning, in her mind's eye, she had an image of Daniel. It was as if he were standing there in front of her. She could see him smiling in that special way he had, never seeming to be serious about anything, the dimple in his cheek endearingly apparent. Somewhere in New York, he was waiting to hear from her. She firmly pushed Mac away.

"Look, if you ever break free, you call me, because I really like you. But I'm your friend, regardless. I promise to do that checking for you on Latimer and your guy

Ray Howard. No strings attached."

"You are a very special man," she said, and meant it.

"Don't start that or I'll forget what a gentleman I am."

Mac left directly, leaving her alone and feeling confused and lost. She had told Daniel there could be no commitment between them. And yet, she did not find herself attracted to Mac the way she did to Daniel. No man had ever made her feel the way Daniel did. It was difficult to render a smoldering volcano extinct simply by an act of will.

She realized that she hadn't called the New York office all day. Would Bertram still be there as he so often was? She called but got the answering the machine. That meant he was probably at home. The second phone call brought results.

"Nothing new at this end," he told her. "Oh, except that your friend Dr. Reiner keeps calling. He wants you to contact him."

"I wish you hadn't told me that just now."

"Are you going to call him?"

"I honestly don't know."

"He's really got it bad for you."

"He's a child."

"Children can be damned appealing," Bertram remarked. There was a small catch in his voice. She wondered if he were thinking of his long-gone young wife, who'd broken Bertram's heart when she'd left him.

"I'll be in touch with you tomorrow," she promised.

In the night, Michelle had disturbingly erotic dreams. She was in Daniel's arms again. He removed a pistol from her hand and placed bloodred roses in their place.

"This is what you really need," he told her.

His kiss was still on her lips when she awoke somewhere near dawn, confused and alone.

At ten o'clock that morning, the telephone rang and it was Mac. She'd been hoping to hear from Ray, but the expectation proved fruitless.

She could tell at once from the businesslike tone of Mac's voice that something was wrong. "Michelle, I got some real lousy news for you."

She felt her breath escape as if she'd been punched. "Is it about Ray? It is, isn't it?"

There was a momentary pause. "Yeah, the fact is, your man, Howard, well, he's turned up dead. Someone whacked him."

She found herself having trouble swallowing. "I don't believe it! Ray could handle himself in any situation."

"Not this time. He was shot to death. His body was left slumped behind the wheel of his car. It was a professional hit. There's no doubt about it. He was shot through the head once, execution style."

"Where?" The word would hardly come out.

"Arlington."

"Anywhere near Charlene Bennett's apartment?"

"Not far from it, as a matter of fact."

"I should have gone to look for him."

"Don't start blaming yourself. He knew what he was doing. I'm going to call his wife. You got the number handy?"

"That's my responsibility. Ray worked for me."

"Whatever you say."

"You'll keep me informed about the investigation?"

"Personal bulletins, okay?"

Going to see Ray's wife, Gwen, was one of the most difficult things she ever had to do. Telling her wasn't the worst part, not even listening to her cry. The worst of it was the accusing look in Gwen's eyes. How could she endure the guilt, the sense of blame?

"All of those crazy hours and that dangerous work. For what? Oh, he thought he was being paid real good, but was it worth his life?"

"I can only say how terrible I feel," Michelle said to the grieving woman. "I realize how inadequate that is."

"Got that right. Get out of my house!"

Michelle left without another word, returning to the asylum that her office offered. Later, she made out a very large, final payment voucher for Gwen. No matter what Ray's widow thought of her personally, she would do right by her financially.

It was time to return to New York, to talk with Nora again, to admit her failure. The day passed as a dream, more like a nightmare. Around seven that evening the phone rang in her apartment, and she answered it.

"My condolences to you," the voice at the other end said. It was a foreign voice, though obviously muffled. "I would be very careful if I were you. The same is true for your friends." There was a click on the line.

The call had startled her. Since all calls were automatically recorded, she played this one back and listened to it again.

Could that possibly be Nastchenkov's voice? It was difficult to tell. Was he behind Ray's death and that of Charlene Bennett? Besides herself, who was being threatened now? She shivered because the room suddenly seemed terribly cold.

# CHAPTER FIFTEEN

Daniel was not having a good day. For one thing, his schedule was hectic. He was booked solidly with patients until eight in the evening. It was his partner's turn to be out of town, and Daniel was filling in with some of Morris's patients as well as ministering to his own.

If his secretary hadn't sent out for a sandwich, he would have completely forgotten about lunch. There really wasn't any time to leave the office anyway. He opened the brown paper bag and found a ham and cheese on soggy white bread oozing with dark brown mustard. It wasn't that he was fussy about food, but this struck him as gross. He pushed the sandwich away and tried the coffee. If possible, it was even worse than the sandwich, bitter in taste as if it had been reheated many times and boiled down to the grounds. It was also cold. So much for lunch.

Who was he kidding? The real reason he felt so miserable was because Michelle had left without a word or a note. Her mysterious departure did not bode well for their relationship. Then again, what relationship? She'd told him flat out she was only having sex with him. It wasn't her fault he'd fallen in love with her, was totally wacko about her. And yet he was certain that her feelings for him were strong as well. But she was fighting them, and her will was plenty strong. Still, obsessing over her wasn't going to help matters any.

He buzzed his secretary and told her to send the next patient in.

"There's a gentleman here to see you. I told him you had no time for him today, but he insists that I announce him to you."

"Who is it?"

"A Colonel Atwood."

He'd never expected to see the man or hear from him again; this visit was a complete surprise. Still, he supposed he had to talk with the colonel. A chat was something owed.

Atwood strode into the room, his erect bearing gave him the semblance of the military even without a uniform. Atwood was distinguished in appearance. His iron-gray hair was slicked back to perfection. Not an ounce of extra fat on him. His black leather shoes were polished to a fanatical glisten.

"Please have a seat, Colonel."

"I only stopped in for a moment. I was attending a conference here in New York. Thought I might tell you in person why we haven't availed ourselves of your services again." There was a severe, disapproving expression on his face.

"Actually, I don't think your work is the sort of thing I want to be involved with anyway."

"That's good because, quite frankly, I was disappointed in what you did for us. As you know, we have a board of psychiatric consultants that work constantly to tighten our agency's psychological assessment program. I thought you might qualify to be one of our people. When we paid your expenses to Europe, it was expected that you would do a first-rate profile of Michelle Hallam for us. I accepted your evaluation and, therefore, did not employ the woman. Later, I discovered that you were personally involved with her. I consider that unethical practice. You were not given her name or any background information about her for a definite reason. As far as I am concerned, you did not fulfill your obligations to us. I thought better of you. I am highly disappointed."

Daniel felt his face grow hot. "I did what I thought was right."

"I suppose you're one of those doctors one reads about who claim they treat their patients by having sex with them."

Daniel tamped down his anger. "First of all, Ms. Hallam was never my patient. And if you remember, I was told to get to know her so that I could do an accurate profile. Later on, she contacted me here in New York."

"The fact remains it was your write-up that convinced me not to use her services. I finally met the woman in question myself. She was just what we needed. For some reason known but to yourself, you did not want us to employ her. Do you deny that?" Atwood's tone of voice made Daniel feel like the accused at a court-martial hearing.

"No, I don't deny it." He looked Atwood straight in the eye.

"What was your reason?"

"Just as you said, it's personal."

Atwood shook his head in disgust. "No one in the intelligence community will ever use you again. You're not to be trusted. You violated the basic tenet of maintaining objectivity. Are you still involved with Ms. Hallam?"

Daniel bitterly resented the man's overbearing manner. "She's an independent woman who prefers to avoid relationships. The only interest we share is in one of my patients who happens to also be her client."

"Nora Parker."

He was surprised. "How did you know?"

"I know a great many things. It's my job to know. However, Ms. Hallam and I did discuss the case. I have an interest in it myself. If there has been a breach in the national security, I want to know about it. Ms. Hallam has promised to keep me informed. But so far I haven't heard from her. Do you have any idea what she's managed to find out?"

So Atwood was here on a fishing expedition. "Ms. Hallam does not confide in me," Daniel said coldly. "And the conversations between Mrs. Parker and me are privileged communications."

"Of course." Daniel had the feeling Atwood would have liked to order his execution in front of a firing squad. Well, he was fairly fed up with the pompous asshole anyway. Screw the bastard!

They said goodbye, parting as strangers who never intend to see each other again. He actually felt a great sense of relief when the colonel left, as if a black cloud had passed by overhead. Atwood and the rest of the cloak-and-dagger people made him very uneasy. He never should have let the fellow woo him in the first place, but at least the seduction had not been total. No doubt if it had been, he would have tripped on the cloak and fallen on the dagger. Meeting Michelle in France had brought him back to his senses.

The three o'clock appointment cancelled out unexpectedly. She called to apologize and told his secretary that she was ill with the flu. She was one of Morris's regular patients and, in all likelihood, didn't feel comfortable confiding in a different doctor. He understood that perfectly well. In any case, the break was appreciated. After telling his secretary that he was going out for a while, he quickly left, walking in the direction of Central Park. Some exercise was just what the doctor ordered and needed.

Along the way, he stopped at a coffee shop, drank a container of milk, and wolfed down a tuna salad sandwich on whole wheat. Well-fortified, he started to walk again. It was a beautiful day, the sky above sparkling like stones of lapis lazuli. But he couldn't help wishing that Michelle was here to share it with him. He wasn't going to give up on her no matter what. She could be stubborn, but he could be equally determined. There was something special between the two of them; it wasn't confined to sex, either, even though he had to admit he'd never experienced such intensely exciting lovemaking with any other woman.

He walked in the direction of the zoo. There were lots of small children with their mothers; some carried brightly colored balloons. He could remember coming here occasionally as a small child, his mother pointing to the seals, him walking along beside her to the animal cages, watching the lions pace and the leopards looking ready to leap out of their cages. Only the sea lions had ever really looked happy, swimming up for the fish which was tossed to them. The zoo wasn't like that anymore, not since they'd changed it with concern for environmental integrity.

He thought about Michelle and her need for freedom. Did she fear he wanted to cage her like an animal in a zoo? Did she find him demanding? He had to talk to her again, to try to understand her feelings and express his own. He knew she had secrets, and if she wanted to keep them, it was her own affair. Trust between people took time to develop, especially with someone as suspicious and complex as Michelle. He could afford to be patient.

Eventually, he glanced at his watch and realized with some reluctance that it was time to be heading back to the office. If he walked briskly, which was what he intended, there was still plenty of time before his next appointment.

Someone fell into stride beside him. Then there was another man flanking him. With his New Yorker's keen instinct for trouble, he knew immediately something wasn't right. Somebody was probably setting him up for a mugging. He broke into a run. But the two men were keeping up with him. Now there was a third man in front of him. In front and in back, big men. One tackled him, jumping on top of him while another held him down. He fought as best he could, managing to kick one of them in the stomach.

Daniel struggled to get up and began shouting for help. Then the third man punched him in the ribs. It was a hard blow, causing him to double over in pain. Strong hands shoved him down to the ground.

In shocked amazement, he zeroed in on the hypodermic needle even before he could try to stand up again. One man held him down while another seized his arm.

The third man, the one who had punched him, was on top of him now applying rigid pressure. One hand was forced over his mouth. The second man bared Daniel's left arm, bending it at the elbow. Searching out a large vein, deftly and expertly, the man injected the hypodermic syringe.

Daniel felt a sharp pain as the steel needle dug deep into his flesh. He tried to shout out, but the hand was clamped too tightly over his mouth. He saw the clear fluid flowing into his body. Then the needle was carefully withdrawn. What had they done to him? What was happening? Terrified, he fought back harder.

To his horror, he thought he could actually feel the drug soaring through his bloodstream. They forced him to stand now. He was having trouble walking. He was suddenly confused, disoriented, dizzy. Daniel realized he had to get away from these men. He shook with panic, outrage.

His mind willed him to run away, but his body would not respond. He felt heavy, lethargic. The first man and the second had him between them. They would not let go. He tried to call out for help, but his voice wouldn't work. By the time he was sitting in the big black car, his mind had begun to float, suspended somewhere in a twilight state that was neither life nor death.

Michelle was feeling terribly depressed. Things had gone wrong ever since she started the Parker investigation. She wondered if Uncle Ted would have approved of what she was trying to do. The truth was she hadn't done a very good job of handling things. Very likely he would have foreseen the difficulties and avoided them. Uncle Ted was first and foremost a field operative. He hadn't wanted her to follow in his footsteps, however. Although Uncle Ted had personally seen to her training, he'd insisted she remain on the administrative end. Perhaps he'd been right. She really tried to cultivate a thick skin, but it wasn't working out well at all.

Ray's death preyed on her mind. And then there was Daniel. She was afraid for him. She decided to call him at his office, since there was no answer at the apartment. His answering service said the doctor was not in and could not be reached. That didn't sound at all like him. Then again, he could have been at the hospital seeing patients. There was no reason to think the worst.

When she couldn't get through to Daniel, she decided to evaluate Nora's situation on her own. There was only one day left before

Nora's release from the hospital. Rather than visit her there again, Michelle determined to ride home with Nora and talk then. Hopefully, she would have something worth discussing by that time.

Bertram came into the office and handed her a cup of cappuccino and a croissant. She accepted his gifts gratefully.

"I just bought these downstairs at that French bread shop."

"Nice and hot. Thank you for breakfast. How did you know I hadn't eaten? I wasn't aware it showed."

"That preoccupied look on your face. I've never seen anyone so unhappy."

"I'm disappointed in myself. I seem to be botching things rather badly."

"You're thinking about your guy in D.C., aren't you? Look, anyone who goes into our line of work understands and accepts the risk, otherwise they would leave. In a way, the excitement is what people like us live for. We crave it. I know I'd be dead without it. Your guy could have been a cop and gotten whacked by a suspect. Point is, he chose what he wanted to do with his life, just like the rest of us."

"I wonder if you wouldn't have been better off if you'd remained at the Bureau."

"I have no regrets. I made my own

choices, too."

She squeezed his hand. "Thank you. I feel less guilty now."

Maureen buzzed, and Michelle put on the intercom. It seemed there was a Mr. Kirson on the line. He insisted that the call was important.

"I'm not in when that vulture calls," she told her secretary.

A moment later, Maureen buzzed her again. "Mr. Kirson says he's got information to share that you'd be very interested in having."

"He wouldn't call if it wasn't important," Bertram observed.

"All right, I'll take the call," she said with a sigh of resignation. She found herself grinding down on her back teeth even before he began to speak.

"Got something hot to tell you," Kirson drawled.

"Really? What is it?"

"Not over the telephone."

"Why not?"

"Are you kidding? Your place is lousy with bugs. Go get it fumigated!"

"All right, where and when?"

"There's a little coffee shop on Broadway at West Fifty-third Street. It's called the Colony. Meet me in front of it in an hour.

Got it?" He clicked off.

"What do you think?" she asked, turning to Bertram, who had been listening attentively.

"Good ol' Wild Bill? He's just one of the boys, and then some. He can be quite a character, but there's no one shrewder."

"You think he's behind this thing?"

"No way to know for certain. He's a master of masks and disguises. I will tell you he's capable of murder though. Once when I was still with the Bureau, I was in this restaurant in the District where a lot of our people hung out after hours. I sat down at the bar and ordered a drink. Kirson was at a table with his wife and another couple. Some guy came over and said hello to his wife in a friendly manner. He appeared to know her very well."

"In the biblical sense?"

Bertram smiled grimly. "Who knows? Anyway, Wild Bill got very upset. He jumped up, started shouting at the guy for making indecent remarks to his wife. Then he punched the man smack in the face. I actually saw him start to reach for his gun, but the other fella who was with him immediately got between them and restrained him. I happened to mention the incident to a friend from the CIA sometime later. He

261

told me Kirson has a reputation for being a jealous husband. There are also other episodes of him having crazy fits of temper."

"So he might have been responsible for whatever happened to Parker, Charlene Bennett, and Ray?"

"I couldn't say. I only know you shouldn't underestimate him."

Michelle was still thinking about what Bertram had told her as she waited for Kirson to arrive. As usual, he was late. Where was that infuriating man? She paced in front of the coffee shop, a sudden breeze putting a chill right through her. She was certain that his lateness was yet another deliberate ploy on his part to subtly put her in her place. The sexist swine had no regard for women, would never consider one his equal. Still, she waited because she had deduced from the way he spoke that he did indeed have something of significance to tell her about the Parker case.

Kirson finally arrived by private limo, a slinky white affair with flashy chrome. The ever-present cigar hung out of his mouth and a cowboy hat sat low over his brow. He made a point of showing the car to her.

"Nice, huh?"

"Shall I buy you a cup of coffee?" she

asked. "Or would that be beneath you?"

He grinned broadly, exposing his nicotine-stained teeth. His suit jacket was unbuttoned, displaying his large paunch as well as his holstered revolver.

"You don't think I was really gonna have anything at a dump like this, do you? Besides, they already got this place wired up. How about we get into the limo and talk?"

"I prefer neutral ground."

"Okay, I'll send the car on ahead. Let's walk over to Avenue of the Americas. I got my eye on one of those pretty little cafés. You ever been to Rockefeller Center? I'm just a tourist when it comes to the big city. I get a big kick out of all those flags. Yep, I'm a sucker for flags."

"You enjoy playing tourist?"

"Sure do. Big city knocks my socks off. See, I'm just a real old-fashioned country boy at heart, born and raised on a ranch."

They began to walk as Kirson continued talking in a casual manner. "I reckon a proper English lady like you must find American life downright crude and vulgar." There was more than a hint of sarcasm in his voice.

"Don't put words in my mouth. We had a townhouse in London and a place in the country. I'm accustomed to either kind of living. All cities have their own character and charm, but they all share one thing in common."

"What's that?"

"The culture of a country is in its cities. There is a great deal of cerebral stimulation to be found here."

"My, aren't you the classy one. Now me, I think the heart of a country is in the land and the people who live close to it. Too many folks leave small towns and come to cities where they don't find nothin' but crime and squalor."

"People can suffer anywhere."

He pointed to several homeless individuals sprawled across the sidewalk. "Never see that in the country. Folks are charitable and neighborly and take care of their own."

"If you say so."

They walked on in silence for a time. At Rockefeller Center, they walked down the steps to a café and seated themselves at a table that overlooked the great golden statue of Prometheus above the fountain. Soon an ice skating rink would be set up for the winter months. It was a particular favorite place of hers, but she could not enjoy it with Kirson.

A waiter came by and brought them menus.

"Order whatever you like, honey; it goes on the expense account."

"Just a cup of tea, and I'll be paying for it myself."

"Whatever you say. Don't object if I order something stronger."

After the waiter had taken their order, he began to talk again. "You like it here in New York, don't you? Pace is too fast for me. People run by each other, never even saying howdy."

She found herself growing very impatient with him. "Please get to the point. You said you had a reason for asking me to meet with you today."

He took a maddeningly long time in responding. He seemed to enjoy holding her in suspense like a cat toying with a mouse.

"I'm doing you a big favor. You ought to be a lot nicer to me."

"You're doing me a favor? That remains to be seen, Mr. Kirson."

He gave her that smug, infuriating smile of his. "I got my reasons for bein' in town, and they don't have much to do with you."

"Fancy that! And I thought they couldn't survive without you full-time at Langley."

"Honey, nobody's indispensable, not even

265

me, though it pains me to admit it. But I do have something to tell you. I think you're gonna thank me for it." Their beverages arrived, and he paused to take a long gulp of beer. "You are a fetchin' woman. There's those that say you're a cold-blooded bitch, got a granite slab for a heart, but I don't think so. No ma'am, I think there's hot blood hidden away somewhere, especially since you took up with that there New York doctor fella. I'll just bet you got some real warm feelings for him."

His leering smile made her stomach churn. "Just what has that got to do with anything?" She found herself talking through clenched teeth.

"Why, it's nothin' to me, but to them foreigners, well, honey, that's another matter entirely."

"What are you getting at?" She was aware that he was continuing to toy with her.

"You gotta learn to be more patient. Live longer if you take life a tad slower." He seemed much too pleased with himself.

"I am very weary of your games. Are we now playing 'I know something you don't know'? If so, please spare me and get to the point. I concede the superiority of CIA information collection."

He leaned forward in his chair. "All right.

I'll tell you straight out, since that's the way you want it. They got him."

"What?" Pressure was developing behind her eyes.

"You heard me. Nastchenkov kidnapped your doctor pal."

She choked on her tea. "Why would he do such a thing? Daniel's a civilian. He knows nothing."

"Parker case, of course. You or Nora Parker must have told him something."

"No, never!" The lemon in her tea left an acrid taste in her mouth.

"Maybe not, but they think he knows something, and you know what that means."

"I suppose you might be privy to where they're holding him?"

He placed a slip of paper in her hand and squeezed her fingers tightly for good measure.

"We must get him away from them."

"Sorry, honey, there's no 'we' in this. It's your problem. The company can't get involved. Just remember, you owe me for giving you the info."

"How did you know?"

"An informant. Don't ask anymore, because I ain't gonna tell you. We do protect our sources, you know."

"When did they take him?"

"Yesterday afternoon."

The bile rose into her throat. Daniel could be dead by now. No, they wouldn't have taken him if they intended to kill him. "I really could use your help."

"Yep, you damn well could! But it would cost you real big." He gave her a smile, now the cat who enjoys tossing around a bird before he kills it.

"What would you want in return?"

"Let's go outside."

They walked out and stood in front of the fountain. Michelle set her eyes on the blazing gold statue before her.

"What will it cost me?"

"Your word you're through looking into the Parker case. I want the book closed permanently on that."

She shook her head vehemently.

"Well, then, you can just go help your friend on your own, sweet lady, 'cause I sure as hell ain't gonna do it for you."

"You bastard!"

She could still hear him chuckling as she turned on her heels and abruptly walked away.

The cab that took her up to the address scrawled on the piece of paper moved ever so slowly through the heavy flow of traffic.

She wished that she could simply walk over. Finally losing patience, she got out three blocks from the building and did exactly that.

It was an old mansion, the architecture of the building reminding her of a fortress. She could probably study the layout of it in detail, but that would take time, and time was something she didn't have.

Was it possible for her to get into the place? But what about getting out with Daniel? She did not even know where they were keeping him or if he were actually in the building. Searching it would take time. And what if he'd been drugged, which seemed very likely. She could hardly carry him out unobserved.

Bertram would assist her, of course. But a project of such enormity would require a detailed, well-thought-out plan. As she saw it, the task was virtually impossible. And unless she acted quickly, Nastchenkov would kill Daniel. He was a vicious, brutal man who would never leave a witness alive to speak out against him if he could help it.

She could not leave Daniel in this unspeakable predicament. The worst part was the knowledge that he would not be in this situation if it weren't for her. She began walking back to her office at the Citicorp building. Walking always seemed to trigger her thought processes. She had to formulate a plan. It wasn't going to be easy, but she had to come up with something foolproof. As Michelle moved briskly through the throngs of people on the street, her mind was totally preoccupied with the examination of possibilities. Finally, a daring idea came to her. It was not something she would normally do or even consider, but this was a desperate situation. She realized there wasn't anything she wouldn't do to save Daniel's life.

Someone was slapping his face none too gently. His mouth . . . God, what an awful taste! There was a terrible pain in his arm. Then Daniel began to remember what had happened, and his heart lurched. He glanced down at the vein in his arm that was still exposed. It had become swollen and discolored. He was having trouble focusing his eyes. There was a hot light directly over him, while the rest of the room was in darkness.

"You are awake now. Respond!"

He didn't speak, and a big man slapped his face again.

"We will talk now." Daniel had seen this short, fat man before somewhere. The eyes were small and mean like a rodent. If only he could think clearly, concentrate. This couldn't be real; it had to be some sort of nightmare. Any moment he would surely wake up.

"Where am I? Who are you?" His voice didn't sound like his own.

The rodent smiled, flashing sharp incisors. "You are in grave danger."

He stared at the man, his sluggish mind shocked into a sudden sense of alertness.

"Do you understand?"

Daniel made no response. There was recognition now. This was the man he and Michelle had met together. What had Michelle told him about the fellow? Exact words would not connect in his immediate state of disorganization. But he knew the rodent was a cold-blooded assassin. Then he did remember something about the guy being compared to Vlad the Impaler, a torturer, or was it a vampire like Dracula? His mind couldn't seem to focus. Daniel felt his leg tremble involuntarily.

"Why have you brought me here?"

"Allow me to introduce myself to you. I am Dimitri Nastchenkov. I am not a man who engages in foolish chatter with people. So I will tell you quite directly what I want from you. You give me the information, and

271

I will let you leave here unharmed."

"I think you've made some kind of a mistake."

Nastchenkov smiled again. "No mistake. You are friend to Michelle Hallam. She has confided in you concerning the Parker investigation. Mrs. Parker has also confided in you. We want to know everything that you have learned. To start with, what has Michelle discovered about Parker's disappearance?"

"I have no idea, Mr. Nasty."

The squat Bulgarian nodded to the huge man beside him. At the signal, a fist came crashing into his face, landing a sharp agonizing blow to his jaw. He reeled in pain.

"In case you wonder, he did not break your jawbone. But the next blow will do that and more. I would advise you speak now while you still are able. Believe me, it is fatherly advice."

Daniel would have laughed at that if he were able. The thought of this man ever being fatherly boggled his imagination.

"Michelle and I didn't discuss her work. I wasn't interested in knowing."

"Ah, of course, she seduced you, promised you heaven with her kisses, but I can assure you she is a false lover who has brought you here to an earthly hell. The woman is a

272

betrayer. It is right for you to tell us all you know of her. She is evil incarnate." As far as Daniel was concerned, the rodent had just described himself.

They waited for him to respond. When he didn't, the big man came toward him again. Daniel cringed.

"Perhaps we will talk a little more before my friend takes over. We know Michelle does not think James Parker was a simple suicide. Does she think he is dead?" The rodent watched him with an intelligence as sharp as his incisors.

"She doesn't know."

"And Nora Parker? What does she think happened to him?"

"She thinks he might still be alive."

That seemed to satisfy Nastchenkov for the moment. But Daniel realized he hadn't told the man anything he didn't already know.

"That is better. However, I must have more precise intelligence about Michelle's activities. She is intimate with you. Therefore, you must know more."

"She was not intimate with me. We are only friends."

The big man hit him again quite unexpectedly, a blow to the stomach that left him groaning on the floor.

"I will restrain Vassilli as best I can. But you see, Doctor, he is not as civilized as you or I. He detests liars. However, he will not touch you again if you cooperate and tell us everything you know. We will even let you off right in front of the zoo as if nothing ever happened."

"Someone must have seen you kidnap me, must have reported the incident to the police." Daniel gritted his teeth, steeling himself to the pain.

The fat man laughed loudly. "One man, a nosy New Yorker, actually had the temerity to ask what was wrong with you. Vassilli explained that you had too much vodka to drink. Once the man understood you to be a foreigner, not an American, he no longer interfered. Americans think we are all alcoholics anyway." He chuckled to himself. "Others just went about their business and ignored the situation, pretending to see nothing. Most people in New York do not involve themselves."

"I've told you the truth. Ms. Hallam is a very careful person. I can't give you any further information." Daniel inhaled, readying himself to be hit again, but strangely, the blow did not come.

Nastchenkov studied him thoughtfully. "Yesterday, I waited for a comrade in front of the main entrance to the New York Public Library building. It is one of many places people may loiter without drawing attention to themselves. The architecture is decadent but interesting. The statues too are interesting. A man seated on a sphinx dominates the north side, supposedly a representation of truth. A woman seated on Pegasus is on the south side, representing beauty. Perhaps you, Doctor Reiner, are the embodiment of truth. As for Michelle, she would qualify as an earthly symbol of beauty. But as we all know, truth is merely relative, and beauty, ah, beauty is fleeting. Such a shame that beautiful things must die. Nothing lasts forever . . ."

"But earth and sky," Daniel interjected.

"I think you do not understand the seriousness of your situation."

"Believe me, I understand."

"In the old days, you would be dead by now. But there are those who do not approve of those methods. They consider me old-fashioned, overly violent."

"How amazing."

"Yes, considering my methods have always been quite effective. These foolish new people call themselves reformers and believe I am some sort of conservative reactionary. But as we agree, nothing lasts forever."

Nastchenkov signaled one of his men. "We will try more civilized methods. I am certain you are familiar with pentothal."

As hard as he struggled, they were too strong for him. The vein in his other arm was used, and in minutes, Daniel found his mind floating once again.

# CHAPTER SIXTEEN

Bertram was waiting for Michelle when she returned. "Thought you might like to know that Kirson was right. I found harmonica bugs inside your phone and mine. The place is swept clean now. Everything checks out."

"And I thought our security was impenetrable."

"I guess it never pays to be overconfident."

"I'd better have the Washington office checked out as well."

"I've already arranged for it," Bertram assured her. "What did Kirson have for you?"

"Something rather shocking." She proceeded to explain what Kirson had told her about Daniel.

"What do you intend to do about it?" he asked her after she had finished.

"I do have a plan. However, I don't want to tell you about it quite yet. The first thing I need is to talk to Dimitri Nastchenkov. How do we do that?"

"I can manage it. I still have my contacts."

"Good, we'll explain that it's urgent, that I have something to exchange with him. That will pique his interest, don't you think?"

"Absolutely," Bertram concurred. "This whole thing is just to draw you out. He'll be pleased to converse with you."

That part of her plan worked well. Nastchenkov was in touch sooner than she'd expected. She waited in the office for his call, and less than an hour after she had left the message for him, her patience was rewarded.

"Michelle, my dear girl, I understand you wish to speak with me?" How polite the cobra could be!

"Yes, so good of you to return my call promptly." Her hand trembled slightly on the receiver, but her voice came out sounding firm and sure. "I believe that you have something that belongs to me — or should I say someone?"

He chuckled unpleasantly. "Ah, dear lady, how quickly news travels in this country."

"Perhaps we might make an exchange."

"That depends. What could you possibly have to offer me?" His voice betrayed amusement.

Be clever, she warned herself. Choose

278

your words carefully. "I have information on the Parker case."

"Very well, what is it?"

Now it was her turn to act amused. She laughed lightly. "Really, Dimitri, give me a bit of credit! I propose that we meet. I will bring certain documents that will be of great interest to your people. An exchange will buy my silence."

"A marvelous suggestion."

"Will you bring Dr. Reiner with you?"

"I regret to say that is not possible."

Her heart was in her mouth. "What have you done to him? If anything has happened to him, you get nothing!"

"He is in excellent health — for the time being."

"Choose a meeting place then."

"Certainly. You know how much I enjoy the ballet. I will be visiting with a friend today, a ballerina who works and practices in New York. We will be lunching at Sonja's Restaurant and Tea Room. Sonja bought many things of quality in Russia including my favorite, a silver samovar. It is rumored to have belonged to Czar Nicolas. A truly extraordinary place. You will see."

"What time shall I come?"

"Meet me there at two-thirty. My friend will have left by then. I warn you, do not arrive early. I detest rushing my meal."

"Fine. I think I can promise you an interesting surprise."

"I can hardly wait. For your friend's sake, I hope you are being truthful."

Had she spoken properly? She meant to sound calm and composed, though inwardly she was in turmoil. Nastchenkov was horribly shrewd and devious. What if he saw through her little ploy? But she doubted that he had. And it could work, especially since he did not appear to sense the extent of her desperation. How she wished she could talk this matter over with her uncle!

One of the few good things about this whole mess was that she could depend on Bertram. He waited for her in his car while she went into Sonja's by herself. It was not crowded, which would make things easier. She had no difficulty spotting Nastchenkov. He was sitting alone, finishing off a plate of beef Stroganoff. He looked up as she sat down at the table.

"Excellent calf's foot jelly today. Care to try some?"

She tried not to gag. Food was the last thing on her mind. Here was a man discussing menu items as if the two of them were old friends sharing a social occasion instead of enemies resolving the fate of another human being, Dr. Daniel Reiner, a unique and special man.

Nastchenkov's small, deep-set eyes followed her every movement with interest. "You have information for me, I believe?" He held out his hand as if summoning a pet poodle.

He appeared to be smugly self-satisfied. Very well, here was a weakness that could be turned to her advantage. She could hear Uncle Ted's voice whispering in her ear. *Discipline, self-control, girl, and you won't blow it.*

"You have perhaps a report for me to peruse?" He continued to hold out his hand in an imperious gesture. "You must give me some reason for releasing your friend."

"Certainly, but there really is no reason to keep Dr. Reiner, regardless."

"Is true?" He raised his thick, bushy eyebrows inquisitively.

"The doctor is an innocent. He knows nothing that would interest you."

"That remains to be seen. We have not as yet finished interrogating him."

"Rubbish! You know as well as I he isn't involved." *Careful,* she warned herself, *you're losing it.* "What is your interest in the Parker disappearance?"

"I ask. You answer. Now where is this

information you are going to give me?"

Michelle reached into her purse. "It's right here."

"Show it to me," he demanded impatiently.

"Of course, but back at my office."

He laughed loudly. "Ridiculous. You insult my intelligence. You are refusing to negotiate. Our meeting is at an end. Your friend will die very slowly." He rose abruptly from the table.

She fell into step alongside him as he started to leave the restaurant. They were an incongruous pair; he was short, fat, balding, and ugly, while she was tall, slender, regal, and attractive.

"I really do have something for you, Dimitri. I have every intention of negotiating. I would just prefer doing it in a more private place. Here, I'll show you what I've got."

Even as he stopped and turned to look at her, she had removed a 9mm Glock mini-pistol from her purse. The barrel was shoved into the fat man's side before he knew what had happened. He let out a surprised grunt and then the ever-ready umbrella began to move. But Michelle was prepared for it. She deftly knocked the weapon from his hand with a quick, swift blow of her free palm. Then she took his arm forcefully. The small pistol she had carefully chosen for this encounter was easily concealed in the short man's plump side.

"If you try anything again, Dimitri, it will be the last move you ever make."

"This is absurd, dear lady."

"My sentiments exactly, but then I did not start this, did I?"

She nodded to Bertram, who was opening the door to the backseat for her and Nastchenkov. Out of the corner of her eye, she saw the bodyguard rapidly approaching.

"Call him off, Dimitri! Tell him you will be dead in seconds if he takes another step toward us or draws his weapon."

"You don't mean that."

She smiled coldly. "Of course, I do. Don't forget, I was trained by my uncle."

"What do you hope to gain from such foolish behavior?"

"The release of Dr. Reiner. Tell your man now!"

Nastchenkov spoke to his bodyguard in a foreign tongue, and the man backed away, all the time eyeing them warily.

Bertram helped her get Nastchenkov into the backseat. Then he quickly took the driver's seat again.

"Where to?" he asked.

"Our office."

Bertram gave her a surprised look.

"Dimitri and I are about to conduct business." She kept the pistol in Nastchenkov's ribs for the entire ride back to the office. She did not relax for even a second, nor did she allow him to move.

Once they were in the office, she sent both secretaries home. Then she had Nastchenkov sit down facing opposite her in her private office.

"Now, Dimitri, I am ready to have our talk, and I will dictate the terms of the agreement. Daniel Reiner will either be released immediately and unharmed or you will die in a most unpleasant manner."

"I cannot believe you would be so asinine. We are professionals, my dear. This is utterly contemptible."

"Those attempts on my life were utterly contemptible. Frankly, I am in a bad mood. Someone who worked for me has been killed. He was quite professional. I don't intend to take any chances with you. You will either give orders to let Daniel go, or you will be dead."

The Bulgarian gazed appraisingly into her eyes. "What are your terms?"

"I want him returned safely to his office, and I don't want any one of your people ever to go near him again. Is that clear? If he is harmed, you have my solemn promise that someone, somewhere, sometime soon will kill you. Even if you manage to murder me, there are those who will carry out my request if you do not follow my instructions to the letter. My firm is well-connected. People owe us favors. Now you must consider whether or not Dr. Reiner's life is as valuable to you as your own."

Nastchenkov lowered his head. "Very well. I will make the necessary call."

She handed him the telephone from across the desk. Nastchenkov dialed a number and spoke to someone in his native tongue. She could not understand any of the conversation. But it seemed as if the correct instructions were being given. That in itself was reassuring. However, she knew better than to underestimate the man sitting opposite her. For one thing, his people knew exactly where he was being held. The building was not a fortress. Anyone could get to her office. Someone would be coming soon, she realized.

Nastchenkov reached nonchalantly into his vest pocket. Her hand was there before his. She twisted his hand with a sure quick movement.

"Stop. I was only reaching for a cigarette."

"I'm aware you don't smoke." She reached

into his pocket and carefully removed two pens and a wicked Swiss Army knife. She knew the fountain pens were loaded with poison he would squirt into the face of a victim if given the opportunity. The knife had well-honed blades.

"Bertram, I believe you have handcuffs for our friend?"

"I can do even better than that."

Bertram disappeared for a few minutes and returned with handcuffs and a length of nylon cord; he used both, binding the Bulgarian's hands and feet.

"I apologize for the inconvenience, but we cannot afford to give you the slightest opportunity for escape. As soon as Dr. Reiner is returned, you will be free to leave here. And I do keep my word."

"That will take at least two hours." Nastchenkov was no longer smiling; his expression appeared somber.

"Why will it take so long? Do your people believe they can liberate you without returning Dr. Reiner?"

"Dear Michelle, how could you think that? No, it is merely that the doctor received a dosage of certain drugs that render him temporarily unable to travel comfortably. However, he is in excellent health," Nastchenkov was hasty to add.

"Let us hope so, since your survival depends on it."

"Michelle, is it necessary to keep pointing that horrid weapon in my face? So uncivilized. I never thought it of you. I myself detest guns and violence. I am somewhat surprised at your lack of subtlety."

"Actually, it's a tribute to you, Dimitri. I have great respect for your remarkable skill and originality. Setting up my shower with toxic gas, for instance. The mark of a real artist. What cleverness! I know with you I must always be prepared. Expect the unexpected. Therefore, I proceed with considerable caution. In your honor, I even exchanged my Colt for this Glock, because it is a more accurate weapon. If I do have to kill you, I want to make certain you're dead with the first shot."

He smiled at her left-handed compliment, enjoying the hint of sarcasm in her voice. "A lady of your beauty and bearing, a goddess, a queen, to descend to such depths for such an ordinary man. I am deeply touched. Humbled, in fact. I have great respect for your abilities, just as I admired your uncle before you. I do not underestimate you. Therefore, I will give you no cause to kill me." His words were polite, but his eyes were hooded like the venomous viper he was.

An hour and a half passed very slowly. Suddenly Bertram motioned to her. Yes, she had heard it, too. There was a slight noise near the door leading out to the corridor. They took up positions on either side of the door, guns drawn. Sure enough, someone was picking the lock. They waited. Two men with automatic weapons drawn came rushing into the office. Bertram instantly disarmed one of them with a sharp blow downward on the man's hand. Her own actions synchronized with his, and both men were quickly at gunpoint.

"You will release Daniel Reiner unharmed, or Mr. Nastchenkov will die very soon. Do you understand?" They stood frozen and expressionless. "Now get out of here."

The two large men scurried out of the office like birds startled into flight. She went back into her office to deal with the Bulgarian.

"No more tricks. Make another phone call. This time give the instructions for real. I'm losing patience. I should kill you right here and worry about disposing of your body later."

"Such a lack of finesse. I am truly shocked. A word of advice. It would be terribly dif-

288

ficult to explain the death of a foreign diplomat in your office, my dear."

"Dimitri, you know very well you wouldn't be found here. Perhaps I will use your own fountain pen to kill you. Perfect justice, don't you think? You, who have murdered so many people with weapons of this kind. A spy should meet his death in an appropriate manner. Everyone would think that you died of a heart attack. No one would even question your passing."

"Yes, we are all mortals, are we not?" he responded with a deep sigh. "What makes you think my people will not call the proper authorities? In which case you will be arrested."

"I very much doubt it. For one thing, you are already implicated in two murders and a kidnapping. I don't think you want the publicity. Being declared *persona non grata* and asked to leave this country would not go over well with your people."

"Such a clever girl! Truly, you are worthy of your uncle. He would have been proud to see you carry on in his footsteps. But you should be aware that I work for myself these days, for those who pay me best. I have become capitalist like you. I have no politics."

"And just who is your current employer?"

"There is no way I would divulge that information, even if I knew. We have had no personal contact."

She moved the pistol closer to his face, but the assassin didn't even flinch.

"Even if you tortured me, I could tell you no more." His voice was dispassionate.

It was best that Nastchenkov remain unaware that she had never killed anyone in cold blood. Frightening a man like him was not easy, but she had to make her point or he would never cooperate. She took a key from a compartment in her desk and then unlocked her private closet. She removed a silencer that had been made for the larger Glock Bertram held. Nastchenkov watched with rapt attention, betraying little emotion as she deftly attached the silencer to the pistol. Then she and Bertram exchanged weapons.

"I will make the call if you will release my hands."

Perhaps she had succeeded in shaking him a bit. "I'll dial for you. This time, talk only in English." She used the speaker so she could listen as he spoke.

The next two hours went by very slowly. The three of them were all extremely tense. But for Michelle the wait seemed interminable. Bertram arranged for a reliable man to wait in Daniel's office and let them know the moment he was returned there. She took to staring at the telephone expectantly, as if that would make it ring more quickly. When it finally did ring, she jumped as if startled from a long sleep.

Dr. Reiner had been returned to his office. In answer to her question regarding his health, Bertram's man put Morris Lerner on the phone.

"Michelle? I've seen him look better, but I believe he's all right. I'm going to take care of him. I'm bringing Dan over to the hospital for a complete physical exam. Here, he wants to talk to you now."

"How are you?" she asked, eager to hear his voice at last.

"Wearing thin, but okay, thanks to you." His words were slurred.

"Are they gone?"

"Yes, but the man who said he was sent by you is still here."

"He's going to stay with you for a while, just as a precaution."

After hanging up the telephone, she turned to Bertram. "Could you please put our friend into a taxi cab?"

Bertram released Nastchenkov's hands and feet, leading the fat man toward the outer office.

"My dear, I regret to say you will know what true suffering is because of the indignity you have put me through today. I shall not forgive or forget."

She accepted the threat stoically. "If I were you, Dimitri, forgiving and forgetting is exactly what I would do. As you can see, we are acting in good faith by releasing you. It should be enough that you are alive and unharmed."

"This is a matter of honor."

"I had hoped you would be more sportsmanlike about this."

He merely glowered at her. "I shall not reconsider."

Bertram arched an eyebrow questioningly. "You still want me to release him?"

"Yes, we gave our word."

"Very well, Michelle, but I hope you won't live to regret your decision."

The important thing was that Daniel was all right. She called his apartment that evening and found he was at home.

"Can I stop by?" she asked, "or are you too exhausted after your ordeal?"

"I'd like to see you," he said.

"Why don't you take a nap, and I'll join you soon?"

■ ■ ■ ■

During the entire trip over to his apartment, all she could think about was whether or not he was really all right. Bertram's man was outside the door when she arrived. She told him that he could leave and paid him extra in cash for his time. Then she decided that rather than ringing the doorbell and disturbing Daniel, she would merely open the door herself and slip in. Since the door was locked, she chose a small pick from her purse and played with the lock until it opened.

Daniel was lying on the couch. His eyes flew open as she entered.

"You really need a better lock," she told him.

"You could have knocked," he said, sitting up.

Michelle came over and sat down beside him. "Just checking the security around here."

She looked at him thoughtfully. His fine, sensitive face was badly bruised. His dark eyes looked weary. He had to be in pain. Yet there was something about his appearance that told her he was undaunted.

"Did I thank you for getting me out of there?"

"You don't have to, since it was because of me they took you in the first place. I apologize for involving you in this horrible business. I never should have sent Nora to you."

"You're not to blame for anything." He took her hands in his own. "You're in danger every moment, aren't you? How can you live that way? How can you be so calm and cool?"

She removed her hand from his. "One acquires a sense of detachment. Don't doctors who work with terminal patients develop a certain objectivity? Otherwise, how can they help their patients?"

He didn't answer her directly. His fingers outlined the lines of her face, touching each part tenderly, reverently. "So you're something of a fatalist?"

"That's right. Death really isn't ever in question, is it? What matters is how we live."

"And how you live, Michelle, are you happy with it?"

"It suits me."

"You or your uncle? Aren't you trying to fit into his mold?"

"No, although I greatly admired him. Actually, his shoes were too large for me to ever fit into. I'm running the business my own way."

"I wonder if it's the right business for you." His intense eyes searched her face.

She turned away from him. He had the uncanny knack of throwing her completely off balance.

"You say you want me, Daniel, but you want me only on your terms."

"Let's not argue again. I'm not up to it. I'm glad you're here. Stay with me tonight. Don't leave."

"If you were smart, you'd tell me to get out and never come back. Look what happened to you simply because we've been seen together."

"You could leave all that behind you. Walk away from that kind of life. Walk into my life. We could make each other very happy."

She looked into his eyes, two candles reflecting darkly in a mirror. How easy it would be just to lose herself in them, and yet she knew that was impossible.

"I only came by to make certain you're all right. I owe it to you. I'd better be leaving now."

His arms were suddenly around her. She felt her heart begin to beat more rapidly.

"Why are you afraid of making a commitment?"

"It's you who should have the sense to be afraid of associating with me." She ought to free herself from him, but somehow she couldn't.

"I won't let you out of my life. Whatever, whoever you are, none of that really matters to me. I want you." He held her tightly in his arms. Her skin was tingling.

"I must go. We should never see each other again."

"We should get married and make beautiful children together."

With his arms wrapped around her, she had no more strength to resist him. He drew her toward him against the warmth of his chest. She gently kissed the bruises on his handsome face. His mouth pressed against her own yielding lips, and she found herself barely able to breathe.

"I want to make love to you right now. I want to give you pleasure and make you happier than you've ever been in your life," he told her.

Her cheeks were damp. She touched them and was shocked to realize that tears were flowing from her eyes. How could that be?

His hands ran slowly along the contours of her body. His mouth was warm and firm against hers. It was hardly what she would have expected after the ordeal he'd been through. His hands moved to the buttons on her blouse. Then she found herself helping him remove her lacy bra. His hands slid to her breasts, sending shivers of excitement through her body.

"I shouldn't let you," she said, trying to sound as if she meant it.

"You know it's what we both want." His hand caressed the fullness of her hip, sliding down on her body.

"You're not in any condition for this. You've suffered too much."

He smiled at her, and the dimple she so adored appeared in his cheek. "For this, I'll somehow summon the strength."

She unbuttoned his shirt and ran her fingers along the silky, dark hair that adorned his bare chest. He reminded her of Michelangelo's statue of David. He brought his lips to her breasts, causing her to gasp with pleasure. All sense of logic was overwhelmed by the great passion she felt for him, her need for him and his for her. She was caught up in a vortex of inescapable feeling. At this moment, they were just two people who needed and wanted the love and comfort each could provide for the other. She pressed herself closely against the velvet of his golden skin, hungry for his touch, overjoyed that he was alive and eager to love

her. All other rational thought was lost to
her.

# CHAPTER SEVENTEEN

It had rained during the night. There was a chill in the air. Michelle moved closer to the warmth of his body, enjoying the intimacy of waking near Daniel. She could tell by the evenness of his breathing that he was still asleep.

Glancing at her watch, which was lying on the end table next to the sofa bed they had slept on, she could see it was ten past eight in the morning. She rarely slept this late. In fact, she rarely slept this well. Having sex with Daniel had caused her to relax mentally and physically. Usually, she woke up in the middle of the night after having a bad dream and was unable to sleep afterward. Being with Daniel was indeed the perfect cure for insomnia.

She turned and studied his face. He was so handsome in repose, even with his bruises. She would let him rest. Knowing he was safe made her feel peaceful inside.

Daniel could not offer her physical protection, yet his presence made her feel emotionally secure. When was the last time she had felt this way? Not since before her parents died. In his own way, Uncle Teddy had tried to make up for the loss. He had taken care of her, taught her how one survives in a cruel and harsh world. But she had never felt truly safe again.

She decided to leave without disturbing Daniel. But as she began to dress, he stirred.

"Michelle?" He reached out for her and she went to him.

"Where are you going?"

"I was planning to stop by my apartment and then go on to visit Nora."

He was suddenly awake and alert. "I'll go with you."

"Don't you want to sleep late today? You must be exhausted."

He smiled at her warmly. "I feel like a buffalo tap-danced on my body, but the only way I'll stay in bed is if you stay here beside me." He grabbed her hand and kissed it. The sheet fell away from his body, displaying his torso.

She caressed his cheek, and the next thing she knew, she was nestled in his lap. She felt his arousal press hard against her core and touched her tongue to his lips. Their bodies entwined, melted together in a molten embrace. For a time, they lay tangled in each other's arms. The languorous satisfaction she felt brought a smile to her lips. She could have stayed with him like this forever. If only it were possible.

She kissed his forehead and then freed herself from his grip. "I really ought to get going," she said, collecting her clothing together. She was aware of him watching her dress, of the hot look in his dark eyes, and it made her terribly self-conscious. "Don't stare at me that way."

"Why not? It's frank admiration." Daniel got out of bed, his well-built body moving stiffly. "Let me fix you some breakfast."

"That's not necessary."

"I want to do it."

She refused again and slipped into the bathroom to finish getting ready to leave. By the time she was completely together, he too was dressed.

"No, it's best if I go alone. It's safer for you not to be seen with me," she told him in a firm manner.

"I don't care about that," he told her.

She was out the door before he could say another word. What had happened between them was not wise. In the cold light of morning, she could be sensible again. She had to stay away from him, at least until the Parker matter was resolved.

When she got outside his building, there were no cabs in sight so she began to walk, thinking to hail a cab on Fifth Avenue. It was then that she heard Daniel's voice calling out to warn her. She turned in time to see a car racing toward her at full speed, seeming to come out of nowhere. Daniel's strong arms were around her, pulling her out of harm's way.

"I could have managed by myself," she said, her voice breathy.

"Isn't that carrying independence just a bit far?"

She heard the car come screeching to a halt and saw it start backing up at full speed, backing up onto the sidewalk. It hit some garbage cans and continued backing up toward them.

"Come on," she said urgently.

They started to run. She steered Daniel toward an alley too narrow for any car to drive down.

The back alley had doors, but each one turned out to be locked. Finally, Daniel pulled one that opened. Michelle ran inside, prepared to pull out her handgun. It turned out that they were in the kitchen of a coffee shop. As they walked through to the front, the counterman stared at them in puzzlement. She realized they must look very strange hurrying through the wrong way, gasping for breath.

"Would you like some breakfast now?" Daniel asked her.

"Just a cup of tea." She turned to the man at the counter, pulling a twenty-dollar bill out of her purse. "This is yours if you'll quickly lock the back door to this establishment."

"Sure thing, lady."

Once that was taken care of, she felt a little more at ease. Daniel ordered coffee, pancakes, and grapefruit, insisting on sharing with her. Several people entered the shop but no one who looked suspicious. She began to relax a little, though she kept her bag close at hand.

"That car looked familiar," Daniel said.

"It should. It's Nastchenkov's. I would recognize that large, black Lincoln Continental with diplomatic plates anywhere. I have truly grown to detest the vehicle."

"My experiences in it weren't too pleasant, either," he agreed.

Obviously the vampire intended to go after her. The terror wasn't over; it was just beginning. Each time a new person walked into the coffee shop, Michelle looked up sharply, but Nastchenkov's people did not enter. When they left the shop, there was no sign of the big, black limo. Daniel hailed a cab.

"I'm going with you," he said in a tone of voice that allowed for no argument. She wasn't in any mood to debate with him. So they went back to her apartment together. Bertram had taken care of the new locks, just as he'd promised. He'd provided her with new keys. She felt better.

"Beautiful place," Daniel said as he looked around. "You have elegant taste in furnishings. I didn't exactly notice last time I was here."

"Toxic gas does rather throw one off one's game. But feel free to look about all you like now. I've been fortunate in having the opportunity to collect things from all over the world. It's one of the few advantages of being in a line of work in which you travel quite a lot."

"Maybe it's time to think of settling in one place," he said. He took her hand and held it, but she pulled away.

"I believe there's tea in the kitchen if you care for a cup. I'm going to shower and change."

"Need anyone to scrub your back?" he asked with a teasing smile. He reached out to touch her, but she carefully moved away from him.

"I'll manage on my own quite nicely." Keeping her distance from him was crucial.

"Probably, but it would be more fun if I helped you."

She ignored his comment and left him in the living room. It took all the courage she could muster to walk into that bathroom again, but she did it. The desire for a shower was stronger than any lingering fear she harbored. She needed to cleanse herself physically and spiritually.

As the hot water hit her body, she considered the most recent attempt on her life. Perhaps it wasn't even a serious attempt. The actual purpose of it could be to throw her out of focus, so off balance that she couldn't think about pursuing her case. Why were people trying so hard to stop her investigation of the Parker matter? What did they fear she would find out?

While Daniel waited, she dressed quickly, selecting a conservative gray wool pantsuit. He surveyed her as she came out of the bedroom.

"Very proper. True Iron Maiden stuff. You look ready to assume the role of prime minister of England."

"Not a half-bad idea. England would fare

better with another woman in charge," she said.

He gave her a quick kiss and then released her. "I'd be very proud of you."

They were getting Nora ready to leave the hospital when Michelle and Daniel arrived. Daniel visited several patients while Michelle talked with Nora. Katherine Matthews was there, too. Nora's daughter bustled around, nervously putting her mother's things in order.

"I want to see you back to the apartment," Michelle said. "Perhaps we might have a private chat."

"Of course," Nora said. She appeared pleased to have Michelle with her.

"I'll take the suitcase down and bring my car around to the emergency entrance," Katherine said. She seemed relieved to leave her mother with Michelle. An attendant helped Nora into a waiting wheelchair. Nora held out her frail hand to Daniel, who had just returned.

"It's good to have both of you here." Nora's eyes were ringed by purple shadows.

They didn't talk much in the car. Daniel sat up front with Katherine. The silence was uneasy. Michelle thought that Katherine was worried about her mother. It showed in the younger woman's face. Katherine had her mother's soft, fine features without the delicate, slight figure. She was tall and broad, like a farm girl. Michelle wondered fleetingly if James Parker had been raised on a farm.

Katherine drove her automobile slowly through the heavy noontime traffic. Sunlight danced on the water as they crossed the Brooklyn Bridge. Finally, they pulled up on Hicks Street. Katherine parked in a nearby lot, and they walked to the converted brownstone. Michelle looked at the building appreciatively. It was a remarkable Victorian structure. She took Nora's arm as they walked up the front stairs.

At her apartment door, Nora turned to her daughter. "I'm not an invalid, dear. I would really prefer to stay in my own apartment."

"No, Mother, we agreed. I'm going to look after you. Just for a little while, until you're feeling better."

"Katherine, I don't know that I will ever be feeling better."

"You will if you let yourself," Daniel said.

It was finally settled that Nora would simply pack up some of her things and stay with her daughter. When they entered the Matthewses' apartment, Michelle sat down with Nora in the comfortable living room. There was a huge brick fireplace, around which the room centered.

"I'll fix us some coffee and sandwiches," Katherine said, consumed by nervous energy. She was clearly grateful to find some excuse to leave her mother for a while.

"She's afraid I'm going to try it again," Nora said perceptively, watching her daughter hurry out of the room.

"And are you?" Daniel asked her. His gaze was direct and uncompromising.

"If I do, I'll manage to do it properly next time." Her voice was quiet and lacking in emotion.

"Nora, it's time we had another talk," Daniel said.

"No. I don't want either of you bothering about me anymore." Her eyes were fixed on the floor.

"You haven't told me everything I need to know. People are trying to kill me. Knowing all the facts is my only possible protection," Michelle said.

"I've told you what I know," Nora responded.

"Not everything. What are you holding back?"

Nora said nothing for a time, and Michelle was about to give up. Nora looked so delicate and vulnerable that Michelle felt guilty badgering her.

"It isn't very easy to talk about, you know. I tried to tell Dr. Reiner. He's so kind and understanding. But I couldn't tell even him." Nora ran her thin, arthritic fingers through her short, graying hair.

"I want to know why you hold yourself responsible for your husband's death. I'm not here to judge you. But I won't leave until we talk about it." Michelle's voice was gentle but firm.

"All right then. He didn't just leave me. I asked him to go."

"Why?" Michelle prodded.

"Because for a long time I knew that there was someone else in his life. James hardly touched me. He wasn't attracted to me anymore. We lived together as man and wife in name only. I wasn't cold to him in the beginning. I tried many times to get him to make love to me, but he just wouldn't. Yet he always insisted that he cared about the children and me. I tried to be patient, but the resentment kept on growing within me. Gradually, he became more and more pre-occupied. We never did discuss his work. Yet I was certain he was worried about something connected with his job. Of course, I couldn't be sure. Eventually, I decided to confront him and resolve the problems in our relationship. I think that was a terrible mistake as I look back on it now. I asked him if we couldn't begin to be more open with each other. I also asked him if there was someone else in his life.

"He finally confirmed my worst fears. He said that he had been involved with another person for quite a while. But he claimed that he wanted to end the relationship. He hadn't been able to do that because the situation became extremely difficult. I pushed him to tell me everything. I told him that he had to make a choice, either end the other relationship or get a divorce. He begged me to be tolerant and understanding. He said it was more complicated than I could possibly understand. I became enraged, demanded to know his reasons.

"When he refused to explain any further, I ordered him out of the house and told him not to come back until he was willing to tell me the whole truth. Well, of course, you both know the rest. He went to her. If I had been a little more understanding, more tolerant, as he asked me to be, maybe everything would be all right now. If I could have just managed to control my temper! I miss him all the time. Not a day goes by that I don't regret my impetuous behavior.

Whatever happened to James, it's my fault. I can only blame myself. I hate myself!"

Nora began to weep, sorrow bursting forth from the depths of her soul.

Daniel tried to comfort her, holding her hand tightly. "When marriages fall apart, no one person is to blame."

"We were married well over a quarter of a century. We had children together. He never did a dishonest or disreputable thing in all that time. He valued his good reputation, and he deserved the respect he got. He was a wonderful man with real integrity. And I threw him away. I handed him over to that woman without a fight. How can I forgive myself? I deserve to die!" She continued to sob, her emaciated fingers pressed tightly over her face.

Should Michelle tell Nora that James had been a spy? Doing so wouldn't help the situation. Besides, Nora most certainly knew. "I'm going to prove to you that you are wrong, that whatever happened to James was not your fault. But you must in turn have faith in me. You must not contemplate suicide again. You must listen to what Daniel tells you and take the medication he gives you. Do you understand? You must wait for me to find out what really happened to James." Michelle spoke to Nora in a strong, compelling voice. "I'm going to leave soon, but I will be back again before I return to Washington. I *will* find out what happened to James. Believe that! We are both committed to the same thing. You must not take a cowardly course of action." She was looking directly into Nora's unfocused eyes. "Do you understand me?"

"Yes," Nora said, but there was still uncertainty in her clouded vision.

Katherine Matthews returned with a tray of coffee and cheese sandwiches cut without the crusts.

"I shouldn't stay," Michelle told Katherine. But the young woman's eyes implored her to remain. "All right, perhaps just a small sandwich," she said.

Katherine smiled gratefully. After they had eaten, Nora announced that she was feeling tired. Katherine led her mother to the guest room and got her settled in. She returned to the cozy living room in short order.

"I hope the nurse we requested arrives soon. Thank you both for coming home with us. You've made it much easier for her and me as well. Will you come by again, Michelle?"

"Tomorrow morning."

"Good. You seem to have a steadying influence on Mother."

"I'll stay here for a little while," Daniel said. "I want to give you a few instructions and write out a new prescription."

Katherine nodded her head solemnly and then removed the lunch dishes to the kitchen.

Daniel turned to Michelle. "I want to take you to dinner tonight."

"I have to decline. I'm going to be much too busy."

"I promise not to take up very much of your time."

"Daniel, I meant it when I said we shouldn't be seeing each other, at least not for the time being."

"And I meant it when I said I refuse to live in fear. I want to be with you and I believe you want to be with me. I don't think we should let anything or anybody get in the way of our feelings for each other."

She touched the lock of brown, wavy hair that fell across his long, sensitive forehead. "I can't believe that you put emotion ahead of logic. And you call yourself a psychiatrist, a mender of minds?"

"Emotions control logic. Everyone knows that. You can't ignore how you feel about certain people. You have to deal with feelings in an honest way or they can destroy you. Look, what you and I think seem to be in opposition. Why don't we just analyze our problem together tonight?"

"Because when we're together, I can't think. I only react." Michelle tried not to look at him. If he refused to control his feelings, then she would have to do it for both of them.

"See what I mean? That's something we need to discuss."

"I have to be back in Washington tomorrow."

"Then I'll go with you."

"That isn't possible."

"I wish you were never leaving New York again, at least not without me."

She bit into her lower lip. "You make everything so difficult for me."

"Just say we can have dinner together. I promise to surprise you. And I'll be on my best behavior, honor bright."

She didn't believe a word of it, but there was something so compelling about him. "All right, you've finally worn me down. Where shall we meet?"

"I'd prefer to pick you up. What can I say? I'm just an old-fashioned kind of guy."

"I don't know where I'll be later. I'll come by for you."

"Modern women! Okay, there's a storefront on Houston Street in the East Village.

A few of us donate time there each week. It's a free clinic we established to help the homeless, addicts, alcoholics — you name it. I'll be there all afternoon."

He wrote out the directions, and she promised to meet him. But he hesitated for a moment.

"The only thing, it's kind of a bad neighborhood for an unescorted woman."

"Daniel, I thought we were through worrying about safety."

"Mine, but not yours."

She laughed at his obvious chauvinism. "Really, I'm much better at self-protection than you are!"

He gave her a quick kiss on the lips. "Then you can be my bodyguard. Everyone will envy me."

"I'll be by around five." With that, she left him at the Matthews apartment.

Bertram was in the office when she arrived. She asked him to come into her private office and closed the door.

"I've been having a bit of a problem with Nastchenkov," she told him directly.

"That's not much of a surprise. Don't you think it's time we took action? He won't be satisfied with anything less than killing you, and probably Dr. Reiner as well."

"He is getting to be something of a nuisance," she agreed.

"It surprises me that you've waited this long. I'll be glad to handle the matter for you if you like."

"That would be most helpful, Bertram. However, it's only fitting that I handle the matter myself. But he won't be easy to get at."

"Michelle, a person with proper training and experience can kill anyone. Presidents of the United States surrounded by so-called top security have been assassinated by amateurs. A smart professional can zap anybody. I'll put Nastchenkov under surveillance right away. Then we can work out something."

She agreed to let Bertram explore the problem. Before they even finished their conversation, there was a caller that Maureen identified as Colonel Atwood.

"Yes, I'll take it," she said.

"How are you, Ms. Hallam?" He sounded as formal as ever.

"Well and content. To what do I owe the honor of this call?" Of course, she knew it had something to do with the Parker investigation, but she wanted him to spell out his intentions directly.

"I've been in New York these last few days.

In fact, I'm going to be leaving for Washington late this evening. Before I go, I thought we might have a talk."

"Concerning what?" she probed.

"James Parker."

"I'm free right now," she told him.

"Unfortunately, I'm not. Can I drop by your office this evening before I leave for the airport?"

She remembered her dinner engagement with Daniel. "I don't believe I can get back to the office this evening. Do you know Monroe's? It's a rather fashionable pub-style bar in the East Eighties?"

"No, but I can find it."

"I estimate that I can meet you there around nine."

"That would be fine."

"Unless you'd be willing to talk on the telephone now? It would save you a lot of extra traveling about the city."

"No, we should talk face to face."

She gave him the address of the pub, wondering what he might have to say to her.

For several hours, the Parker investigation was shunted aside as calls came in from England and the Continent, and Bertram asked for input on work they were doing for other clients.

■ ■ ■ ■

It was already growing dark by the time she got out of the cab in the East Village. She looked in the storefront where Daniel was working. She could see him inside sitting and talking to a young woman with stringy, blond hair. Michelle glanced at her watch. She would give him a little more time.

She walked partway up the block and looked around. The street seemed incredibly dirty and sinister. Graffiti artists had been hard at work redecorating the old buildings. Bags of garbage overflowed trash cans.

She was suddenly aware of two mean-looking youths approaching her, and she turned and started walking back quickly toward Daniel's clinic. It was always best to avoid trouble whenever possible. Without warning, there was a hand on her shoulder and a switchblade at her throat.

"You want money?" she asked in a soft, calm voice.

They looked like members of a street gang. She took them for muggers.

"Hey, dude, remember what the freakin' foreigner said, if we make it look like robbery when we off her, we get double."

"I would pay you more not to do anything," she said, trying to reach into her purse.

The second man attempted to wrestle her purse away, but when she held tight, the first nicked her throat with the knife and snatched the handbag away.

"Let's do her now," the second youth said.

With her feet planted firmly and her knees slightly bent, she moved her hips to the left and quickly struck the abdomen of the man holding her with her right elbow as hard as she could. Slipping her right arm around his waist, under his left arm, she grasped his right sleeve with her left hand and threw him over. He took a hard fall on the concrete and grunted. The second attacker picked up the knife before she could get at it and started moving toward her with a sweeping motion of the blade. As he swung at her, she pulled her body out of the path of the knife, moving to the outside of his knife hand in a position that left her less vulnerable. Then she blocked his slashing motion with the center of her forearms, her right palm making contact with his right wrist. Her left forearm was just above his elbow. She slid her right thumb under his wrist and grabbed it, turning the knife away. She maintained a steady force on the pressure point just above his right elbow. She clearly heard the cracking sound as his arm broke. He let out a deep groan of agony.

The first attacker came lunging at her again. She let out a loud, clear yell, forced from the center of her body through her diaphragm, and then drew up her knee, thrusting it sharply into her assailant's groin. She pushed him to the ground and snatched back her purse. Both men were lying on the pavement now, no longer a threat to anyone. She opened her purse and removed a handkerchief, using it to pick up the knife from the pavement. Carefully, she wrapped the weapon and placed it into her bag. Then she removed the automatic she was carrying and pointed it at the two men.

"I ought to kill both of you," she said.

They stared at her, cringing in fear.

"No, lady, it was all a mistake!"

They were very nervous now, she observed with satisfaction.

"Your mistake, not mine. Who hired you?"

"Nobody. We wasn't really gonna hurt you." She kicked the first assailant in the knee.

"I repeat my question. Who?"

"Just some guy. He gets calls from people. Sometimes he gives us work. I don't know nothing."

This was a waste of time, she realized. "Since you're both so innocent, I'll give you a chance to get out of here before I make a call to the police."

They ran away like a pair of antelopes eluding a hunter's rifle.

Her neck hurt. She touched her throat. Her hand came away with blood. There was a lovely scarf in the pocket of her suit jacket. She brought it out now and arranged the accessory to hide the unsightly cut.

She walked back to the clinic. Daniel was just finishing with his patient. The girl he was talking with was biting her nails, oblivious to everything around her except Daniel, her face pale and intense. Michelle could see the girl was a lot younger than she had at first realized.

"I know what you want me to do, Doc, but I just can't call my folks." Michelle noticed how emaciated and unwell the girl looked.

"It's not what I want, it's what you want."

"They don't care. They're glad I ran away."

"Maybe they're not. Anyway, how can you be sure what they'll think or feel until you've spoken with them again?"

She shook her head. "Can't do it."

"Look, Teri, you give me the number, and

I'll call them for you just to let them know you're okay."

The conversation went back and forth for several more minutes, and finally the girl agreed. Daniel was persuasive, Michelle realized. Teri finally wrote out her family's name, address, and telephone number on the small pad Daniel handed her. Daniel gave her another appointment, and the girl passed Michelle, her eyes barely focusing.

Daniel saw Michelle standing there and immediately came toward her.

"Finished for today?"

"Ready to leave." He picked up his suit jacket and unrolled his shirtsleeves.

"That girl was a drug addict?"

"Street hooker on crack. The pimps wait for girls like her to get off the bus and they swoop down on them like vultures. I'm doing what I can to help her. Let's get out of here."

"Did you have any special place in mind?" she asked.

"I did promise you a surprise." His eyes twinkled.

"Let me guess. Is it the French place we ate at last time?"

He shook his head. "We practically came to blows there. Besides, it's much too ordinary. No, I've got this excellent place in mind with a unique atmosphere and warm, friendly service. You might say it's intimately family style."

She laughed dubiously. "You aren't going to tell me any more than that, after piquing my curiosity?"

"Two can play at the mystery game, my darling." Holding the door open for her, he leaned over and kissed her on the tip of her nose. Suddenly, he looked alarmed. "What happened to your throat?"

She looked down and realized that the scarf had loosened and the cut was showing. His hands moved the scarf away from her neck.

"It's nothing," she said.

He eyed her professionally. "Deep gash and it's still bleeding. I've got my medical bag with me. I'll take care of that before we leave here."

His hands were magic. He cleaned the wound, applied antiseptic and a bandage with quick, competent movements, finishing before she even realized he was done.

"There," he said. "That's better."

"You should have been a surgeon," she said, carefully reapplying the scarf at her neck. "You have wonderful hands."

"Glad you think so." He caressed her cheek. "Let's get going," he said. "I don't handle compliments any better than you do and I'm also very hungry. If I don't get some food soon, I'm going to start nibbling on you."

"Is that supposed to be a threat?"

She was happy to discover he had a car parked close by. As he drove, she realized how terribly tired she was. He turned on the radio and found some music that was pleasant and relaxing. She closed her eyes and let her mind drift. It was peculiar how comfortable she felt with him, even when they didn't speak. She realized that some time ago she'd begun to trust Daniel absolutely and completely, a rare occurrence in her life.

At one point, she opened her eyes and realized they were on a bridge, gliding over water in the moonlight.

"Where are we?" she asked dreamily.

"Leaving Manhattan," he said.

"Whatever for?"

"We're almost there," he said evasively.

She realized she must have dozed off when the car came to an abrupt stop and she was again fully alert.

"How do you like it?"

She looked around at the unfamiliar surroundings. They were on a tree-lined avenue with lots of brick homes interspersed with apartment buildings.

"Exactly where are we?" she demanded.

"Ocean Parkway in Brooklyn."

She gasped. "Let me guess. Where your grandparents live?"

He gave her a big smile, displaying his dimpled cheek. "What a clever girl! You can catch the brass ring on the merry-go-round over by the boardwalk on Coney Island."

"Is there really one?"

"Would I lie to you? My grandparents used to take me over to Coney Island to ride it every Saturday when I was four or five."

"How incredible to think of you as a little boy. And did you ever catch the brass ring?"

"All the time," he said with a boyish smile.

"And you're also terribly modest."

"Glad you noticed."

"Daniel, don't you think you should have told them we were coming tonight."

"Oh, they know all about it."

She was furious with him. "How dare you not tell me?"

"You wouldn't have come."

She admitted to herself in the interest of fairness that he was right.

"There's a saying: it's easier to ask for forgiveness than permission. I kind of subscribe to that philosophy."

She opened the car door, got out, and slammed it behind her. "How could you? You had no right! I'm leaving. I'll find my own transportation back to the city."

"This is part of New York City." He took her hand. "They're expecting us, you know."

"You're really impossible."

"I love you," he said.

She pulled away from him. "That doesn't excuse anything. And I wish you'd stop saying it."

"Come with me, please." He held his hand out to her.

She turned her back to him. "I'm really no good at this sort of thing. I don't have any family, and I'm not comfortable with those of other people."

"Please do it for me." He stroked her back, sending a shiver down her spine.

"You're totally unfair. You're fighting dirty."

"What are you so afraid of, darling?" He turned her toward him. His dark eyes caught her own and held them fast with riveting intensity. "You need human contact. No man or woman is an island. It's wrong to try to cut yourself off from your feelings."

She found herself trembling. "All right, I agree to meet your family, but I'm still quite angry with you."

"Michelle, we have something very special. Let's hold on to it. I want you to get to know my family. Is that so terrible?"

Daniel took her hand firmly and guided her toward the brick apartment building where his grandparents resided. She found herself unable to speak. What was there about Daniel that stopped her from thinking sensibly? Why was she so drawn to him?

# CHAPTER EIGHTEEN

It was apparent to Daniel that his grandmother's initial reaction to Michelle was one of disapproval. Although he thought that it would not have been obvious to anyone but him, since she was careful not to let it show. Michelle, however, was not just anybody. She flashed him a look that told him she understood the situation perfectly, and it was just what she expected.

He marveled at her perceptiveness. That was one of the things that made her so attractive. Michelle's outward toughness came not from a lack of sensitivity but, in actuality, too much of it. She was like a tortoise, compensating for her tender skin by developing a hard outer shell. He sometimes had the feeling he understood her better than she understood herself.

"Your face, what happened? Let me get an ice pack to put on it."

"I'm okay, Grandma," he assured her.

"Just a little accident. Tell you what? Can we have some of your outstanding chicken soup? I told Michelle it was a cure for everything that ails a person."

"Of course. I made a fresh pot this morning."

He watched his grandmother nervously smoothing her apron over her ample hips. "What lovely gloves you're wearing!" she remarked to Michelle, clearly searching for something polite to say.

Michelle acknowledged the compliment with a polite nod of her head.

"So come into the kitchen. The two of you must be starving to death. You'll have some soup while I serve up the meal." She brought out a steaming pot of chicken broth with vegetables plus barley and ladled it into plates at the neatly set table. Michelle seated herself opposite Daniel in the small but immaculate kitchen. There was no formal dining room in the old-fashioned apartment. However, there was no need for one. The atmosphere in the kitchen was homey and warm.

"Seltzer?" his grandfather asked, bringing out a chilled bottle.

"Tonic water! Certainly, I'll have some."

"So you're English?" his grandmother asked.

"I hold dual citizenship actually, Mrs. Lupinsky."

"Please, call me Ethel, and my husband is Joe. We try to be modern."

"Michelle travels a great deal," Daniel told them. He still had hopes that they would like her once they got to know her. Their opinion mattered to him. But regardless, nothing would change his feelings for her.

His grandmother placed a plate of hors d'ouevres in front of them. Michelle self-consciously removed her gloves and selected a miniature potato pancake.

"Delicious," she said appreciatively.

His grandmother smiled at the compliment. Then she began staring at the hard, callused area along the ridge of Michelle's right palm.

"You play a musical instrument of some kind?"

Michelle smiled tolerantly. "I believe you're thinking of guitar players. They develop calluses on their fingertips. I practice martial arts, not musical arts. Although I must say I am appreciative of good music."

He saw the look that passed between his grandparents and squirmed in his chair.

"Jujitsu? Like in the movies?" his grandfather asked.

Michelle laughed airily. "Not like in the

kung fu movies, no! The karate I practice is essentially used for self-protection. All women should learn it, at least the basics."

"You're so right! A woman isn't safe walking the streets of this city alone," Daniel's grandmother agreed.

"You set a lovely table. I can't remember when I've been treated so graciously."

His grandmother looked genuinely pleased. "Such good manners! It isn't often we have a charming world traveler in our home. So I guess your life is exciting?"

"Sometimes, too exciting," Michelle conceded.

"I'll bet you're a fashion model," Daniel's grandmother said. "You're so tall and slim."

Michelle smiled. "Hardly."

"A stewardess then?" His grandfather said.

"Joe, they're called flight attendants these days. You'll offend our guest."

"I wouldn't be offended, I assure you, but as it happens I'm not in that line of work either."

"So what line of work are you in?"

Daniel sighed deeply. His grandmother did not give up easily when she wanted to know something.

"I run a consulting firm."

"You make a living from that?" His grandfather's question was embarrassing, but Michelle seemed to take it in stride.

"We do well enough. I can't take much of the credit. My uncle created the firm. I took it over when he passed on. It runs rather autonomously now."

"Grandpa, why don't you pour Michelle some wine?" Daniel interjected.

While they drank a glass of sweet red wine together, Daniel's grandmother told Michelle about how hard he'd studied to become a doctor.

"Daniel was such a good student. He earned scholarships and worked his way through school. I wish we could have given him more. I always knew he was meant to be a doctor. Daniel cares about people." Ethel turned to her husband. "Joe, remember how people always used to talk to him and tell him their problems, even total strangers on the subway?" She turned back to Michelle. "He has such sympathetic eyes, don't you think?"

Michelle smiled over at him. He could tell she realized how uncomfortable the conversation was making him.

"And he's so modest. He got straight As in school. He was always studying, never thought he knew enough. He'd come home from taking an exam and think he'd done badly. Then his grades would be the highest in the class."

"It's always the intelligent, well-educated people who think they know very little," Michelle observed. "Stupid, ignorant individuals are convinced they know everything, or at the very least, all they need to know."

"You're right about that," Ethel agreed.

"Is the roast chicken ready?" Daniel asked, eager to change the subject. The last thing he wanted was for his grandmother to continue to brag about him.

Grandma Ethel returned to setting food into plates. "I didn't know you were waiting for it. Let me know if you like the glaze. It's my own special recipe."

"Fresh, crisp vegetables," Michelle said. "Marvelous!" Her great green eyes sparkled with remarkable clarity.

"I try to cook old recipes in the modern way."

Michelle was a perfect guest. She was pleasant and polite. The atmosphere soon became more relaxed. Daniel would not have believed it, but everyone was having a good time. He thought at first that they were all trying especially hard for his benefit. In a sense, that was probably true. But Michelle managed to win his grandparents over. She was like a gemstone, a multi-faceted woman, always surprising him with a new aspect. As Shakespeare said of Cleopatra: a woman of infinite variety.

Daniel smiled; his grandmother was definitely warming to Michelle. When his grandfather began telling some of his stories, Daniel knew they'd accepted her completely. The evening passed quickly.

"You be careful going out on the street tonight," Grandma Ethel admonished as they got ready to leave. "Mr. Bernard two floors above us was beaten and robbed right at the corner."

"Your grandmother blames the Russian mob that's taken over in Brighton. They call it Little Odessa because hardly any English is spoken. All the shops are owned by Russians."

Daniel almost said that with Michelle by his side, he had his own personal bodyguard, but he knew such a remark would only pose new questions. Instead, he gave his grandmother an affectionate kiss on the cheek.

"I'm always careful."

"No, you're not. Just look at your face!"

"Ethel, the boy is right," Joe Lupinsky's blue eyes twinkled brightly. "He shouldn't be fearful the way we were taught to be."

His grandmother stubbornly folded her arms over her full breasts. "It's just common sense. People must be streetwise. Otherwise, how will they survive in a big city like New York?"

"Actually, I agree completely. I'm always cautious," Michelle said. "I'll make certain your grandson is, as well."

Ethel's face beamed appreciatively. "I'm glad Daniel met such a sensible young woman."

It was nearly eight by the time Daniel drove Michelle back to Manhattan. She hardly spoke on the drive, and he thought that she was probably tired.

"So are you glad I drove tonight?"

"I'm surprised you keep a car in the city," she said.

"It's my one real luxury. Comes in very handy when I leave Manhattan. Your apartment or mine?"

"Neither. You'll have to drop me off at Monroe's. I have an appointment there."

"Will it take long? I could meet you afterward."

"I'll let you know."

"I hope the evening wasn't too unpleasant for you," he said, glancing over at her momentarily.

"Your grandparents are very nice people, good people. I like them."

"I'm glad you feel that way, because you

certainly won them over. And I want them to love the woman I'm going to marry."

He could see her face flush as he glanced over at her.

"Daniel, I can't believe the things you say!"

"I'm just being candid."

"We hardly know each other."

"I mean for that to change, Michelle." He glanced over at her. "I know it's not easy for you to trust other people."

"That's right. Believe me when I say I have my reasons, good reasons, actually."

"I accept that," he said, gently kissing her hand. "I don't mind doing the talking. I told you I was raised by my grandparents after my mother died. Mom was a beautiful woman, loving and vital. She developed ovarian cancer and died too young. I was only five years old at the time, but I knew then that I wanted to be a doctor and save as many lives as possible. I found out years later that surgery just wasn't for me. So I set out to heal people's minds instead of their bodies."

"The desire to help other people is always a worthy ambition, and there are many ways to help. Are you in contact with your father at all?"

"Every now and then, I get a postcard,

but there's been no real communication for years."

"I can see how that must have hurt you."

"I was lucky to have my grandparents. They've given me their love and devotion. But they weren't born in this country. They grew up with fear. Their parents suffered because of prejudice. They worry about me too much. I don't intend to spend my entire life living in fear, no matter what. When Nasty and his crew kidnapped me, I was terrified, but I didn't cower. There's a book called *The Red Badge of Courage.* Did you ever read it?"

She shook her head. "I've heard of it."

"Well, the point that Stephen Crane made was you never know if you really have courage until you're faced with a situation where you need it. I found out I'm not a coward. So you don't have to be afraid for me."

She didn't answer him, and he had no idea what she was thinking. He drove her to Monroe's, which was just two blocks away from her apartment on East 82nd Street.

"I'd like to continue our conversation," he said before she got out.

"All right, why don't you take my keys and wait for me in the apartment. I shouldn't be very long." She placed her keys

337

in his hand and then quickly got out of the car.

It took him twenty minutes to find a place to park. Then he went into Michelle's building. It felt strange going up to her apartment without her. Her living room seemed impersonal without her in it. He studied the carpeting, royal blue, velvet plush, luxurious, and expensive. The elegant room was impressive, and yet cold, almost sterile. There were no family photos, no mementos, nothing to differentiate the place from a hotel suite.

He closed his eyes and rested. He had never felt quite so tired. His experience with Nastchenkov had been more frightening than he cared to admit to Michelle. He was far from recovered physically or mentally.

He must have dozed off for a while, for when he was fully awake again, he heard someone ringing the doorbell and realized that Michelle had returned.

He went and let her in immediately. Her facial expression looked odd, off. There was something about the eyes, a masklike quality. It made him feel uneasy.

"Time for our talk?" he asked.

"Yes, and then some. I haven't been completely honest with you," she said. She brushed a few strands of copper bright hair away from her face.

"I think you've been very open."

She turned and faced him squarely. "No. You see, I haven't told you everything about myself. After all, you've been entirely open with me, haven't you?" Her great, green eyes probed his like searchlights.

She was in a strange mood, he decided. When he didn't answer her question, she continued to speak. "Everything I told you about my work was true. The firm does private investigations of a sensitive nature. I refuse all espionage activities in the ordinary sense. For example, we do not steal secrets or pass clandestine messages. We avoid the really sordid stuff. What I omitted to mention was that Uncle Ted was something of a specialist — in political assassination." She paused as if to let what she'd said sink in. Suddenly, it hit him with the force of a mortar.

"Michelle, are you saying that you —"

She interrupted him impatiently. "I'm saying that Uncle Ted was a professional assassin. It began when he worked for British intelligence. Then when he left, he decided to branch out on his own. It wasn't difficult, because he had all the right contacts."

She was in a peculiarly volatile mood, emotionally charged, and he sensed that she wanted to talk on. He said nothing, waiting for her to continue.

"I told you that my parents died. I did not tell you that they were, in fact, murdered, viciously shot to death in an Arab marketplace by terrorists because they were British diplomats. That was when my uncle decided to work freelance. His first assignment was to find those who had assassinated my parents and kill them. He swore revenge, and he made good on his promise to himself and me."

"But you're not a killer."

He stared into her eyes, which looked as wild as a storm at sea.

"My uncle trained me. I know many ways to kill. I am highly skilled. But no, since his death, I haven't allowed the firm to accept those sorts of assignments. But there is something you should understand. Although I have never had to kill anyone, if and when it became necessary, I wouldn't hesitate."

"You mean in self-defense. Given the right circumstances, anyone could kill."

"Would *you* be capable?"

He stared at her, not able to answer her question.

"If it's any comfort to you, I never take on an assignment unless I believe it's right. Uncle Ted never did either. There are always moral and ethical considerations I weigh very carefully. Uncle Ted was an avowed antiterrorist who wanted to remove human vermin from the world. I am in sympathy with that goal."

"God protect us from zealots."

She faced him angrily. "I believe in what Uncle Ted was trying to do. He wanted to make the world better for everyone. This world needs more people like him."

"I'm sorry, but your uncle sounds like he was something of a fanatic."

"Now you're the one who is standing in judgment." She pointed her finger at him. "But are you so pure? Tell me, love, just how honest have you been with me? Wasn't there something you might not have told me?"

Her accusing tone of voice made him wonder. "Who did you see at Monroe's tonight?"

"Take a guess!"

Suddenly he knew. "Colonel Atwood?"

"Give the man a brass ring!"

"If they give one out for stupidity, I certainly deserve it."

She folded her arms; her mobile mouth was set in a hard line. "If we don't have trust, Daniel, we have nothing. You told me to trust you, but you lied to me. We really didn't meet in the South of France by accident, did we?"

He realized that he should have told her the whole truth long ago. Not doing so had been a serious mistake, an error in judgment. But somehow, he'd known all along she would react like this. It was what he'd feared. That was why he'd put off telling Michelle. Damn Atwood! Why did he have to tell her now? Daniel took a deep breath and plunged in like a swimmer diving into an uncharted ocean, aware that Atwood would have put the ugliest spin possible on his actions.

"I was recruited by agents from the National Security Agency during my senior year of medical school. They interviewed me, explained how they needed psychiatrists in a capacity to help protect the national welfare in the war against terrorism. I was pretty green, I guess. Anyway, I bought into what they were selling. I thought I should do something for my country, serve in my own capacity. When I was asked to take an expense-paid trip to Europe on behalf of the NSA, I didn't question it. I was required to do certain things for them. One of those things related to you. Colonel Atwood ordered me to do a profile. I was told where to go and when to be there. I was given your description. They were considering you for some sort of special assignment. I wasn't told anything else."

"I was never contacted."

He lowered his eyes. "I know. I didn't recommend you. After we met, I didn't want them involving you in whatever cloak-and-dagger activity they were planning. I cared for you too much."

"So on your own you decided to protect me? Is that it?"

He saw the color rising in her cheeks.

"How charmingly chauvinistic! How dare you presume to make such a decision for me! Who gave you the right to act as judge?"

"I admit to being wrongheaded. I had no right. If it's any consolation, I never worked for them again. And I know I should have been truthful with you from the beginning."

"But you weren't! And there can't be anything real between us without trust."

"So what are you saying? We can't have a relationship?"

She ran her long, slender fingers through her copper tresses. "We're wrong for each other in every possible way."

He tried to reach for her, but she eluded his grasp. "I love you, and I think you love me in spite of everything else."

"My work leaves no place in my life for a serious involvement with anyone. When we went to your grandparents' flat tonight I had a glimpse of the world you come from and what you need. We're so different! Let us just say goodbye and part on friendly terms. I want good memories of the time we spent together, brief though it may have been. You must find yourself a woman of similar background who will devote herself to you. But that woman can never be me."

He realized that his body was shaking with emotion. "So you think that we can just be casual friends? Maybe when we bump into each other occasionally we can just exchange a casual peck on the cheek. Something like this?" He took her forcefully into his arms and kissed her on the mouth with all the passion he felt for her in his soul. For a fraction of a moment, she responded urgently. Then she pushed him away with violence.

"Don't you dare do that ever again!"

He saw the tears well up in her eyes, although she did her best to hide them.

"Get out of here, Daniel, and don't ever come back!" She shoved him toward the door with incredible strength and then slammed the door in his face. He stood there, his body still shaking, more confused than ever about Michelle and his feelings for her. He could hear her sobbing right through the door.

"Michelle!" he called out. He pounded on her door, anger fueling his intensity. But she did not answer. "I'm not giving up on you or us. I'll find a way to reach you."

"Go away!" he heard her cry out.

He felt totally drained. All he knew was that there was feeling within him for her that ran so deep, it pierced the marrow of his being.

# CHAPTER NINETEEN

Michelle could not sleep, tossing and turning the entire night. Try as she might, she could not stop thinking about Daniel. Her attraction to him was like a dread disease. She knew she had to put him out of her mind but such a thing seemed impossible.

And yet every time she thought of Daniel, she recalled what Atwood had told her the previous evening. At first, it had been a friendly chat — as friendly as a man of Atwood's stern disposition could manage. Then he'd gotten down to business.

"How is your investigation of the Parker matter coming?"

She'd answered that there wasn't much clear-cut information regarding the man's disappearance.

"I can help you if you like. All you have to do is ask."

"Thank you. I'll keep that in mind, I assure you."

"There's something you should know. I feel I've been remiss in a sense. I spoke to your friend Dr. Reiner a few days ago."

"I wasn't aware you knew him." She'd been genuinely surprised.

"Actually, I hired him to do some psychological evaluations for us. Yours was one of them." He gave her a moment to let the information sink in. "He recommended we not hire your agency. We followed his advice. When I finally met you, Ms. Hallam, I realized you were just the sort of person we wanted on our payroll. I must say, Dr. Reiner proved to be quite a disappointment. I can only believe that he has his own agenda. Who knows? Perhaps there are others who have employed him? Think carefully about trusting the man. And I do hope you will reconsider working for us. I could put you on immediately at a generous salary."

She felt cold and hot simultaneously. It was as if she'd been dealt a lethal blow. She thanked Colonel Atwood and politely refused his offer of employment, then quickly made an excuse to leave.

Daniel was the one person she'd believed to be completely honest and decent; how could she have been so wrong about him? He was just an ordinary man as capable of deceit as the next person. Their entire friendship was built on a network of lies. How horribly foolish she'd been! He hadn't made love to her—he'd fucked her.

Bertram was not in the office when she arrived at ten in the morning. He'd left a message on her desk that he was "working on her problem." She understood that to mean he was personally shadowing Nastchenkov. It was just the sort of thing Bertram would do.

Michelle thought back to when she'd hired him. Bertram had just retired from the Bureau after twenty-five years of service, his wife had left him and he was at loose ends. Michelle knew his work well. He had done counterintelligence for the New York Field Office. She'd first met Bertram at an embassy party when he was temporarily assigned to the legal attaché in London. He and her uncle had hit it off right away.

"Now, there's a clever fellow," her uncle had said. "We need more people like him working for us."

Uncle Ted would have been pleased to know that Bertram was with the firm.

At eleven, Bertram phoned the office. "Just thought I'd check in and let you know what I've been up to."

"Where are you? Do you need any help?"

"You'd be recognized. By the way, Nastchenkov has a chauffeur and a bodyguard, both young and tough. He's not easy to get at."

"He's many things but not a fool."

"I've kept two of our own people on him. We've followed every move. The main problem seems to be that Nastchenkov's protection is so strong. I think the key to solving our little problem lies with the car."

"Bertram, be careful." She thought of Ray.

"Of course, I will. I've got a plan in mind. Call you back later and let you know if it works out. Don't worry."

With that, the phone conversation came to an abrupt conclusion. There was no point waiting at the office for him to call back. Michelle decided to call Katherine Matthews and see if she could meet with Nora Parker again before she left for Washington.

Katherine encouraged her to visit. Michelle was welcomed at the apartment, in fact, like a long lost sister. Michelle's hope was to learn anything new or helpful, however small, that might enable her to continue the investigation productively.

Katherine invited her to sit in the lovely living room. Michelle looked around, appreciating the walnut wainscoting, parquet floors, stained-glass windows and marble mantled brick fireplace. There were large green hanging spider plants greedily absorbing sunlight. It was hard to imagine that Nora could have felt anything but happy and secure in such a place.

"Did Nora have a good night?" she asked Katherine.

"I caught her in the bathroom about two in the morning rummaging through the medicine cabinet. I started to yell at her. I didn't mean to, but she frightened me. I'm beginning to think that Dr. Reiner is right. Maybe she should be confined temporarily for her own safety. Honestly, I just don't know what to think or do anymore where she's concerned."

"Does she have an appointment with Dr. Reiner today?"

"Yes, at two o'clock in the afternoon."

"Make certain she keeps it. He's a very compassionate man and he may be able to help her." Strange, even mentioning Daniel's name brought her pain.

"I'll be bringing her personally to his office. I'll get Mother for you."

Michelle walked to the front window and looked out. She liked this area. Brooklyn Heights reminded her of Greenwich Village in that it shared a bohemian atmosphere and was populated to a large extent by artists and writers. But the area was cleaner than the Village and it had a nicer view. The Matthewses' brownstone was situated near the esplanade and had a breathtaking view of the Brooklyn Bridge and the Manhattan skyline.

There was a knock at the door. Since no one else was nearby, Michelle answered it herself.

"What are you doing here?" She stared at Daniel as if he were a ghost.

"I had some time and figured it might be better for Nora if I dropped by here rather than have her travel to Manhattan in her present condition."

"How considerate of you," she said with biting sarcasm. "And of course you had no idea I would be here."

"As a matter of fact, I didn't, but I don't suppose you'll believe me, will you? From now on, everything I say is going to be suspect." His dark eyes flashed angrily.

"How dare you act self-righteous with me! Why don't you come back later, after I've spoken with my client?"

"I think it's just as important for me to speak with my patient."

"Bugger off, Doctor." They were toe to toe, eyeball to eyeball. She wasn't going to hit him, but the desire was certainly strong.

Nora entered the room wearing a china blue pantsuit. In the soft, silk outfit, she looked as fragile and vulnerable as a child. She'd clearly lost more weight.

"How good to have you both here." She appeared oblivious to the tension in the room.

"We both care about you," Daniel said. He was looking meaningfully at Michelle rather than Nora.

She felt herself flush with heat all the way from her throat to her hairline; he had a knack of making her feel small and petty. "Are you up to taking a walk?" Michelle asked the older woman. "It's a magnificent day out there."

They did not talk while they strolled along. There was a river walk with benches. In the brilliant light, the skyscrapers stood out clearly. She could see the straight lines of warehouses and railroad sidings, and farther out, the movements of ferries and barges crossing the river into the bay.

Nora, leaning heavily on Daniel for support, looked up at the sky. "When I was a child, I used to think splendid white clouds like that were either made of cotton candy or scoops of vanilla ice cream." She lowered her head. "Life was so simple then. Now

I'm past the age of illusions." Nora fixed her eyes thoughtfully on the bridge.

It was time to dig more deeply, to ferret for the truth. "Professor Latimer thought James might be in Russia."

Nora gasped. "That's impossible! James was not a traitor! He would never sell out his country. He was a man of honor."

"The professor seemed very certain about James being a spy. I spoke with Colonel Atwood of NSA. He also believes James was a spy. He even believes that James might have been a mole planted by the Soviets long ago."

Nora was becoming increasingly agitated. "James was not a mole. I'm certain of that. And he would never willingly spy for the Russians or any foreign power. He had too much integrity." Nora was wringing her hands.

Daniel tried to soothe her. "There's no proof they're right. You knew him better than they did."

"Be patient," Michelle said. "Let me find out the truth. I feel that I'm close to it now. However, you have to wait for me." She took Nora's hand gently in her own.

"All right, I'll do what you ask. But I want a promise from you. If you should find out that James was murdered and you are able to discover who did it, I want you to kill that person for me. I want you to exact justice. An eye for an eye."

"I won't make a promise of that kind. But I do promise that justice will be done."

They began walking back toward the house in solemn silence.

"You'll have to make a promise too, Nora," said Michelle. "You must take care of yourself while I'm gone."

Nora's eyes seemed clearer and more focused now.

"No more of this suicide nonsense. You're frightening your daughter to death."

When they got to the house, Katherine was waiting anxiously.

"Your mother and I have talked. She's going to behave herself. I'll be back in a few days, hopefully, with some substantial information."

Katherine's open face registered relief. After Daniel took Nora inside, Katherine turned to Michelle.

"Thank you. I feel better now. You've been very good to both Mother and me. I know we're related distantly by blood, but more important, you've become a true friend to us."

Michelle was taken aback by the reference to friendship. She had no friends. The people who worked for her, like Bertram, were as close as she came to friendship, but that wasn't quite the same thing. Bertram was extremely well paid for his efforts and his loyalty. In reality, she avoided forming close attachments with people. It was something that Uncle Ted had warned her about, and she knew that he was right.

She thought of Daniel. He had wanted a good deal more from her than friendship, but in return she would've had to give up her freedom. The thought of his betrayal hurt beyond measure. No, she must put him entirely out of her mind. It was her work that mattered and nothing else.

"Before I leave, Katherine, there's a personal question I must ask. Please don't be offended by it. Did you have knowledge of your father's affair with Charlene Bennett?"

Katherine's expression was one of perplexity. Her pretty face was as round and undeceiving as a cabbage. "Did I see them together, you mean? No, I can't say that. I might have killed him myself if I had."

"Was he seeing anyone else that you were aware of?"

Katherine was pensive. "I don't think so. Although there was this one evening. I was visiting my parents at their home in Virginia.

Accidentally, I overheard a conversation. I happened to pick up the extension in the study about the same time Dad picked up the telephone in his bedroom. On the other end of the line was a male voice. He asked my father if Dad was coming by the apartment. Father said he would make it if he could. Then the man mentioned he thought they might work out together at the gym. It wasn't so much what they were saying. It was the way they spoke to each other. Very familiar, even affectionate. I don't know, at the time it struck me as being a little peculiar somehow. Father wasn't a warm man. He found it difficult to display love or emotion in general, at least with us children."

"Did you mention overhearing the conversation to your father?"

"Are you joking? Of course not! He would have been furious and accused me of eavesdropping. My father was a very private sort of man. He had many secrets and he kept them all to himself."

"How long ago did this conversation occur?"

Katherine thought for a time. "More than a year and a half ago. In fact, it was probably more like two years ago. I never really thought about it again. I mean, my father wasn't at all the type of man who would — well, you know." Katherine's voice trailed off in embarrassment. "He just wasn't like that. But still, there was that special tone of voice between them. I don't know. It probably didn't mean anything. Anyway, I never mentioned it to Mother. I would rather you didn't either."

"No, I won't if I can help it."

"Will you join us for lunch?" Katherine asked.

"I can't stay. I have a few things to attend to before I leave for Washington again."

"Shall I tell Dr. Reiner you're leaving now?"

"No," she said hurriedly. "I'd rather not disturb him while he's with your mother."

"Any message you want me to give him?"

Michelle thought for a moment. "Just say goodbye."

From Brooklyn Heights, Michelle traveled back to the office. She found Bertram sitting at his desk.

"I have something for you," he said. He handed her a brown paper bag. "Well, aren't you going to open it?"

"A little early for Christmas, isn't it?"

"Never too early for a present like this."

She opened the bag and looked inside.

There was a narrow, twisted piece of metal shaped very much like a tailpipe.

"Is this what I think it is?"

Bertram smiled at her grimly. "Exactly. But you were right. It wasn't easy. The main problem, according to my people who were watching him, was that the bodyguard always remained close to Nastchenkov, especially after what happened in the restaurant with you and him. They weren't going to take any chances. The chauffeur stayed with the car. So both Nastchenkov and the car were normally under careful surveillance." Bertram cleared his throat.

"I followed Nastchenkov to Lincoln Center and then over to the restaurant. The chauffeur never left the car. The bodyguard kept in the background but you bet your sweet ass he was watching everything. So there seemed to be only one way to handle it."

"Which was?"

"Blowing up the car with all three of them in it. Not very subtle, I have to admit, but I was looking for results. I also wanted there to be no clues. I didn't want the explosion traced back to us."

"You used a plastic explosive?"

"I considered something like C-4 because it's putty-like and can be molded around an object, but eventually I decided on something simpler and quicker to install. Dynamite and an electrical blasting cap."

Michelle's training had included the technical aspects of car bombs. She followed what he'd done with interest. "But how did you get the opportunity?"

"I waited. When they left the restaurant, I followed them around the city. The bomb was pre-wired and ready so I just continued to wait. They went to the Russian delegation offices. Then the driver waited around for hours. I was about ready to give up when finally the driver was attracted by something in a shop window a short distance from where he was parked. He glanced around then went inside. That was it. Three seconds with the alligator clips and the bomb was installed."

"You didn't wait around?"

"I most certainly did. Nastchenkov and his bodyguard returned in about half an hour. All three of them got into the car. The chauffeur tried to turn over the engine but it didn't take the first time. That was when I started to sweat. If nothing happened, he would have checked out the engine. But the second time the driver turned the key in the ignition, the engine turned over and there was a simultaneous explosion. The car burst into flames. Boom! You should have seen it!"

"No doubt I will see it on the news tonight." Michelle looked down at the twisted piece of metal in her hand. "So this is what is left of our friend Nastchenkov."

Bertram looked at her steadily. "I know you're sick to your stomach. But you realize it had to be done."

"Pity there wasn't another way. I hope no innocent people were injured or killed by the explosion."

"I was careful," Bertram said. "No one else was harmed. The street was pretty much deserted."

As she sat turning the piece of scorched tailpipe in her hand, Michelle wondered what Daniel would have thought if he could have heard the conversation between Bertram and herself. Would he have been shocked to hear them coolly dissect and analyze the murder of a fellow human being? Probably. When had she begun to see things through Daniel's eyes? That could prove dangerous to her survival.

"It's always a shame that people have to die, but don't expect me to feel anything for Nastchenkov. He was a total bastard." Bertram's brow creased with a frown.

"We agree on that," she said. "Unfortunately, I'm still left with the problem of finding out who hired him. This individual is obviously well-connected. He or she could very well hire someone else."

Bertram was thoughtful. "I didn't think of that. We could have had Nastchenkov followed and listened in on him, see who he contacted."

"I was the one who should have considered it. I'm too green at field work. Still, Nastchenkov told us he didn't know who was giving the orders. I'm inclined to believe he told the truth. He was just hired help. Fortunately, there are still some other leads to pursue."

"You'll be in D.C.?"

She nodded her head, in no mood for many words.

"I don't suppose I have to tell you to be careful."

"Of course not. Anyway, I have a feeling that we'll be wrapping the Parker case in a matter of a few days."

"Let's hope you're right. It's turned out to be a lot more trouble than expected."

She couldn't disagree with that.

"Call if you need me, day or night."

During the plane trip to Washington, Michelle felt oddly drained and emotionally worn out. The first move she made on the case was the following morning, when she again phoned Georgetown University to find out if anyone there had heard from Professor Latimer. As before, the faculty office had no idea where the professor could be reached. They too were disturbed by his disappearance. She tried his home phone but got no answer; not even an answering machine picked up. What had become of Latimer? Was he another victim? Or was he in hiding somewhere?

The only hope of finding the professor quickly was with the help of Doug Maclaren. He actually looked happy to see her when she walked into his office. He extended his hand to her and then invited her to sit down.

"How you been, Michelle?"

"Fine."

He looked at her thoughtfully. "You look a little thinner and kind of pale."

"I'm always pale."

He grinned at her. "Still hunting for info on the Parker case?"

"Naturally."

His smile was warm. She decided that she liked his face. He had a good, strong face with a square-set chin. "I'm yours for as long as you want me." His voice was half-teasing, half-serious.

"I'll keep that in mind," she said dryly.

"What about the other guy?"

"We're through."

"Yeah? You don't sound like you're so sure of that."

"I forgot how perceptive you are."

"Some people think I'm just a dumb ex-jock."

"Some people are quite wrong. But I don't really have much time for a social life at the moment."

"Too bad," he said. "Well, if you ever decide you crave good pizza and friendly conversation, look me up."

"I'd like a little friendly conversation right now."

"That so?" he said. "Parker case? If it is, I haven't turned up anything new. Otherwise I'd have called you."

"I thought you were still investigating Ray's death as well as Charlene Bennett's demise."

He sat down wearily behind his desk. "Officially, I was removed from both cases. Charlene's death was ruled accidental. We didn't have a clue with Ray Howard. It was too clean a hit. Let's just say it's out of my jurisdiction now."

"All right, but you must have found something. You're much too good an investigator to come up totally empty."

"Compliments will get you," he said cheerfully. He went to his file cabinet and brought out some papers, mulling them over reflectively.

"Yeah, here's something that struck me as being pretty weird. When Parker left his wife, he didn't move in with Charlene Bennett for quite a while. He went to stay at the apartment of a friend. And who do you think that friend was?"

"Professor Latimer I presume."

Mac looked surprised. "How did you know?"

"Parker had only one close friend as far as we've been able to determine."

"And here I thought you had E.S.P. There's something else. Charlene lived in the same apartment building as Latimer. And get this, the Washington building they lived in also housed eleven employees of the Russian embassy. Latimer just happened to live on the eighth floor where seven of the Russians also had their apartments. You believe in coincidence?"

"Not since jolly old Santa and I parted company. Perhaps I've been underestimating the importance of Professor Latimer.

364

He looks more and more important. It was he who told me that Parker was a mole in the first place."

"Come again?"

"A spy who had ferreted deep into the bureaucratic structure. Latimer told me Parker would turn up in Moscow. Apparently, that was a deliberate attempt to plant misinformation. Perhaps Latimer is actually what he accused Parker of being."

"You think he's a spy?" Maclaren looked surprised.

"Why not? It does happen. But Latimer's disappeared. Can you help me find him?"

Maclaren ran his fingers through his closely cropped hair. "Sure, I'll do what I can. Of course, I've been ordered to stay out of this Parker mess. As far as the state police are concerned, the case is strictly a closed matter."

"Do you know why?"

"It's not hard to figure, right? That Latimer guy is still a consultant to the CIA. No matter what he's done, they protect their own. Chances are he's making a deal with them right now. He'll end up coming out of this pure as the driven snow, even if his hands are covered with shit."

Or blood, she thought grimly.

Mac loosened the shirt collar around his

thickly corded neck. "Makes me sick to see people like that getting away with crimes!" A vein was pulsing at his temple.

Whatever else, at least she knew one dedicated law enforcement officer. She was certain Mac could be counted on to help her if she needed it.

"I wish I had more people like you working for me," she told him.

"Is that a job offer?"

"It would be if I thought I could lure you away from here."

"I'm flattered, but I don't think so."

She pressed his hand gingerly. "That's all right. I don't require any immediate answer, Mac. I believe that good people are worth waiting for."

He smiled and touched her cheek. "Funny, I was thinking the very same thing in connection to you."

"In your investigation of Latimer, did you ever find out any other places he might have frequented other than his apartment or the university?"

He checked the files for her carefully. "Here's something. Latimer had a boat registered."

She felt a surge of excitement. "You have the name?"

"Would you believe the *Coup d'Etat*? But

then an egghead like that would choose something weird, wouldn't he?"

"Where's the boat docked?"

He checked his notes. She could see that they were sloppy and had been hastily written, but he always seemed to know what he was doing.

"The boat's at a private pier at a marina in Lusby, Maryland."

"Thanks. I'll go have a look."

"I'll go along with you."

"No, Mac, I don't want you having any problems with your superiors on my account."

"And I don't think you should be going alone."

"I'll get hold of an investigator."

"Promise?" His genuine concern moved her.

"Yes, it'll be fine. I'll call you if there's a real lead or anything develops. I have my cell phone with me."

He agreed reluctantly. The truth was, she didn't want him along. To obtain information, she might have to do things that he couldn't legally permit. Besides, she worked best alone. However, she did call the office and tell her secretary exactly where she was going. That was only good procedure. As to putting an investigator on the case, she wanted to act immediately herself and not wait.

Michelle drove her Corvette at full speed down the Beltway into Maryland. Was Latimer a spy? He certainly knew a great deal more than he'd been willing to tell her. But it would be different now. She could question him much more effectively — assuming she could find him. The boat seemed a logical place for him to have gone if he were trying to avoid people. Yet she could not ignore the vague sense of apprehension that gnawed at her stomach. She hadn't forgotten that Parker had also owned a boat.

The drive to the marina seemed to take forever. There was no one on the pier. It appeared to be deserted. It took her quite a while to locate the right boat, which turned out to be a cabin cruiser. Why had she expected a small sailboat? Probably because Parker had a sloop. She looked around. The yacht did not seem luxurious, but there was no doubt that it had been expensive. The motor was of the inboard variety with diesel engines. The boat was at least forty feet in length, she calculated. There was a cabin, and above that, a separately enclosed wheelhouse. Even from her limited knowledge of boats, she could see that it was a sturdy, well-built vessel. Latimer had obviously taken this ship out into deep water.

She continued to look around. The craft still seemed deserted. There was no reply when she called out. Perhaps she had made a mistake in thinking that Latimer might be here. He could be long gone, possibly even in Russia, if he'd really been a mole. She prowled around the cabin. The door was locked. But it looked easy enough to open. No jimmy guards on it. There was only a spring latch. Michelle removed a credit card from her wallet. Loiding the latch, she easily opened the door. As she entered the darkened cabin, a clicking noise caught her ear. She looked up. Situated in the opposite top corner of the cabin was a camera setup. Her picture had been taken.

She found a chair in one corner and climbed up. It was not too difficult to figure out how to open the camera and remove the film. She then exposed the film and placed it back in the camera. After stepping down, she began looking around the cabin in earnest.

There was a great deal of radio equipment, sophisticated, short wave stuff. She remembered that Parker had similar equipment aboard his sloop. Hadn't Parker been trained as a radio operator? Might he not have trained his friend Latimer? She was frustrated. Too many questions without clear-cut answers.

Suddenly, she heard footsteps and hid herself behind some cartons stacked in a corner. They were a man's steps, firm and sure. So Latimer was here at last! She opened her purse and gripped the handle of the Glock she'd brought with her, and found herself face to face with the unexpected.

# CHAPTER TWENTY

"Michelle?"

It couldn't be! She was so surprised that as she came out from behind the boxes, she clumsily knocked half of them over. Quickly, she slipped the automatic back into her purse.

"What are *you* doing here? Are you insane?"

"You asked me that before, and no, I don't think I am."

"How did you ever find me?"

"I knew you were in Washington so I went directly to your office. I prevailed on your secretary to tell me where you were."

"I can't believe she told you. I should fire her."

"It wasn't her fault. I explained how urgent it was for me to get in touch with you."

"Has something happened to Nora?" she asked.

"Let's just go someplace where we can talk privately." Daniel tried to take her arm.

"No, I'm waiting for someone."

"Then we can wait together. I'll talk to you right here and now."

Michelle was not happy to see Daniel. His presence represented an unwelcome complication. "Please leave! This is no place for a personal discussion, if that's what you were planning."

"I didn't say it was personal, did I?" His manner was nonchalant, as if they'd gone for a stroll in the park.

"You are the most infuriating man."

His eyes were compelling in their earnestness. "I intend to remain with you no matter what."

She realized that he would not leave unless she left with him. "All right, let's get out of here quickly before anyone sees us. I hope I haven't already blown any chance of finding Latimer."

"Him again?"

"Yes. I believe he holds the answer to the enigma of what happened to James Parker."

"Like I said, I'll wait with you. I'm in this too."

"No, there isn't any sign of him. Let's just go."

They walked back to her car and got in.

She turned and looked at him. His dark good looks were emphasized by a gray tweed sports jacket and neat charcoal slacks. The bruises on his face had lightened in color but were a reminder of why he absolutely should not be further involved.

"You don't belong here, Daniel. And, quite frankly, I can't think of anything we have to say to each other. There really isn't a thing you can tell me that I want to hear."

"So I came all this way, and you don't even want to listen to what I have to say?" There was an ironic smile on his lips.

He obviously wasn't taking any of this seriously. She found his entire attitude terribly annoying.

"You're jolly well not going to make me feel guilty or unreasonable." She folded her arms over her breasts.

"Wouldn't think of it." His eyes met hers directly. "I'm not trying to lay a guilt trip on you."

"Good, because I happen to be immune to that sort of coercion. Your charm doesn't work on me anymore either."

"Of course not." His smile was warm..

She averted her gaze. "I'm considering your safety. This could turn out to be a very dangerous location. You've already had enough happen to you."

"So you still care for me after all. I'm touched." He moved close to her. The proximity of his body was an overwhelming distraction. He was dangerous, for her.

She felt his body heat; his breath sent peculiar tingling feelings against her neck. "Please, stay away from me! Just tell me why you're here."

"Not to be insulted again. I'm not into sadomasochism. I told you that I'd help with your investigation. Nora had a break-through yesterday. I worked with her after you left. She's finally beginning to open up. I think it was your doing. Incidentally, I'm not betraying doctor/patient confidentiality because she gave me permission to discuss this with you. Anyway, she spoke again about her guilt feelings. Nora led us to believe that the person James was involved with was a woman — or at least she thought he was involved with another woman. The truth is, she later found out that it was a man. Apparently, Parker had homosexual tendencies. According to Nora, the other man seduced him. They had been intimate for some time when Nora asked James to choose. She still maintains that James claimed he couldn't break off with the other man, although he would have done so if it were possible. But he wouldn't explain why."

"Then you're saying she deliberately misled me into thinking that Charlene Bennett was the cause of their break-up? Why would she do such a thing? I can't fathom her reasoning!"

"You have to understand. Nora is a very proud woman. She didn't want it known that her husband had a homosexual affair. She was ashamed of it, just as James himself was. His good name meant a lot to both of them. I don't know if this bit of information will help your investigation any, but I wanted to make certain you received it."

"Very old school, the both of them. You just confirmed what I already suspected."

"Now if you want me to leave, I will."

"I'll drive back you back to the office. I owe you an apology and a decent meal for the time and trouble you've taken — but don't get any ideas beyond that."

He looked at her innocently. "Of course not. Purely business."

On the drive back to Washington, she didn't speak to him very much. She didn't want to forgive him. She glanced at him out of the corner of her eye once or twice and caught him staring at her. His intense gaze made her uneasy. She wondered what he was thinking.

"So you believe the liaison was between

Latimer and Parker?" Daniel finally asked.

"It seems likely. In fact, there are all sorts of implications. If Latimer seduced Parker, he may have done it to blackmail Parker into providing secret information. Latimer might have been a mole, or merely a dupe himself."

"Which do you think?" he asked her.

She shook her head. "I honestly don't know."

"Whose boat were we on?"

"It belongs to Latimer — or at least it's registered in his name."

When they got back to the office, Michelle collected her messages. Since there was nothing that looked particularly important, she decided to order out for lunch.

"What sort of sandwich would you like?" she asked him.

"I've got a better idea. Play hooky for a little while. You said yourself, your leads have dried up. Getting away might help you get fresh insight and perspective."

"Daniel, you might as well know, I intend to put you on the first plane back to New York. I'm certain your patients need you."

"Morris is handling things."

"Haven't you imposed on him enough already?"

He smiled at her. "Probably, but I

wouldn't be any good for anyone else if I didn't straighten things out with you first."

"There's nothing to straighten out."

"I think there is. But all right, you want me back in New York, I'll go willingly if you'll spend lunch hour with me at a place of my choice."

"Fine. Remember you gave me your word."

"Honor bright." He raised his right hand, gesturing as if he were a boy scout.

She was dubious, but chose to go along with his show of integrity. "Very good then, I'll drive wherever you like."

Lunch turned out to be hot dogs at the zoo. Daniel insisted on seeing the pandas, among other things. She tried very hard not to enjoy herself, to be stern and stiff, but it was difficult to be with him and not have fun. He was just too enthusiastic. He even insisted on buying her a red balloon.

"I knew I could make you smile if I tried hard enough. You know what your problem is, Ms. Hallam? You had a deprived childhood. It's never too late."

"Thank you for your diagnosis, Doctor, but if you think that being well-adjusted means acting as childish as you do, then I prefer to be deprived."

"And I prefer to be depraved." He gave her a seductive look.

"Do you ever take anything seriously?"

"Everything. That's why I have to joke about things so much."

"I really don't understand you," she said with a deep sigh.

"Good. You might not find me so wildly exciting if you did." His dark brown eyes were warm as toast.

She had to look away. "I'm taking you to the airport now."

"What? I was just beginning to enjoy Washington. Nice city for tourists and patriots. I wouldn't mind seeing more of it."

"Go home, Daniel, I have a case to solve."

"Now you're back to frowning in disapproval at me. I left my attaché case in your office when I was there the first time. It has some important files inside."

"This is just a device to stay with me, isn't it?" she seethed. "You're quite impossible."

He held up his hand in a placating gesture. "No, it's the truth. I really did forget it. Look, I'll just pick it up and then get a cab to the airport. I'm not trying to make your life more difficult."

He started to whistle a tune as she drove back to the office. She shook her head. That boyish quality of his helped him get away with too much.

"What you need, Michelle, *ma belle,* is less work and more fun."

"Do stop analyzing me."

"Can't help myself." He kissed her cheek sending a shiver of recognition down her spine.

"I made a mistake ever allowing intimacy with you. It will never happen again."

"I think it will. I know you want me and I'm crazy for you."

"Crazy is the operative word here. One of us has to behave like an adult. I made a mistake letting passion rule."

"You're in denial."

She shot him a sharp look. "Don't try to use your psychobabble on me, you charlatan!"

His hand snaked over and pressed the swell of her breasts beneath her windbreaker. "No matter what you think, I did not betray you. Trust me, you really don't want anything to do with Atwood."

"That was not your decision to make, Daniel. You behaved in an arbitrary manner and you weren't honest with me. That's what hurts." She pushed his hand away.

He hung his head. "All right, I was wrong and I'm sorry."

"How sorry? You'd probably do the very same thing again if the opportunity presented itself."

She'd been checking her rearview mirror from time to time and was alarmed to find that her car was being followed by a nondescript vehicle. There were two men in the car, neither of whom she recognized.

"Something wrong?" Daniel asked.

"What makes you think that?"

"You've got a frown on your face and you're watching the traffic behind you in your mirror."

"It's nothing." Privately, she admitted the worst: Nastchenkov had been replaced.

A phone call had come while she was out, but the man hadn't left a message. There was another call for her before she could even usher Daniel out of the office.

"You were on my boat today," the well-cultured voice said.

Her spine stiffened. "How did you know?"

"I keep it under surveillance," the disembodied voice said.

"You haven't been honest with me, Professor."

"There was no need for me to be, was there?"

"Actually, there was. You were James

Parker's friend, weren't you? His best friend. Didn't you want to help me find out the truth about his disappearance?"

"I told you the truth before. James was a spy. He faked his death and he's somewhere in Russia now. End of matter. I just solved your little problem for you. Why don't you take that information back to Nora and then forget the whole thing?"

"That seems to be the general consensus. Everyone wants me to forget about James Parker. Why is that?"

"What's the point? If you continue with this, you're going to end up dead."

"Let's meet one last time, Professor. I really think we should talk in person."

"I don't see the need for it."

"Let's just say I still have a few pertinent questions. Perhaps you're right, but I'd feel better if we met once more face to face."

Latimer hesitated, but only for a moment. "I'll agree, but you're to be alone. I'll be parked in my car near the dock where you found my boat. Be there at three o'clock." He quickly hung up.

"Latimer agreed to meet you?" Daniel inquired.

"Yes. I have just enough time to get you to the airport if we hurry, and then I'll go out to meet him at the dock."

"If he is a spy, this could be very dangerous for you. Shouldn't you get some backup?"

Perhaps, but who should she phone? Certainly not Kirson. Colonel Atwood? She preferred to avoid him. The only person she did trust was Maclaren, except she really shouldn't involve him.

"I trust myself."

"I don't like this. I'm going along with you."

She studied his fine profile. "No, you're not! I'm putting you on a plane."

"I can take care of that myself. Go to your meeting. But Michelle, one last thing."

She turned and faced him. "What is it?"

He pulled her into his arms and kissed her hard. When they came apart, she could scarcely breathe.

She left him in her office and took off without uttering another word. She had neither time nor energy to argue further with Daniel. The truth she hated to admit to herself was that being with him made her heartsick. She could not forgive him, but neither could she stop feeling strong emotion for him no matter how hard she tried to feel nothing.

It was just before three when she arrived at

the dock. As before, it seemed deserted. She sat in her car and waited, thinking that Latimer had not yet arrived. When it got to be three-twenty, she decided to get out of her car and check the boat again.

She looked around and found no sign of Latimer anywhere. What could have happened to him? Had he changed his mind about meeting her?

Suddenly, she heard footsteps and turned to look around. "Not you again!"

"Is that any welcome for a man who's willing to put his life on the line for you?" Daniel proffered his hand to her, which she ignored.

"I thought you were on your way to New York."

"I must have given the cab driver wrong directions."

She took his arm as if to guide him. "Come on."

"Where to?"

"For you, anywhere but here. I cannot believe you've behaved so foolishly."

"I don't look at it that way. I want to redeem myself in your eyes. I want to be your knight in shining armor."

"So putting yourself into terrible danger for some absurd romantic notion is supposed to impress me?" She shook her head.

"I won't have it."

"You don't have any choice." He pulled her into his arms and kissed her.

When she would have pulled away from him, he deepened the kiss. She pushed him away breathlessly. "You have to go," she said in a husky whisper. "You're distracting me, impairing my judgment. You could get us both killed. This is no game. Once and for all, you're getting out of here!"

But as she started to lead him off the boat, she saw a man coming toward them. No, it was not Professor Latimer as she had hoped but someone she definitely did not expect.

# CHAPTER TWENTY-ONE

"What are you doing here?"

She managed to keep her composure. "I might ask you the very same question, Colonel."

"I'm looking for Professor Latimer."

"Then we share a common purpose," she said.

Colonel Atwood walked forward, his bearing rigid and erect. His thin face was pale and severe. The iron gray hair was parted down the middle, and though an autumn breeze was blowing, not one hair moved out of place.

"After our talk the other night, Ms. Hallam, I began to think that Latimer was something of a loose end, and that it would be best to put my people on him."

"I wasn't thinking about the professor at that time," she said in mild surprise. "But everything does seem to point back to him."

"So you did see the connection eventually, just as I knew you would." He smiled at her tolerantly. Then he looked over at Daniel and his smile vanished.

"What are you doing here, Reiner? Aren't there enough society matrons in Manhattan for quacks like you to fleece?"

Michelle was stunned by the hostility of the colonel's remark. She hadn't realized until now just how much he disliked Daniel, perhaps because Atwood was so good at hiding his feelings. But she'd learned that in espionage work, nothing was ever as it appeared.

Daniel did not respond, asserting an amazing level of self-control.

"Let's have a look around the cabin while we're waiting for Professor Latimer to put in an appearance, shall we?" Atwood was not making a suggestion so much as giving a command.

"He may be watching the boat and be frightened away if he sees you here, Colonel."

The colonel jutted his square chin. "That's always a possibility, but worth the risk in this case. You don't mind if I look around, do you, Ms. Hallam?"

"It's not my boat, Colonel." Her manner was regal in its formality.

Atwood went ahead and she heard him

examining the contents of the cardboard boxes. He returned after a time.

"With the kind of equipment in those boxes, it's possible for a trained person to make a phone patch and couple the CIA computer into any other computer he would have access to. He could empty out all of the CIA's secrets within minutes."

Michelle and Daniel exchanged looks. They followed the colonel and watched as he further examined the contents of the boxes.

"I believe I've solved your mystery for you. Parker had access to all the computers and digital codes. It's my guess Latimer somehow managed to obtain Parker's help. This equipment matches what's used to transmit and intercept communication by both NSA and CIA operatives. Using this, Latimer was capable of intercepting secret communications at sea." The colonel spoke with absolute authority as he continued to study the equipment.

"Unbelievable!" The colonel's eyes filled with horror. "There are special devices here that can send burst transmissions, even a high speed telegraph key is included. CIA field agents are given those in order to avoid detection while they send and receive coded messages." Atwood continued rummaging through the stacked cartons. "Incredible."

"What is it?" Michelle asked.

"There are a number of telephone line intercept devices that would allow Latimer to tap the CIA computer for information. The digital codes stored in our NSA computers could have easily been transmitted to locations where they would be reconstructed into photographs by computer. If foreign agents obtained this knowledge, they could learn to bypass the system. In short, it's quite possible that we no longer have any defense secrets whatsoever."

The day that had started out to be so brilliant and sunny had begun to darken. Storm clouds were gathering overhead.

"I'm glad that we made the discovery. Now that it's all out in the open, perhaps you can do something about it," Michelle said.

"My dear, we owe you a great debt of gratitude. I intend to have a generous check made out to you. And you need not stay on. Latimer won't come back here, but we'll find him — if at all possible. We want to know what he's passed along."

"Then you believe Parker is dead?" Michelle asked.

"I have a strong suspicion Latimer disposed of Parker, knowing that I was becoming suspicious of their operation. That way he could make it appear Parker and only Parker was a spy. He even planted false reports concerning Parker to make him seem particularly suspicious."

"Like the FBI report on Parker's background?"

"Precisely. Latimer was a brilliant man. We must not underestimate him."

"I suppose not."

Michelle and Daniel left the cabin, trailing behind Atwood. He turned and waited so that he could walk along beside them. He did not speak to Daniel, and Daniel completely ignored Atwood, which made the situation very uncomfortable for her.

"Allow me to escort you to your car," Atwood said.

Three men waited on the dock near the boat. They were dressed in a similar manner, Armani-style unstructured suits and casual shirts. She turned a questioning look on Atwood.

"I brought some leverage with me," he explained. "Those are NSA agents. Apparently I won't be needing them after all. It doesn't seem that Latimer is going to show up."

"He said he would. I expected him earlier. But after what we learned, I'm surprised that he called me at all."

"He was probably planning to kill you and dispose of your body at sea, as he did with Parker."

"He hardly seemed the sort of fellow to go about murdering people," she observed thoughtfully.

"One never knows," the colonel said. His smile never reached his eyes.

Sea gulls flew above them, screaming shrill warnings. Altostratus clouds, like twisted strands of old rope, formed and reformed above them. A sharp wind blew through her. The boat rolled unexpectedly for a moment, and she lost her balance, slipping toward some cans of varnish. She felt something shatter beneath her heel. Looking down, she caught sight of an object lying cracked on the deck. It was a pair of eyeglasses, unusually thick lenses in dark frames.

The glasses seemed familiar. Suddenly she remembered where she had seen them before. Professor Latimer had worn them when they met. Should she tell Atwood? Perhaps Latimer was somewhere on board the boat after all. But Latimer could not see without his glasses. He would not have simply thrown them on the deck. She felt certain something had happened to the professor.

Something was very wrong here. She decided to say nothing to Atwood and pretend she hadn't noticed anything out of the ordinary. Time enough to decide what to do when she had an opportunity for reflection.

She looked over at Daniel. The look on his face told her that he too had recognized the eyeglasses. He shook his head solemnly as if to warn her not to mention the matter.

"Well, goodbye, Colonel. We'll be going now. Thank you for your help. I'm glad we've solved the Parker matter." She kept her face a perfect mask with no inflection whatever to her voice.

Atwood nodded grimly, his eyes intense, unnaturally bright. He took her gloved hand as if to shake it, but then seized her in a painful, viselike grip.

"What are you doing!" Daniel came at the colonel, but a man appeared and knocked him to the ground.

Atwood tried to grab her purse as Michelle fought back. The fellow who knocked Daniel down suddenly pulled out an automatic weapon and pointed it at her. The men who'd been standing on the pier came around and faced them with drawn pistols as well. One man seized Daniel, pulling him to his feet and twisting his right arm behind his back.

Michelle kicked the gun from the first man's hand, then used a series of rapid blows on Atwood in an attempt to free herself. But immediately there was another assailant to contend with. Daniel was doing his best. Unfortunately, these people were well-trained in martial arts. She swung around to engage the new attacker. However, he was shrewd enough to keep his distance; his semi-automatic weapon aimed directly at her heart.

"They will not hesitate to kill you or your friend, Ms. Hallam," Atwood said in a breathless voice.

Michelle raised her hands in a gesture of surrender. Atwood seized her purse and opened it, removing her Glock.

"Not a bad little weapon, although I prefer something with more firepower. But I'll borrow this for now. I don't think you're in any position to object."

Atwood nodded to the first man who had come to his aid. She saw now he was Asian.

"Give my friend your windbreaker, Ms. Hallam. I'm not naïve enough to believe this is your only weapon. Then raise your arms and keep them up."

She removed her jacket and gave it to the man. Atwood handed over her weapon to the Asian and began patting her down himself.

"Keep your filthy hands off her!" Daniel tried to break free of the man who held him.

"It's all right. Don't give them reason to hurt you," Michelle said to Daniel.

"Excellent advice."

Daniel's outburst had distracted Atwood, and to her relief, he stopped his search.

"Were you really planning to let us go?" She seized the advantage, however slight.

"Before you made the mistake of stepping on the professor's eyeglasses. I did want a reliable witness that would tell the story exactly as I laid it out. I think I had you convinced, until you saw those glasses. You both recognized them, didn't you? Once you thought about it, you would have realized that my interpretation wasn't accurate. What a terrible shame!"

"I thought we hid it rather well."

"Not to a trained observer's eye. It was that look that passed between the two of you." Atwood smiled coldly. He spoke with the authority of a man in total charge of the situation.

"Surely those agents realize that you are a traitor who intends to kill us?" She spoke loudly and with emphasis.

Atwood laughed with gleeful amusement.

"They are my employees, bought and paid for. These men will do whatever I ask of them. Two of them are fanatics, terrorists who are eager to destroy this country and Western culture. Why, they would work for free and willingly sacrifice their lives to kill as many of you as possible. No, Ms. Hallam, you are not going to get away, nor is your annoying friend. But if it's any consolation, I wish your particular death was not necessary."

"Then perhaps you should reconsider."

Atwood shook his head with vigor. "I have no other options."

"Perhaps we could come to some sort of an arrangement?"

"I think not. You would betray me. I am not a stupid man. Under other circumstances, you and I might have dealt well together." He turned and gave Daniel a hard look.

"I suppose it was you all along," she said, thinking out loud.

"Of course," he acknowledged. "I knew from the first that you would simply not be satisfied with obvious explanations. That was why I had Latimer tell you about Parker. I thought the information he gave would satisfy you. Too bad it didn't. You should have ended the investigation right there and then. You should have been glad. You had been given all the answers you needed. Why couldn't you just accept them? Anyone else would have been frightened by the nearly successful attempts on their life. Any normal investigator would have closed the case right there. But you proved to be entirely too persistent. You chose to keep digging into matters that were never meant to see the light of day."

"So you sent Nastchenkov after Michelle and me," Daniel said, entering the conversation.

Atwood smiled smugly. "Yes, he was good up to a point. I must give you credit, Ms. Hallam. No one else ever proved a match for that man. He was diabolical. But you won't win with me."

"I had a feeling that James Parker was really dead, in spite of your attempt to cloud the issue. You were the one who changed the original FBI report on Parker and saw to it that most of his records were destroyed."

"That's right. I had it done, Ms. Hallam. I killed Parker myself and made certain that he would be found only after the body was so badly decomposed that a clear identification could not be made. I wanted Parker to be thought of as a mole. There had been rumblings about a spy and the launching of a secret investigation to uncover him. I didn't want it to go past the talking stage. And Parker had already threatened to talk."

"But why did you kill Ray Howard?"

"You were to blame for that. You upset Charlene. She thought she could blackmail Latimer. I was forced to have her disposed of. Howard was snooping around. He found out more than he should have. Latimer was foolish enough to go to Charlene's apartment, looking for evidence she claimed she had. Your man saw him there. Of course, we always kept someone on Latimer. We were able to remedy the situation immediately by getting rid of your associate. Latimer was so pathetic. The man was easily frightened. He actually believed what Charlene told him, that she had some sort of documented proof she had hidden which would be turned in to the authorities if anything happened to her. The fool was determined to find out if it were true. Your man caught him going through Charlene's things."

"Charlene was never really important to Parker, was she?"

"Merely window dressing. She did what we told her to do as long as she was paid. She amused Parker for a time. That's all."

"I hope you won't mind answering another question for me. Professional curiosity. Did Latimer work for you from the beginning?"

The sun arabesqued crazily off the barrel of the automatic that was pointed at her body.

"Latimer was a homosexual. He and Parker were good friends. When they came to work at NSA two years ago, I had their backgrounds fully investigated. That was when I realized that I could effectively use them. I blackmailed Latimer, told him I would expose his background if he didn't help me. I got him to move into a building where he could be under constant surveillance. Then I had hidden cameras set up in his bedroom. Every word, every action in that apartment was recorded. It was easy enough to get Latimer to set up his friend. The professor was, as I've told you, a very weak man.

"Parker was too ashamed to refuse me. I blackmailed him into doing my bidding since he valued his reputation as much as Latimer did. But one fine day, Parker developed an attack of conscience. He told both Charlene and Latimer that he was going to expose the entire operation. Obviously, his usefulness had come to an end."

"So you killed him?" Michelle asked quietly.

"We met at sea. Parker actually thought his wife would forgive him if he made a full confession. The fool!"

"And you took the papers he was working on."

"Of course."

"Parker was right," Daniel said pensively. "Nora would have forgiven him."

Atwood's cold eyes glistened. "You'll soon be joining him, Dr. Reiner. If it weren't for you, Ms. Hallam would have been working for me, and neither of you would be in this position."

Daniel took Michelle's hand and held it tightly. "What are you planning for us?"

"An ocean voyage would be appropriate. Unfortunately, you won't be making a return trip."

"More suicides?" Michelle questioned.

"A boating accident. They won't be finding your bodies." Atwood smiled as if the thought gave him a great deal of personal satisfaction.

Atwood signaled his men. "You will be escorted below."

One burly character shoved them in the direction of the stairs leading below deck. It was so dark that Michelle nearly tripped.

Surprisingly, there was full standing room. She and Daniel were pushed toward a door that the lumbering man indicated. Once inside, the first man was joined by a second who tied their hands and feet securely with ropes and then knotted them tightly. Neither of these powerfully built men bothered to speak. Michelle and Daniel were forced into yet a smaller space, a tiny area that obviously served as a storage hold of sorts. There was a fishy odor as if tackle and bait had once been kept here.

Once the door of the storage room was shut, there was absolutely no light. The feeling of confinement almost made Michelle panic, but she held tightly to her self-control, knowing she must keep her wits about her. Suddenly she felt movement and then vibration. She could guess what was happening and didn't like it a bit. The engines had started; they were moving.

How could they possibly escape at sea? She must think of something, a way out, or they were dead. In her entire life, she had never known such desperation. *I will not give in to my fear! I will not panic!*

She took a deep breath and forced herself to meditate to clear her mind. She was on a tranquil pond. No movement could disturb the water. There was not so much as a ripple. Her peace was complete. She was able to control her physical and mental energy and channel it. She reached out for enlightenment.

"Michelle, are you all right?"

"What? Yes, I'm fine now." She took another deep breath and exhaled it slowly.

"It seemed like you weren't with me for a while."

"I wasn't. Let's concentrate on a way out of here."

"Sounds good to me."

The fear had left her. She wasn't really calm. Certainly she could feel her adrenaline flowing. But that was good. She was ready to act. She tried to move her hands and feet. They were bound so tightly that they were beginning to numb. Also, her hands were tied behind her back as were Daniel's, further restricting movement.

"Daniel, see if you can reach your hands under my shirt."

"I don't think right now is the best time for that sort of thing, though ordinarily I'd love to oblige."

It amazed her how he never seemed to lose his sense of humor. "I wasn't suggesting anything kinky."

"I'm disappointed. Here I have you all to myself in a dark, private place. We could be thinking of ways to stimulate our sexual fantasies."

"I'm afraid there's nothing amusing about our situation. There are some useful tools tucked away in a special lining in my shirt." She situated herself so they were back to back and guided his hands as best she could.

"That's it!" She had moved his hand to the small of her back and pressed it within, guiding him to the compartment that had been stitched into the special lining of her oversized shirt.

"Can you pull out a small knife?"

"Got it! Oh, no!"

"What's wrong?"

"Dropped it. My fingers are losing feeling."

They groped around in the dark, touching the floor in close proximity. She moved toward the corner. Suddenly, she touched something that made her gasp in horror.

"Michelle, what is it?"

"Dear God, I think I just found Professor Latimer."

# CHAPTER TWENTY-TWO

The clammy hand she held fell limply from her grasp. Michelle groped the body and felt wet, warm liquid. She knew the smell and feel of blood. She knew the smell of death. Even in the total darkness, she was certain this was a dead body.

Daniel moved in beside her. "Here, I'll check him out. Maybe there's something I can do."

"I believe he's past your help."

"I'll feel for a pulse."

She heard Daniel rustling around in the darkness.

"He is dead, isn't he?"

"I can't find a pulse at the wrist or throat."

"That's it then," she said with a fatalistic sigh. "Help me find that little knife."

She pulled away from Latimer's body and began skidding along the floor again. It was exhausting and ridiculously demeaning, but at least the room was so tiny she could cover the entire area quickly and efficiently. Almost immediately, her fingers touched something cold and metallic.

"Got it," she told him.

They had to return to sitting back to back. Her fingers moved stiffly, awkwardly. The ropes were cutting deeply into the flesh at her wrists. She even had difficulty opening the folded knife. Finally, she was able to start cutting Daniel's ties.

"Think that miniature blade can handle these ropes?" he asked.

"Of course, the blade is made from the best, tempered German steel available."

A few minutes later, she had Daniel's hands free. He took the knife from her; quickly and expertly, he cut through her bonds.

"Wonderful surgical technique, Doctor."

"Thank you. Just for that, I'll do the same thing for your feet." He cut away the rest of their ropes then handed her back the knife.

It took a while to get the circulation going again. The skin near her ankles was particularly raw and aching.

"What now?" he asked quietly. "We're still in a locked room."

"That's the least of it." She put her hands to her hair. The special hairpin was secure, just as she knew it would be. Long ago, it had been a gift from Uncle Ted, who had seen to it that she not only had the best possible survival training for working in the field, but quality tools as well.

Her little hairpin was a special steel pick, a professional burglar tool that helped her move in and out of places with the least amount of difficulty. It was inconspicuous and did not call attention to itself. She removed it now from her thick curls and carefully put it into the lock on the door. It took a few minutes because of the darkness, but the lock opened without difficulty. At that point, she carefully replaced the pin in her hair. The knife was still in her hand, the blade folded so that the weapon was carefully concealed as she tentatively opened the door.

As her eyes adjusted to the light, she gasped involuntarily. In front of her stood one of Atwood's men, huge, powerful, a wide forehead wrinkling savagely. What light there was gleamed off his shaved head. He had a dragon tattoo that twisted from his neck under his shirt. The thug held up an automatic weapon and pointed it directly at her head. Small, piggy eyes narrowed meanly. She raised her hands in a gesture of surrender, still concealing the small knife in her closed fist. As she turned as if to go back into the room, her hand quickly and deftly opened the knife. She clutched the carved wooden handle convulsively. Her entire body shook.

Michelle turned back with a smooth, decisive movement, and, with her left hand outstretched, she dealt a swift, smashing blow, disarming the gun from the man's hand. Then she plunged the steel blade into the man's chest. The aim was purposeful and exact. He groaned and stared at her in disbelief. He tried to come toward her, to seize her, but before he could touch her, she struck again, this time with a thrust to the throat. His eyes began to roll wildly as a gurgling sound brought blood spurting through the gushing wound at his throat. He finally collapsed and fell to the ground writhing.

Daniel was next to her now. "God, was that really necessary!"

"Only if you want to survive. And if it's any comfort to you, I've never done anything like this before and wish I hadn't been forced to do it now."

The man no longer moved. Daniel got down on his knees and did a quick examination. "He's dead." Daniel studied her. "You're trembling." He stood and took her into his arms, holding her, comforting her.

His lips brushed her pulsing temple. He kissed her gently.

She wished never to have to leave his arms again. But she knew better. "We have to even out the odds."

"You mean more killing?" He let go of her, looking appalled.

"Yes, if it's necessary." She was fairly certain it would be. She wished he'd stop looking at her that way, as if she'd just confessed to being a serial killer.

"Daniel, I don't know if we're going to get out of this alive. So please don't start to preach middle class morality to me. We simply can't afford it. This man was our enemy." She touched the dead man with the toe of her shoe. "He would have killed us without a thought if given the opportunity. Atwood and his remaining cohorts are exactly the same. The taking of our lives is a bloody impersonal matter to them, just business as usual. Do you understand?"

"I'm sorry, but to my way of thinking, there's more to life than mere survival."

"And what would that be?" She was growing impatient with him.

"Surviving with a certain amount of dignity and integrity."

"There is little that is dignified about death in my opinion."

"I don't think that way," he said.

"This entire discussion may be purely academic," she told him, lifting the dead man's automatic from the floor and struggling to retrieve her knife from the body. "There's a good chance we won't remain alive to continue our debate."

She realized Daniel wasn't going to be much help to her. If anything, with his overwhelming sense of conscience, he could easily get in the way and cost her the edge she so desperately needed.

"When we go above, promise that you'll do exactly as you're told. Do you swear?"

"I hardly swear at all and especially not in the presence of a beautiful lady."

She let out a sigh of frustration. "Don't joke about this, Daniel. I want your word of honor you'll do as I say. I'm the professional here, as you may recall. It could mean the difference between life and death. *Our* life and death."

"All right, whatever you say."

"I saw a dinghy up there. I want you to get to it and cut the ropes. It's terribly important, our one chance to escape. But they can't see you or know what you're doing." Her gaze was direct. Yes, he was listening attentively.

"Now take the knife." She quickly wiped

the bloody blade against her jeans and handed it to him. "Please use it on the ropes. I'm going to the cabin and will attempt to radio the Coast Guard for help. One other thing, are you a strong swimmer?"

"You don't have to ask a boy who grew up in Coney Island that."

"Then we have a chance. Last matter, I'm sorry I am not the woman you believed me to be. I know I'm a good deal more ruthless than you ever imagined, but I did try to warn you about romantic illusions." She touched his handsome face gently with her callused hand. She could not read the look in his dark eyes that seemed to have no bottom.

"Whoever, whatever you are, I do love you. No one's perfect, not even me — although I come pretty close." He gave her an irreverent smile.

"I haven't forgotten this mess we're in is my fault."

He took her hand and kissed the palm. "Sweetheart, stop beating yourself up — especially when there are other people around who can do it so much better. We're going to get through this together. I have faith. You should too."

It amazed her how wonderfully supportive

he could be. "Thank you," she said. She kissed his cheek, a tear glistening unshed in her eye. "There isn't much time. I suppose we best get to it. We must go up quietly and cautiously, staying very low. I'll point out where the dinghy is located. Don't let it go over the side until I signal you to send it over. If anything happens to me, just go on alone. Do not try to help me, because you can't. Save yourself. Do you understand?"

He didn't answer.

"Please do as I say." She listened and watched, but no one else was near. She kept hold of Daniel's hand and they slowly came up on deck.

Daniel followed her directions, keeping low and making certain he was well hidden as he went to work cutting the ropes that held the small boat to the larger one.

She peeped through the cabin window. Inside, one of Atwood's flunkies was using the radio. She crouched down and waited silently, her stomach in a vortex of agitation. She could feel the boat still moving out to sea. Soon it would stop and they would go below deck looking for her and Daniel. She had to move quickly.

She tightly gripped the gun in her hand. It was a foreign made weapon of Eastern European origin. She wondered if it would have the same accuracy in performance she was accustomed to, but under the circumstances, she chose not to be ungrateful. Her hand was sweating and her heart was palpitating.

She heard the man leaving the cabin, closing the door behind him. His footsteps moved toward the front of the boat and then faded away. She took a deep, cleansing breath and walked around from the side of the cabin to the front, careful to keep low. No one was near. She went inside. The door was no longer kept locked. Immediately, she went to the transmitter. The machine presented only a minimal amount of difficulty for her. She tried to send an S.O.S. message, but there was a great deal of static. Was the Coast Guard picking up on it? If only she could radio their location! But she had no idea where they were or where they were headed. Instead of getting better, the static grew worse. It sounded as if a storm front might be heading in their direction.

She heard footsteps approaching and tried to hide herself in the corner behind a stack of cartons.

"It's no use, Ms. Hallam. You might as well come out. I have your friend here, and I know this is the only place you would be."

At first she didn't move, thinking that Atwood was bluffing.

"If you don't come out, I'll be forced to kill Dr. Reiner right now."

What would Uncle Ted have done? She tried to think. But she knew with certainty. He would let Atwood kill Daniel. There would never be a choice involved for him. Uncle Ted would not have given up his weapon or sacrificed his advantage. But she couldn't just follow in her uncle's footsteps. Uncle Ted would consider Daniel expendable; she could not. Did she love him? She'd savagely fought having feelings for him, but faced with this situation, it was impossible to deny how much she cared. Suddenly she knew what Daniel said was true: mere survival was not enough. Maybe it had been for Uncle Ted, but it could not be for her. Daniel, damn his magnificent humane heart, had irrevocably changed that part of her.

"I can't wait any longer for your decision," Atwood called to her. "Are you coming out?"

As if in a nightmare, she stood up and walked out of the cabin.

"The gun please."

She dropped the weapon at Atwood's feet. All the time, she could hear Uncle Ted's voice in her head, telling her what a foolish thing she was doing.

Atwood smiled and pushed Daniel away from him. His gun was pointed in her direction. "That's so much better, Ms. Hallam. I foolishly underestimated you. Now I'm going to ask you to strip off all of your clothing, just to make certain you aren't carrying any more concealed weapons. I should have searched you more thoroughly. I apologize for the lack of professionalism."

"Quite all right, but I'm very modest, so forgive me if I refuse to undress for you, Colonel."

"You're not in a position to refuse me anything," Atwood said waving the gun for effect.

"Don't you dare touch her!" Daniel exploded hotly.

"Now, Doctor, don't be so naïve. We all know the sort of woman she is. I'm certain she would compromise her virtue, if she had any, without a second thought."

She saw Daniel's cheeks redden. He charged wildly at the Colonel. As Atwood turned to aim his gun at Daniel, she brought the edge of her palm downward, chopping the weapon from his hand. For a fleeting moment, she thought that they would be free. Then two of Atwood's henchmen came upon them. One punched Daniel in the stomach. Daniel came back surprisingly well considering the punishment he had sustained and threw a sharp blow to the other man's jaw. But the Asian stood at a safe distance holding an automatic weapon. She knew there was no chance now and stepped between Daniel and his adversary.

"It's over," she said before the other man could hit Daniel again.

"Certainly," Atwood agreed, signaling his man to back off. "But first, why don't you just admit to your lover that you're nothing better than a slut. Isn't it time his eyes were opened? Enlightenment before death."

She spat contemptuously in Atwood's face, catching him on the left cheek. "If there's anyone here who knows about selling out for money, it's most certainly you. No, Colonel, you're the bloody whore, not I."

Atwood's face went livid. Color drained from his cheeks like wine escaping a shattered decanter. He brought his hand up as if to slap her face. She ducked successfully, noting that he was off-balance. She drew up her knee sharply and kicked Atwood in the groin, pushing him to the ground. Then she turned toward the wiry Asian. But she was not quick enough. She saw the gun barrel, heard the explosion, and felt the pain. She

413

was aware of her shoulder bleeding. Daniel was suddenly beside her now, holding her in his arms in an effort to comfort her agony and pressing on her wound to stanch the flow of blood.

Stoically, Michelle didn't allow herself to speak or cry out. She realized that she'd acted foolishly out of emotion when cold logical planning was called for. It was costing her dearly.

"Atwood, you're the lowest kind of scum," Daniel said.

"You're both going to die shortly," Atwood said, rising unsteadily from the deck. His face was ashen and he was gritting his teeth. "Just for the record, I didn't do it for the money alone. I gave everything for this country and what did I have to show for it? I was passed over twice for promotion. Twice! Do you understand what that means?" His eyes burned with an unnatural glow.

She didn't need Daniel to tell her that Colonel Atwood wasn't quite sane.

"I should have been a general, but they cheated me!"

"You held an important position at NSA," she said.

"That job was a mere token. I deserved so much more, and they knew it. Now the score is finally settled."

The pain in her shoulder was increasing. It was getting more difficult for her to think clearly. Daniel leaned over her, continuing to apply pressure to the wound in order to stop the bleeding.

"Such touching compassion and tenderness, Doctor. Pity it's being wasted. You're both as good as dead." Atwood motioned at them with his automatic to walk ahead of him. "If either of you makes another threatening move, you'll be shot dead on the spot."

"Like Professor Latimer?"

Atwood smiled. "Exactly like Latimer. Such a weak and foolish man. In his case, death was justice."

The man who had wounded her was calling to Atwood from the wheelhouse above. He was steering the vessel now. His voice was animated. She couldn't comprehend what he was saying.

Atwood turned to them. "There's a storm approaching. We seem to be in its path."

She looked up at the sky. The clouds were dark and angry. The wind was strong and as they walked forward, her face was graced by foam and spray. Looking out to sea, she observed that the waves were long with white-capped crests. At least the storm would slow Atwood's progress to his destination, although she could not honestly welcome its advent. If they had any opportunity to escape and sail away in the dinghy as she hoped, their chances for survival were that much more diminished by bad weather conditions. She wondered fleetingly if her message had been picked up by the Coast Guard. If only she had been able to transmit a little longer!

Atwood left them and climbed up to the wheelhouse. That left only one man guarding them. She was certain that just as soon as Atwood returned, he would shoot them both. This was their only chance, their only hope. The bullet wound in her shoulder made it much more difficult, but she must try.

What to do? She had to turn the immediate situation to her advantage. She fell down on the deck, pretending she had fainted and was unconscious. As she dropped, her hand moved into position. When the thug bent over her, the side of her palm chopped a sharp blow across his eyes. He got off one wild shot. But her next blow was to the carotid artery in his neck which cut off the blood flow from the neck to the brain and rendered him unconscious.

"Get the dinghy into the water and jump!"

she yelled at Daniel. She could see he wanted to wait for her. "Remember your promise to me."

Atwood was after her now. He had brought up his gun, but she brought her body back and hurled into him at full force before he could get off a shot. She knocked the gun from his hand with a blow of her outstretched palm. They both lunged for the weapon. The colonel was a seasoned soldier; he could and did defend himself. He hit a hard sharp blow against her wounded shoulder.

Michelle bit down on her lower lip so hard she tasted blood in her mouth, her head reeling from the agonizing pain. Atwood called to the man at the helm to stop the boat. He obviously wasn't going to let Daniel escape either.

Daniel was already in the water, and that gave her the courage she needed to continue fighting Atwood. She used her feet against him now instead of her hands. She kicked the gun from his hand. But he continued to come at her, a lean, well-muscled man in marvelous condition for someone in middle age. She kicked him with all the force she had left, a smashing blow to the right knee, and then she began to run.

She knew her strength was failing. If the

man at the helm came to Atwood's aid as she expected, she was finished. She had to act quickly. There was really only one thing left to do. The kick had slowed Atwood's pursuit of her just long enough. She removed what was the last and at the same time most potent weapon in her small arsenal.

It looked deceptively like an ordinary wristwatch. But in reality it was something quite deadly. Uncle Ted had given it to her as a present on the last Christmas Eve they shared together.

"It's a saboteur's weapon," he had told her, "developed originally during World War II, but refined considerably since then. Save it for a special occasion. Until then, use it as a watch. It does keep excellent time."

Atwood was gaining on her. She saw that he had his gun once more and the other man was running down the steps.

*I've got to hurry, hardly any time left!* Her head felt dizzy and light as if she were going to pass out. She fought to remain alert, running toward the back of the boat as fast as she was able. As Michelle moved, she pulled the pin out of the watch as one would a grenade. Then she threw it on a piling of ropes. Had they seen her do it? No, she didn't think so. She jumped over the side of the boat, tumbling into the icy depths of the ocean. Once in the water, she began swimming as fast as she could. It was difficult because of the pain in her shoulder, but she knew she had to keep moving.

They were shooting at her. Where was Daniel? How far had he gotten? And the boat? She didn't see the dinghy. Fear choked her throat.

Suddenly, she caught sight of Daniel in the water and began swimming toward him. But before she could reach him, she felt a sudden pain in her side. This new pain pierced her, knocking the last of her strength and breath out of her. So they had managed to hit her again! She ducked under the water for a moment, continuing to move relentlessly in the direction of Daniel. Her stomach felt strange. She was chilled and yet hot simultaneously.

*I've got to reach him!* She knew the watch bomb had a delayed detonator. There was approximately a minute and a half before she could expect a large explosion to occur. Unless Atwood had seen her drop the watch, the boat was destined to blow up in seconds.

They were still shooting at her but now it seemed that she was past the range of their bullets. She felt strong arms encircle her.

419

"Michelle, you're badly hurt!"

"No, I'm all right. We've got to keep swimming. Get far away." The thought that they could have found the bomb haunted her. She went over her movements in her mind. The toss had been done with finesse. No, they couldn't have known — could they?

She felt Daniel's hands, strong, firm and loving. He was supporting her in the water. Everything hurt as she swam, but she knew that to stop meant certain death for both of them. She willed herself to continue. Jabbing needles of pain thrust through her shoulder and stomach.

And then it happened. A great explosion rocked the water like an earthquake. The ocean roared up into an angry tidal wave. She was under for a time, struggling to reach the surface and breathe again.

Finally, she could see. But where was Daniel? Gasping for air, she tried to call out his name. Only a weak, inarticulate sound left her lips. There was fire on the water and debris was scattered everywhere. She felt a sense of confusion and disorientation. Someone was touching her. She turned quickly. It was Daniel. So he was all right. She felt a sense of relief. They swam together for what seemed an interminable length of time. She was finding it increasingly difficult to remain alert. So cold, so tired, so much pain. If she could just go to sleep. She needed to rest. Several times, she felt herself lapsing and determined not to give in to the feeling.

"They're going to come for us, darling. We'll be saved. Just hold onto me. I won't let anything or anyone hurt you again. I won't let go of you."

She wanted to answer him, but she couldn't speak. He was so comforting. She wanted to tell him how much she loved him too, but words wouldn't come.

On the horizon, there was a roll of thunder followed by a charge of lightning. A galelike wind blew around them. But the impending storm did not frighten her. Michelle felt too tired and sleepy to care. A sense of peace washed over her. And then merciful darkness.

# CHAPTER TWENTY-THREE

"Daniel?"

"Right here, sweetheart." He tightened his hold on her.

"I-I hurt."

"I know, honey. But you're going to be all right."

"If I'm not . . ."

"You will be." He tried to reassure her. "I'm taking care of you."

"I was supposed to protect you. Instead you're protecting me. Ironic, isn't it? I'm so very tired." She closed her eyes and drifted out of consciousness again.

She was probably better off. Under the circumstances, there wasn't much he could do for her. He concentrated on keeping them afloat. In his youth, he'd had some training as a lifeguard working one summer at the beach. How did a head-carry work? He tried his best to remember. Daniel took a position behind her, placing one hand on each side of Michelle's head, palms covering her ears, fingers extending along her jaw, thumbs under the temples. He had her securely now. He assumed a half-sitting position in the water, stroking vigorously with his legs and using a scissors kick. He watched vigilantly to make certain her face stayed above water.

A strong swimmer accustomed to the ocean, he was able to support her effortlessly. He decided to conserve his strength and just tread water for a time, all the while looking for the dinghy. Just as Michelle told him to do, he'd pushed the boat over the side. It couldn't have gotten too far away. But in which direction? There were a great many things floating in the water and the sea was choppy.

He studied Michelle with his practiced eye. She was losing some blood from the shoulder wound but that seemed superficial. It was the second bullet that worried him. He was afraid she'd sustained internal damage and he couldn't tell to what extent. Everything depended on the chance course the bullet had taken. Every minute that went by diminished her chances for survival. The sense of helplessness he felt was about to unhinge him.

The waves became larger and the sea

increasingly violent. Off in the distance, he could hear the ominous rumblings of thunder. Flashes of lightning continued to slash the sky with indifferent brutality. The cold water had begun to numb his extremities. Still, he kept calm, telling himself that at any moment another boat would come by and rescue them. Over and over, he told Michelle how much he loved her and promised he would take care of her. He knew she couldn't actually hear him, but it didn't really matter.

He couldn't be certain of the exact moment he sighted them. Of course, he'd read about them in books, but he'd never actually expected to see one with his own eyes. And now he was seeing not one but several. They weren't exactly large, but damn it, what sharp, ugly teeth they had! No, there was no mistake; he could tell by the fins. It was the blood, he realized. There were parts of bodies floating in the water. And then there was the bleeding from Michelle's wounds. The smell had brought them here to hungrily congregate for a meal. They were ready for a feast, a frenzied orgy of eating delight. And they were getting closer. Daniel shuddered.

His heart hammered uncontrollably. He could never outswim them, not with Michelle in tow. He felt the terror in his mouth and throat, but forced himself to stay very still so as not to attract them more quickly.

Desperately, he scanned the surface. And then as if in answer to his silent prayers, he saw it! The dinghy was nearby. At first he believed it was just a mirage, the vivid dream of a doomed man. But he swam toward it with everything he had, keeping a tight grip on Michelle. It really was there! So close now. They had to make it! He swam with all the strength he had left, giving it his final burst of energy, the last rally, switching to a breast stroke style kick. His heart felt ready to burst as he reached the little boat. He lifted Michelle up on his shoulders and lowered her into the bottom of the boat. One of the sharks was so near that its teeth snapped upward toward Michelle's limp leg. He took his fist and smashed it for all it was worth downward on the creature's snout. He was not a violent man, but at that moment, he felt a savage rage, an uncontrollable rush of anger. The shark moved away. Daniel climbed hurriedly into the dinghy, thinking that was the end of it.

But the blow had only stunned the shark momentarily. It circled and returned followed by others. He found an oar inside the boat and began hitting at the sharks repeatedly with it. They actually managed to lob off a fair chunk of the oar. He used the second oar he found in the dinghy to paddle away as quickly as possible, expecting that they would follow.

Soon he realized that the sharks were losing interest. Something else appeared to have attracted their attention. It was the debris from the explosion. It wasn't a very pretty sight. He turned his eyes away. He was a doctor and should have a certain objectivity in relation to such things, but he could not prevent a spasm of nausea from overtaking his stomach at the feeding frenzy. There wouldn't be much left of Atwood and his comrades after these scavengers got through with them. It was ironic, he realized, this was exactly what Atwood had planned for them.

Momentarily spent, he collapsed into the bottom of the boat beside Michelle. He warmed her body with his own, afraid she would soon go into shock. He brought his lips to hers and breathed life into her senseless form. He kissed her with all the passionate desperation he was feeling.

The storm's intensity was fierce. Above them, great dark clouds hung low and threatening. He was weak and terribly cold, but fear kept him going. Terror tore at his throat like an attack dog. A hard, driving rain began to beat down on them. He continued to shield Michelle's body with his own and prayed that the boat would not capsize. Adrenaline kicked in.

The rain water felt refreshing against his parched lips. But the boat rocked treacherously. He tried to keep the movements of the dinghy steady with his one remaining oar. That proved impossible, and finally the oar was swept away.

His strength completely depleted, he stretched his body out flat against Michelle in the bottom of the boat and closed his eyes. All he could do was try to keep her warm and protect her from the storm.

Eventually, the turbulence rolled by and the sea gradually became calmer. The dark day deepened into twilight. With a great sigh of relief, he fell into a sleep born of bone-rending exhaustion.

What it was that woke him, he could not be certain. There was initially only a mild awareness. Then he was fully alert. He could hear voices coming through a bullhorn. His own voice choked with emotion as he shouted in a hoarse yell.

"Help us! We're here."

# CHAPTER TWENTY-FOUR

Michelle felt a cool hand on her forehead and opened her eyes. The unpleasant odor of antiseptic assailed her nostrils.

"Where am I?" Her voice was a hoarse whisper. Her throat was parched and her lips felt cracked and dry.

"You're in the hospital. Don't try to speak yet. Just rest."

The cool hand went to her wrist. She was beginning to focus now. There was a nurse standing over her, checking her pulse. The nurse's eyes were a clear blue and reminded her of Professor Latimer. Memory returned with a sharp vision. She remembered everything vividly now. It all came back to her. The nurse left without saying another word.

A few minutes later, the nurse returned with a young doctor who smiled at Michelle.

"How are we feeling?" he asked sympathetically.

"I wouldn't know about you, but I've felt a lot better."

He nodded his head in agreement. "Sounds reasonable."

"Suppose you tell me how I am."

He looked at the medical chart hanging at the foot of her bed.

"Well, you were pretty bad off when they brought you in here. You needed transfusions before we could operate, but the prognosis is good."

"What sort of operation?" She somehow managed to keep her voice calm.

"There were two bullet wounds. The damage done to your shoulder was easy to repair. The other was tricky. We had to perform a splenectomy."

"What precisely is that?" It hurt so to speak. She gritted her teeth.

"Damage was done to your spleen. The bullet ruptured it, and your spleen had to be removed."

"And am I all right now?"

"I'd say so. Fortunately, a person can live quite well without a spleen. You're a very lucky woman."

She closed her eyes and went back to sleep. The next time she woke up, there was a different nurse examining her, but the same doctor returned.

As her mind cleared, she thought of Daniel. Where was he? What had happened to him? She remembered his arms around her, supporting and comforting her.

"Is Doctor Reiner here?" she asked. "Is he all right?"

"He was mainly suffering from exposure. He's been demanding to see you. We'll let him come visit you soon," the nurse said.

But it was Bertram who turned out to be her first actual visitor. He wore a look of relief as he saw her alert expression.

"I told them we were related so that I could get in," he said. He handed her a bouquet of assorted flowers.

"Lovely. However, it really wasn't necessary to bring flowers. It's not my funeral yet."

"From what I understand, it nearly was." He frowned deeply.

A nurse took the flowers to put in water, and they were left alone. Bertram sat down on a chair beside her bed. His homely features looked weary.

"I ought to fill you in on what's been happening in New York. There hasn't been much flack over the demise of our pal Nastchenkov. It seems the man had become an embarrassment to certain Eastern European officials."

"Only because he was not successful. Failure breeds contempt."

They talked for a while, but when Bertram thought she seemed tired, he quickly left.

She must have dozed off for a time because the next thing she knew, Doug Maclaren was sitting beside her. His large hand with its thick, muscular wrist held her own. How pale her skin looked next to his!

"Have you been sitting here long?" she asked. Like Bertram, his eyes betrayed concern.

"Just a few minutes. I wanted to see for myself how you were doing. I used a little pull to get in. Hope you don't mind."

"Not at all."

"How are you feeling?"

"A bit weak, but otherwise all right."

"I'm sore at you. You were supposed to call me for help."

She lowered her eyes. "Colonel Atwood took me by surprise."

"Yeah, he kind of surprised a lot of people. Well, I brought you some candy." He placed a large, gift-wrapped box down beside her.

"Why don't you open it for me and act as the official taste tester."

"Are you sure?" He looked pleased.

"Of course," she said wearily.

"These are great. Want to try one?"

She shook her head. "Not right now."

Mac loosened the tight, white collar that was cutting into his thick, muscular neck. "I partly blame myself for what happened. Atwood came to see me several times when I was working on the Parker case. I was really fooled by him. He was the one who warned me about you. Now I know why he asked the questions he did. Guess I wasn't very smart."

"I believed Atwood too. He was very good."

"Yeah, too damned good." Mac stayed for a while and when it was time for him to leave, he gave her an affectionate kiss on the forehead.

"Call me day or night," he said. "For you I'm always available."

Daniel hadn't been in yet. She wondered if he still felt the same way about her. Maybe he'd decided her way of life was all too much for him. After the experience they'd had, it was entirely possible that his feelings had changed. If they had, it was for the best. And yet she ached to see him, to be near him, to have him tease her, to have him touch her.

■ ■ ■ ■

It was early evening when Daniel finally walked into the room. He looked wan and tired, but when he smiled, it lit up the room. He sat down beside her and took her hand in his.

"How long have we been here?"

"You were in intensive care for two days."

"I seem to have lost track of time."

"You were a very sick girl," he said.

"Were you worried?"

"Very worried." His eyes heated.

"I'm all right now."

"I know." He leaned over and brushed her lips with a gentle kiss.

"I probably look ghastly."

"Told you before, you're even more beautiful without makeup."

She laughed at his obvious attempt at flattery, but appreciated it all the same.

"I wanted to talk to you about us. That is, when you're ready." His expression became serious.

There was a knock at the door that startled her slightly. Wild Bill Kirson sauntered into the room.

"How y'all feelin', honey?" he drawled.

"What do you want?" She wasn't feeling

hospitable.

"That any way to talk to someone who wants to do you a good turn?" He smiled through his ugly, nicotine-stained teeth.

"I'm not up to fencing with you."

"Just a short talk."

"Please leave."

"This is important," he said, inching closer to her bed.

"Want me to throw him out of here?" Daniel asked. He actually glared menacingly at the cowboy. How brave and handsome he was!

"Hey, that wouldn't be easy to do, son. Besides, I got top security clearance. I can always tell them you're wanted by the CIA. Hells bells, nobody throws me out of anywhere!" He tossed his Stetson down at the foot of her bed for emphasis.

"I'll do just that if Michelle wants it," Daniel said, facing Kirson.

"Son, I don't take on puny sick people. It don't do well for my image."

"Don't bother with him, Daniel. He isn't worth your trouble. Just say whatever it is you came to say and then please leave, Mr. Kirson."

"That's no way to talk, girl. Show a little respect for your elders. We're gonna have ourselves a conversation now, but your

434

boyfriend waits outside."

Daniel turned to her, his brow cocked in a question. Michelle nodded her head.

"It's all right, Daniel. Really."

"I'll be right outside the door if you need me," he called over his shoulder and abruptly left the room.

Kirson waited until the door closed behind Daniel before he spoke again. He approached her bedside.

"Please, don't come any closer. You still smell like a human ashtray."

He pretended to be offended. "Okay, darlin', if that's the way you want to treat a friend."

"It's no thanks to you that I'm still alive."

He gave her a wide grin. "Now wait. I warned you plenty of times that you were in over your head. Anyway, you don't look too bad, considerin'. Just a little pasty white in the face like the belly color of a dead catfish."

"How reassuring," she said sarcastically.

He laughed. "Sassy as ever."

"You're very fortunate that I'm still too weak to get out of this bed."

"That's good, 'cause I got a few things to tell you, and I don't much cotton to you walking out on me. First off, you had this thing all wrong from the beginning. I was suspicious of Atwood for a long time. Parker had a first class record until he went over to work for NSA. That was around the time things started getting stolen. The thief could only have been someone with a top security clearance in both agencies. Atwood was Parker's immediate superior. We only pretended to close the Parker case. It ain't easy investigatin' secretly when you're dealing with people near the top. And Atwood was real careful. He covered himself good. He thought he was safe. 'Course, that's what I wanted him to think. Then you entered the picture and messed everything up."

"Why didn't you tell me what you knew or suspected?"

"And what were you going to do with it? Run and tell Parker's widow? No, I had no intention of risking my investigation by blabbing what I knew to you." Kirson sat down on the chair near her bed. "Screw amateurs."

"Thanks for the vote of confidence."

"Information like that is strictly disseminated on a need to know basis. You did become useful though. When Atwood had his people start going after you, I realized that you were the perfect blind. You had some facts, enough to frighten them. Maybe even enough to bring them out in the open where they'd make some mistakes. Wherever you went, we were there too. We even had your boyfriend followed."

"Do you know how many times they tried to kill me?"

Kirson smiled broadly. "Yeah, I know all about it. But then, nobody forced you to go on with the case, did they? You could have quit at any time."

An alarming thought flashed through her mind. "Did you send Nora to me in the first place?"

"What do you think? Of course not! I didn't want outsiders involved, not in the beginning at least. But I got to hand it to you. I never thought you'd stay alive. Glad I didn't take bets! For the record, I was the one who sent the Coast Guard out after that cabin cruiser. As soon as my people transmitted the information back to me about you meeting up with Atwood on the boat, I knew you were in real trouble. I sent out an alert. They'd of gotten to you sooner if it hadn't been for the bad weather. And I want you to know you're being paid for the job right well, just as if you were on the payroll from the beginning. We're picking up the hospital bill too. Nothing but the best for our brave girl. Notice the private room?

Classy right? The big shots think a lot of you. You'll get more work sent your way. You've proved yourself. Now what do you think of that, honey?" He waited for her reply.

"Kirson, you can go straight to hell," she said.

He laughed wickedly. "Now, darlin', you better watch out 'cause hell's surely where we're both headed."

"I'm not like you."

"Aren't you? Took out that Russky pretty good, didn't you? Yes, sir, I do respect a woman with spirit! Be seeing you around, cutie. Maybe you'll be more grateful when you're feelin' better."

He left her alone with her own thoughts. So Kirson had used her to flush Atwood out into the open. She resented being used that way. But it was true: Kirson had warned her.

Someone knocked at the door. It was a nurse who announced that there were flowers being delivered. She watched in astonishment as dozen after dozen of lush red roses in vases were brought into her room and put in every free space. A card was placed on the table beside her bed. She took it from its envelope. The message was brief;

printed on the card were the words GUNS AND ROSES.

Daniel walked back into the room. She turned her head to one side in a gesture of appraisal.

"Yours?" she asked.

"Thought you might like them." He smiled and the dimple she so loved appeared in his cheek.

"You've turned the room into a greenhouse."

"Hope you're not allergic to flowers."

"No, and I do adore roses," she said. "Quite a grand gesture."

"They'll help you get better sooner." He sat down next to her on the bed. Then he took her into his arms and kissed her very gently on the lips.

"That was very nice."

"Just nice?"

He kissed her again, showering her face with many tender kisses.

"Did you send all these flowers because you thought I might die?"

"Just the opposite. I'm celebrating the fact that you're going to live." He squeezed her hand. "I love you."

"I thought that might have changed."

He smiled. "Not a chance. When are you going to talk the talk, lady?"

"It's not easy for me. After my parents died, I began to look on caring for other people as a weakness or an affliction."

"Great, so you put loving me on a par with getting cancer."

She shook her head. "You do have a way of making a joke out of everything. Mock me if you will, but I'm just being honest."

"All I'm saying is that your uncle might have been right about a lot of things but love isn't one of them. Loving and sharing your life with another person just makes it better. We have something real here. Don't be afraid of it."

But she was afraid. In fact, she was terrified. She'd never considered herself a coward, but in this regard, she was one. "You've turned this hospital room into a very romantic place, a veritable rose garden."

Daniel, however, was not so easily put off the subject. "Sweetheart, just consider this: if you're sick, I've got the cure."

"I'll keep that in mind," she said in a throaty voice.

"You mean everything to me. Marry me."

She looked directly into his deep, dark eyes. "That's impossible."

"Why can't we get married?"

"You can't live with what I do for a living."

"I've accepted your life."

"Have you? Can you truthfully say it doesn't matter?" Her eyes searched his.

"Of course, I'd be delighted if you gave it up. Tell the truth. Don't you feel just a tiny bit burned out right about now?"

"And then what would I do?"

He smiled amiably. "Well, I could think of a few things." He gave her a meaningful look.

"Be serious!"

"I am. I love you more than anyone or anything in this entire world. I want you for my wife. I'm prepared to employ you on a full-time basis, and I promise some incredible fringe benefits."

She could feel an ache stirring within her. "I can't accept." She nearly choked on the words.

"Sure you can!" His hand took hers and held them tightly. "Look, do you know that sixty-eight per cent of British women change their occupation at least once by the time they're thirty?"

"Really?"

"No," he grinned irresistibly. "I just made that up to impress you, but it does sound true, doesn't it? Good, I finally got you to smile." He brushed the auburn curls back from her face with the tips of his fingers.

"I'll go along with whatever makes you happy, but you've got to promise me that you'll really give this whole thing a lot of hard thought."

The touch of his hands on her face made her skin tingle. She couldn't give in to the feeling — could she?

"It's just that we're so different, I don't see how we could make a go of it. The odds are against us."

"The odds were against us when we were out on that ocean too, but we made it back alive. You're forcing me to play dirty. I wasn't going to mention this but the fact is, you do owe me your life. My body warmth saved you. I thought Brits were honorable and paid up their debts."

"Of course. What do I owe you?"

He smiled again. "I've already told you. I don't expect much, not your money, not your thanks, merely the rest of your life dedicated to me and servicing my lustful needs."

Now it was her turn to smile. "You don't demand much, do you?"

"I'll take a token payment for now, just to show good faith."

The kiss was gentle yet passionate, the warmth of his lips making her heart pound.

"I can be very stubborn, just as strong-willed as you are. You and I belong to each other. I won't live without you and I won't let you live without me. We can't be separated anymore."

"But you expect me to give up my work?"

"We'll figure something out. A compromise. We're going to be very happy together."

He placed a sensual kiss on the sensitive curve of her neck and she quivered like gelatin.

"I suppose I could take an entirely administrative role, stay out of the field. Fieldwork doesn't seem to be my strong suit anyway. Uncle Ted actually did expect me to run the company from the office."

"I promise to make our nights together as intriguingly dangerous as possible to make up for it."

"I do love you," she said, running her hands through his thick, dark hair.

His eyes lit up. "I knew you'd get around to admitting it eventually."

Then he kissed her again, and she forgot about everything else, including the living and the dead.

# ABOUT THE AUTHOR

Multiple award-winning author **Jacqueline Seewald** has taught writing courses at the university level as well as high school English. She also worked as an academic librarian and school librarian. Eleven of her books of fiction have been published. Her short stories, poems, essays, reviews and articles have appeared in hundreds of diverse publications. She enjoys spending time with family and friends when she isn't writing. In addition, she is a playwright, a landscape artist and loves many types of music.